PRAISE FOR CAROLYN BROWN

Hummingbird Lane

"Brown's (*The Daydream Cabin*) gentle story of a woman finding strength within a tight-knit community has just a touch of romance at the end. Recommended for readers who enjoy heartwarming stories about women overcoming obstacles."

—*Library Journal*

Miss Janie's Girls

"[A] heartfelt tale of familial love and self-acceptance."

—*Publishers Weekly*

"Heartfelt moments and family drama collide in this saga about sisters."

—*Woman's World*

The Banty House

"Brown throws together a colorful cast of characters to excellent effect and maximum charm in this small-town contemporary romance . . . This first-rate romance will delight readers young and old."

—*Publishers Weekly*

The Family Journal

HOLT Medallion Finalist

"Reading a Carolyn Brown book is like coming home again."

—*Harlequin Junkie* (top pick)

The Empty Nesters

"A delightful journey of hope and healing."

—*Woman's World*

"The story is full of emotion . . . and the joy of friendship and family. Carolyn Brown is known for her strong, loving characters, and this book is full of them."

—*Harlequin Junkie*

"Carolyn Brown takes us back to small-town Texas with a story about women, friendships, love, loss, and hope for the future."

—*Storeybook Reviews*

"Ms. Brown has fast become one of my favorite authors!"

—*Romance Junkies*

The Perfect Dress

"Fans of Brown will swoon for this sweet contemporary, which skillfully pairs a shy small-town bridal shop owner and a softhearted car dealership owner . . . The expected but welcomed happily ever after for all involved will make readers of all ages sigh with satisfaction."

—*Publishers Weekly*

"Carolyn Brown writes the best comfort-for-the-soul, heartwarming stories, and she never disappoints . . . You won't go wrong with *The Perfect Dress*!"

—*Harlequin Junkie*

The Magnolia Inn

"The author does a first-rate job of depicting the devastating stages of grief, provides a simple but appealing plot with a sympathetic hero and heroine and a cast of lovable supporting characters, and wraps it all up with a happily ever after to cheer for."

—*Publishers Weekly*

"*The Magnolia Inn* by Carolyn Brown is a feel-good story about friendship, fighting your demons, and finding love, and maybe just a little bit of magic."

—*Harlequin Junkie*

"Chock-full of Carolyn Brown's signature country charm, *The Magnolia Inn* is a sweet and heartwarming story of two people trying to make the most of their lives, even when they have no idea what exactly is at stake."

—*Fresh Fiction*

Small Town Rumors

"Carolyn Brown is a master at writing warm, complex characters who find their way into your heart."

—*Harlequin Junkie*

The Sometimes Sisters

"Carolyn Brown continues her streak of winning, heartfelt novels with *The Sometimes Sisters*, a story of estranged sisters and frustrated romance."

—All About Romance

"This is an amazing feel-good story that will make you wish you were a part of this amazing family."

—*Harlequin Junkie* (top pick)

The Wild Card

ALSO BY CAROLYN BROWN

Contemporary Romances

The Party Line

The Sawmill Book Club

Meadow Falls

The Lucky Shamrock

The Devine Doughnut Shop

The Sandcastle Hurricane

Riverbend Reunion

The Bluebonnet Battle

The Sunshine Club

The Hope Chest

Hummingbird Lane

The Daydream Cabin

Miss Janie's Girls

The Banty House

The Family Journal

The Empty Nesters

The Perfect Dress

The Magnolia Inn

Small Town Rumors

The Sometimes Sisters

The Strawberry Hearts Diner

The Lilac Bouquet

The Barefoot Summer

The Lullaby Sky

The Wedding Pearls

The Yellow Rose Beauty Shop

The Ladies' Room

Hidden Secrets

Long, Hot Texas Summer

Daisies in the Canyon

Trouble in Paradise

Contemporary Series

The Broken Roads Series

To Trust

To Commit

To Believe

To Dream

To Hope

Three Magic Words Trilogy

A Forever Thing

In Shining Whatever

Life After Wife

Historical Romances

The Paradise Petition

Historical Romance Series

The Black Swan Trilogy

Pushin' Up Daisies

From Thin Air

Come High Water

The Drifters and Dreamers Trilogy

Morning Glory

Sweet Tilly

Evening Star

The Love's Valley Series

Choices

Absolution

Chances

Redemption

Promises

The Wild Card

CAROLYN BROWN

This is a work of fiction. Names, characters, organizations, places, events, and incidents are either products of the author's imagination or are used fictitiously. Otherwise, any resemblance to actual persons, living or dead, is purely coincidental.

Published by Montlake, Seattle
www.apub.com

EU product safety contact:
Amazon Media EU S. à r.l.
38, avenue John F. Kennedy, L-1855 Luxembourg
amazonpublishing-gpsr@amazon.com

ISBN-13: 9781662528750 (paperback)
ISBN-13: 9781662528743 (digital)

Cover design by Mumtaz Mustafa
Cover image: © Hundley Photography / Shutterstock; © Raymond Forbes LLC / Stocksy

Printed in the United States of America

This one is to
my agent and my friend,
Erin Cartwright Niumata,
who has believed in me for more than twenty-five years.

Chapter One

Lady Luck had deserted me.

We had been best friends since the first time I beat ol' Frank at Texas Hold'em and won all the pennies, nickels, and dimes in the middle of a tiny table in a cheap hotel room. Poor loser that he was, he never played poker with me again. But to give him a little credit for being my mentor when it came to the game, at least he kept enough seed money in his pocket to buy each of us a burger and fries.

Lady Luck had sat on my shoulder and told me not to go to that poker game, but I had gotten so high and mighty in my success that I didn't listen to her. Tucson was a nice little stopover on my way to a high-stakes game in Vegas, and I could use a few more bucks to stuff into my lockbox. A big, big mistake that I will never make again.

My name is Carla Wilson, and I am thirty years old. Ol' Frank always said that I was his wild card . . . his good luck charm. Frank wouldn't think that if he was with me today. Not after last night. He would probably say I was the joker. I have been a professional gambler for more than a decade. I don't need a house, an apartment, or even a travel trailer. Everything I own is in the back of my SUV, and I live in whatever hotel I can find that is close to where my next game—legal or otherwise—is being held.

The punishment for not obeying what the Lady had laid on my heart was that I lost all my money for the high-stakes Vegas game. And to add insult to injury, I lost it all in a seedy little room in the back of an auto repair shop in a ratty part of town. My cash was always hidden in a lockbox, but after the game that night it was totally empty.

So now I had a full tank of gas, a package of stale peanut butter crackers, and almost ten dollars in change that I had thrown into the console of my SUV. Well, that, and the quitclaim deed to a café in some godforsaken place east of El Paso that a tall, skinny guy with a horse-shaped face had thrown on the table as part of a bet. His unkempt goatee made his face look even longer, so I'd named him the Goat while we were playing cards. When I'd gotten a whiff of his cheap cologne, bad breath, and body odor, the name seemed to fit even better.

In all the years I had been playing, I'd never walked away from a game flat broke. The only choice I had now was to drive to the café and live in it until I could sell the place for enough money to start all over again. Traveling and playing cards was all I knew.

I cussed everything from the potholes in the road to the empty lockbox in the back of my SUV as I drove the few blocks to the motel on the same side of town as the auto shop. Just as I stepped out of my vehicle, a rat the size of a possum ran across the toe of my high-heeled shoe.

Luckily no one was awake that hour, because I was sure I looked like I'd had one drink too many. But the very idea of a rat touching even my shoe gave me a case of the heebie-jeebies. I stomped the gravel parking lot so hard that the spiked heel of my shoe popped off, and I kicked the tainted shoe to the side. No way would I ever wear that pair again. I kept one eye on the ground for any more varmints and hobbled on tiptoe to my room with one bare foot. I opened the door with a key instead of a card, switched on the overhead light, and a roach crawled up the toe of my other shoe. I did a dance right there on the brown tile floor that would rival any breakdancing contest, but the bug hung on and kept going right up my bare leg.

Instinct took over, and I brushed the pest away with the back of my hand. It landed on the edge of the bedspread and disappeared under a pillow. I removed my good shoe and set it on the pillow. "There! You can have it."

I went straight to the bathroom, stripped out of my clothes, and hung them on the towel rack, then started to step into the shower to get the feel of rat and roach off my skin. A spider looked up at me with evil eyes from inside the tub. Lady Luck had deserted me in more ways than just the poker game.

"That does it!" I screamed, and grabbed a washcloth from the hook.

"I have to wash the creepy feeling off," I muttered as I kept an eye on the spider, who was slowly making its way out of the tub. I imagined it humming the theme song to a horror movie. I didn't even take time to wring the washcloth out, but let water drip across the floor to where my suitcase sat on the dresser. After thoroughly scrubbing my feet, legs, and hands, I got dressed in a pair of jeans and a T-shirt. Then I tucked what I had worn to the poker game in a plastic bag and tied the top shut with two knots. I zipped up my suitcase and pulled it outside.

With self-pity draped around my shoulders, I jogged across the lot and dropped my key in an outside slot beside a barred office window. Maybe that was why the Lady had waved goodbye to me—she had grown accustomed to fine hotels with a minibar, soft sheets, and room service. I was sure she didn't like rats, roaches, and spiders any better than I did.

"I'm sorry," I apologized, but the feeling in my heart said that she was gone. Quite possibly for good.

Since I had to have someone to blame for the predicament, it all landed on my friend who had suggested I make a stop in Tucson. Maybe I should have said he was my *former* friend, because as of that night, he topped the list of people I would never speak to again.

"You can clean all those guys out," he had promised with a broad wink during the game in Amarillo. "I've got a sister in Hobbs, New Mexico, that I'm going to stay with a couple of days. But I'll see you in Vegas. Be prepared to lose."

Had he known at that time that the stars were lined up against me to lose—not in Vegas, but in Tucson? Had he promised Lady Luck fine hotel rooms with no ugly critters if she would desert me and be his BFF?

As I pulled out of that parking lot, I envisioned strangling my ex-friend and watching his pretty blue eyes pop out and roll around on the floor like marbles. Until my temper cooled down, that man would do well to keep several hundred miles between the two of us. Poker players, like most of the guys who played football, were a superstitious lot. They clipped their toenails at a certain time of the morning, touched their ear seven times, or did something else that would bring them luck. As for me, I shuffled the same deck of cards we used the night I beat Frank. I had even shuffled my lucky deck of cards twice that night and had gone into that game full of confidence that I would walk away with all the money.

I hoped the Arizona Highway Patrol officers were cuddled up with their wives in the early-morning hours, because my foot, right along with my eyelids, got heavier with every passing mile. Glaring at the deck of well-worn cards sitting on the passenger seat fired up the anger and kept me awake for a while longer.

Other than a brief two-hour nap I'd managed to squeeze in before I went to the poker game, I hadn't slept since Tuesday night, when Lady Luck and I had cashed out at a casino in Amarillo and gone to a nice hotel to sleep in a soft king-size bed.

Now it was Thursday morning, New Year's Day, and Frank had a superstition that said whatever we did on the first day of the year, we would be doing all year. So we usually traveled from one casino to another, but we never hit the poker tables until after the clock ticked off 12:01 a.m. on January 2. If we lost, that meant we would be losers all year. I had lost everything and won a diner in a place called Tumbleweed three minutes past midnight on New Year's Day—point proven, thank you very much, Frank.

Hey, don't blame me. You should have left that game before midnight. His voice was loud and clear in my head.

The first hint of morning light appeared at the same time I passed a sign that said the First Baptist Church welcomed me to Picacho Hills, and a few hundred yards on, another sign told me it was fifty miles to El Paso, Texas. I pulled into one of those open-all-night truck stops, got out, and went to the bathroom, where I washed my face and did fifty jumping jacks to wake myself up. According to the address on the deed and the GPS on my phone, I still had 140 miles to go.

"Then I'm going to lay down and sleep for twenty hours, even if it's on the floor with my duffel bag for a pillow," I promised myself as I filled my empty water bottle at the sink.

The chemistry teacher I'd had in public school once told us to each bring water from our homes, and we looked at it under the microscopes. Every one of them had stuff in it that was downright disgusting. I forced myself not to think about all the microscopic germs coming out of the faucet that were invisible to the naked eye.

The pretzels and beer I'd had at the poker game from hell had long since vanished, and my stomach growled as I made my way back through the store. The aroma of breakfast *taquitos* and sausage biscuits floating through the room smelled oh-so good. But for the first time in my life, I didn't even have the money to buy one candy bar or a small bag of chips from the racks I walked past on the way outside.

When I got back to my vehicle and started the engine, the low-fuel light flashed. I pulled up to a gas pump, counted all the loose coins in the console, and put $9.43 worth into the tank. The lady at the cash register frowned when I handed her all that change—but hey, pennies are money, right? According to the gauge, I could go 150 miles on what fuel I had. That meant I would slide into the parking lot of an empty café building on fumes and prayers.

By rationing my stale peanut butter crackers to one every ten minutes, I made it all the way through El Paso. My eyes got heavier and heavier with each passing mile—until a norther hit. That's what Southern folks call a hard north wind that drops the temperature by several degrees and tries to blow the hair right off a person's head. I had to concentrate just to keep the SUV on the road, because the wind seemed hell-bent on pushing me south all the way to Corpus Christi.

My arms and shoulders ached, but I mentally patted myself on the back. Then, out of nowhere, something that looked like a full-grown bull slammed into my windshield. I braked hard, then finally came to a stop on the side of the road. Gravel was still settling all around me when I forced the door open and pushed against the wind as I walked back about fifty yards to where I expected to see a mangled body lying.

I forgot about being hungry and sleepy, and my shoes felt like they were filled with concrete. My heart thumped around in my chest so fast that I thought surely it would pop out and blow away like a tumbleweed. Visions of jail cells and orange jumpsuits flitted through my mind. That color had never looked good on me, and I doubted the inmates had any money to bet with, either.

No money, starving, and I had just killed a hitchhiker. Would a pro bono lawyer argue that thumbing rides was illegal anyway, or would the judge just throw the book at me for involuntary manslaughter? Then the bottle of water with wiggly things in it hit, and I had to pee. I could see a yucca plant close by, but it wasn't big enough to hide me if I squatted behind it.

I was still imagining a bloody, mangled body when I found a semi-flattened tumbleweed the size of a small Angus bull lying in the middle of the road. I was so mad that I kicked it, and the damn thing magically resurrected and headed south with the next gust of wind. The words that came out of my mouth when it danced across the flat land were not pretty. They bordered on sending me straight to hell to sit on a hot barbed wire fence for all eternity.

"At least it was just a tumbleweed." I jerked my jeans down and hoped there were no chiggers or poison ivy the cold weather had not killed. If the state of Texas was as great as everyone said, then why didn't they at least have a port-a-potty along the side of the road every twenty miles? If I was ever elected to be in office, that would be my first bill. Fifty miles with no bathroom was downright cruel.

I am not a skinny girl—more what folks call *curvy*—yet when I was squatting there on the side of the road, that norther did its best to throw me into a race with the tumbleweed I almost murdered. When I was done, I trudged back to my vehicle and got inside. Exhaustion had set in several hours ago, but so much adrenaline rushed through my body that I didn't have to worry about falling asleep behind the wheel anymore.

Two miles down the road, what I first thought was fog or smoke turned out to be dust with a heavy dose of even more tumbleweeds flying through it like the flying monkeys in *The Wizard of Oz*. Those things had scared the bejesus out of me when I watched the movie as a child.

Another one, even bigger than the one I'd almost killed, hit my windshield. "Rats, roaches, and spiders—and now flying tumbleweeds that have faces like those monkeys."

Gravel crunched under my tires when I swerved to miss the next army of them. Trying to get back on the road was no easy feat, and there was no way to dodge the hundreds of tumbleweeds blowing against the side of my SUV. One even hitched a ride on the side mirror and stayed with me for several miles before it finally dislodged and went on its way. By then I didn't give a damn how many I slaughtered.

"I see now why the place that I now own is called the Tumbleweed Bus Stop and Diner. I wonder how big the town is. I didn't get a key with the deed, so if I'm lucky it will still be open for business. Maybe in six months, I can save up enough money to . . . Damn it!" The granddaddy of all tumbleweeds hit the windshield and got hung up in the wiper blade.

A Class 5 tornado couldn't have dislodged it, so I had to pull over again and manhandle the thing off the SUV, all the while trying to avoid a scorpion that seemed to have its eye on my hand. The dust was thicker than any fog I had ever seen, and by the time I slid back under the steering wheel, I was coughing like a three-pack-a-day smoker.

When I finally got control of my breath, I remembered what Larry Dimson, the Goat and previous owner of the café, had said when I won the pot that included the deed to the Tumbleweed Bus Stop and Diner. "Now that eyesore is your responsibility. It's been bad luck for me since the day my Aunt Matilda left it to me."

"I believe you, but it's all I've got," I said between clenched teeth. *And there's my answer as to why Lady Luck divorced me after twenty years of blissful friendship.*

She didn't want to stand too close to anything with the stink of bad fortune on it.

If I'd had any other option, I would have tossed that deed out the window for one of the tumbleweeds to haul off to points south. But I did not have a choice in the matter. I had to sell the place before I could get back to the lifestyle I knew.

"Since Lady Luck has deserted me, the café will probably be a defunct building with a front door swinging on one hinge and letting all kinds of varmints into the place." Talking to myself had always kept me awake, but that morning, with the sun shining in my eyes, it didn't help much—not with the vision of vermin and insects roaming through the café.

"I'll have to sleep in the car if that's the case, and hope that the town is big enough I can find a job. Not that I'm skilled in anything but poker. God, what am I doing? I'm going crazy from sleep deprivation, hunger, and fighting the dust and these damn tumbleweeds," I swore. "I could sleep anywhere—even in a broom closet. Come on, Carla, it's only another twenty miles. I know I'm breaking my vow to never do anything but play poker—but like Mama told me before she died, 'Never say never.'"

The tinny voice of the GPS lady announced that I had arrived, just as a flashing warning light on the dashboard told me I was dangerously low on gas. The clock said it was 7:13 a.m. Normally, those were my lucky numbers, but I thought that Lady Luck was simply playing tricks on me that morning.

Surprise is the only word that came to my mind when I looked up. Since Larry had said the café was for sale, I had thought it might be an empty building. I was so glad I had been wrong that if I'd had the energy, I would have done a little dance the minute I saw the OPEN sign blinking in the window. There was also a FOR SALE sign, but I guessed we wouldn't need that for now.

I parked beside a Greyhound bus, got out of my SUV, and held my breath to keep from breathing in more dust. I kicked half a dozen tumbleweeds out of the path and froze when I heard a squeaking noise. I was sure a huge rat would run out from the corner of the café, but it was the TUMBLEWEED BUS STOP AND DINER sign that hung between two rusted metal poles. I studied the place and wondered if it had been Pepto-Bismol pink at one time, because no one in their right mind would ever paint a place of business the horrible shade of a shriveled-up grapefruit. My mind went back to my bedroom in the house where I'd lived until I was eight years old. The walls were the same color as this café.

Was that an omen? Was I stepping back in time rather than going forward? No answers floated by me on a tumbleweed, so I opened the door and stepped inside a warm dining room. I really thought I might drop in a dead faint when the aroma of food slapped me right in the face.

"Have a seat anywhere. Be with you as soon as I get this table cleaned off," a woman said. SCARLETT was embroidered above the picture of a tumbleweed on her shirt. Her strawberry-blond hair was twisted up on top of her head, and her crystal blue eyes sparkled. A big dose of jealousy shot through my body at her peaches-and-cream complexion. I'd never liked my eight million freckles, which no amount of makeup could cover.

According to Frank, reading what was in a person's eyes was my biggest talent. If that was the truth, what I saw said that she wouldn't last long in a poker game. She was way too open and way too friendly.

"Are you the manager?" I asked.

"No, ma'am," she answered on her way to carry a tray of food to a table. "That would be Rosie. She's in the kitchen, but she doesn't like folks to come back there. Larry is the owner, but he's not here right now, so if you're looking for a job, you'll have to come back on Monday. That's the day he usually drops by."

I brushed dust from the shoulders of my denim jacket and walked around the end of the counter and through the swinging doors into the kitchen, where a short, round woman stood at a grill.

"Hey, didn't you hear me?" Scarlett yelled.

"I did, thanks," I called over my shoulder and then focused on the lady flipping pancakes.

The woman turned and gave me a look meant to kill me dead on the spot. She wore loose-fitting jeans, a T-shirt with ROSALIE embroidered on the right shoulder, and a bonnet printed with big sunflowers on her head. She reminded me of Dr. Loretta Wade, the coroner on *NCIS: New Orleans*. She was shorter than me—and I'm only five feet four inches tall—and had a round face that was still scowling at me. Her body had probably been curvy about twenty pounds ago, but I would place a fifty-dollar bet on her if it came to a fight. She wouldn't have to lift a finger. Her glare alone would send anyone running for the hills.

"Get out of my kitchen," she growled.

God Himself couldn't have made me take a step back rather than forward to look at those perfectly round pancakes. Not even the dark-brown eyes that were still glaring at me could put me out of a room with food in it. Especially when I owned the place.

Rosalie shook her long-handled spatula at me. "I said get out!"

"I'm broke, hungry, tired, and angry, and I want food," I said.

"I don't take in strays—not any kind, two legged or four," she declared.

"I'm sorry," I apologized. "I should have introduced myself. I'm Carla Wilson, the new owner of this place, and I am starving."

"So, Larry finally found a buyer for the place, did he?" She tucked a strand of black hair up under the bonnet-looking thing on her head.

"No, he didn't," I answered. "I won it in a poker game."

She made the sign of the cross over her chest, sighed loudly, and looked up at the ceiling. Her lips moved, but no words came out. When she focused back on me, her brown eyes were mere slits. "How do I know you are telling the truth?"

I set my purse on the table in the middle of the kitchen and brought out the quitclaim deed Larry had given me and handed it to her. "If this is good, I'm the new owner. If it isn't, then I'm about to ask for a job. Like I said before, I'm dead broke and I am hungry. And I'm out of fuel in my SUV, so I can't go any farther."

She picked it up and studied it for what seemed like hours before she handed it back to me and yelled through the service window, "Hey, Scarlett, come on back here and meet the new owner."

Scarlett was as pale as vanilla pudding when she came through the swinging doors. "Are we out of a job?"

"No, ma'am, you are not," I told her. "Is it all right for me to eat while we talk?"

"I'm the only one who is allowed near my stove or my cooking pots, so you tell me what you want for breakfast and I'll make it," Rosalie said.

"I don't like onions, but anything else is fine," I told her. "Are you two the only ones who work here?"

"That's right," Rosalie answered as she cracked eggs in a bowl and whipped them into a froth. "Larry breezed through on Monday to pick up the money and go to the bank, but other than that, we're on our own. We manage."

Scarlett peeked out over the swinging doors at the customers. "So, you are not selling the café or closing it until a buyer comes along?"

"Not right now," I answered. "How long has it been up for sale?"

"Since the day Larry took ownership," Rosalie said without even turning around.

"Just how big is Tumbleweed, anyway? I guess this place is on the outskirts, right?"

Scarlett laughed out loud. "You are looking at it. Since you got here, the population has risen to three. It never was a real town, just a wide place in the road."

Rosalie chuckled. "It's never had a post office or a school."

"Or a liquor store, which makes Rosie a happy woman," Scarlett added.

"You have got to be kiddin' me." I was sure they were just yanking me around and that there was a real town named Tumbleweed not too far up the road.

"Nope." Rosalie set a platter of eggs, bacon, hash browns, and biscuits in front of me, then slid another plate of pancakes covered in melted butter and a mug of coffee beside it. "Everything else you might need is right there." She pointed to a condiment tray in the middle of the small wooden table in the kitchen. "If you want a town, you have to drive about fifteen miles north to Dell City."

"I'm not sure you can call it a town," Scarlett said, "but it does have a post office, a school, and a convenience store for the folks to buy gas, milk, bread, and that kind of thing. I've got to go refill drinks. We can talk later when the bus crowd clears out, but welcome to Tumbleweed." She pushed through the doors and back out to the dining area.

"Dell City is a tiny town with only about three hundred people living there, but there is a church up there where I can go to Mass. So I'm not complaining one bit." Rosalie made the sign of the cross again and sat down across from me.

Her gaze made me shift positions in my chair, twice, as I ate my eggs. From her expression, it didn't take a genius to know that no one messed with her religion—or her kitchen.

I stood up, refilled my coffee mug, and then went back to finish my breakfast. "Well, this place sure got the right name. I had to fight tumbleweeds blowing around all the way from El Paso."

"It's that time of year," Rosalie said.

I dove into the pancakes like a hungry hound dog with a big soupbone. That vision almost put a smile on my face, but it soon faded when I remembered that Frank often said that very thing when we stopped at a place to eat. I didn't want anything to remind me of him or his wife or the two little boys they'd produced. He called them my brothers when he talked to me on my birthday each year, but I felt more of a kinship to the two women in this café than I did for those two kids, whom I had met only one time. And that was at the Thanksgiving family reunion in Kentucky—a disaster I did not plan on going through again.

I must've had a strange look on my face, because Rosalie studied me with an odd expression. "January is our worst month for tumbleweeds. The folks on the buses that stop here think they're cute. If they had to deal with them every day, they wouldn't be taking the things home with them to use for decorations."

"Are you serious? They really take them home?"

"Yes, they do," Rosalie answered with a nod. "I tell them to be careful and watch out for thorns. And to be sure that a scorpion or two haven't hitched a free ride in the middle of one to get from one place to another."

I tried not to shiver—I really did—but there was no controlling it when I remembered the curly-tailed thing on the tumbleweed I'd had to remove from the wiper blade.

"But nobody listens to me," Rosalie went on. "Where were you playing poker with Larry, anyway?"

"Tucson—and for the first time in my life, I walked away broke, except for owning this place." Another shudder chased down my spine and made me wonder if all the previous owners of the café had bad luck or if it was just Larry. "Are you trying to scare me, or are there really lots of scorpions in this part of the state? And why is the dining room suddenly quiet? What's going on?"

Rosalie refilled her coffee mug. "We will be slow until closer to lunchtime, when the next bus comes through here. Matilda—that's the former owner, the one before Larry—said that in the beginning of days here at the Tumbleweed, it was really a bus stop. One where folks could get a ticket to go west toward El Paso or east to Dallas, but that ended years ago. And yes, I am serious about the scorpions, and the lizards that manage to sneak into both the café and the house. Not to mention the snakes that come out to pester us in the spring."

Mice, roaches, and spiders were the only things I hated worse than bugs and snakes. Lizards could possibly land on the list if I didn't make enough money in the next six months to get out of this godforsaken place. I didn't care if it did have a church fifteen miles up the road.

"Do buses come through every day?"

"Twice a day," Rosalie answered. "Once in the morning for the breakfast rush and then around noon. The rest of the time, we only see a few folks from the RV park, or maybe a traveler who stops on their way across this part of the state."

The bell above the door jingled, and Scarlett's voice drifted back to the kitchen. "Good mornin', Miz Ada Lou. How are things at the RV park?"

"Cold and it's spittin' snow, but the weatherman says that the sun will come out tomorrow, so I'm not worried." The voice belonged to an elderly woman. "I'll have my usual brunch."

"Coffee coming right up," Scarlett said. "And we'll have those pancakes and sausage out soon."

I stood up and peeked out the window into the dining area. Miz Ada Lou was a wisp-thin little lady with a bright-red streak in her chin-length gray hair.

"That's our regular customer," Rosalie said as she went to the grill and poured out batter for three pancakes. "She's here every morning after the bus crew leaves, and has pancakes, sausage, and coffee."

"Is the café ever closed?" Seven days a week did not sound good—but then, that would bring in more money, which meant I could possibly leave the place sooner.

"No, but we are only open for breakfast and lunch. We're usually done with everything by three o'clock," Rosalie told me. "Have you ever worked in a diner?"

"When I was sixteen, I waited tables for a few months." Not a happy memory.

Frank had remarried that year. *He'd* decided we were both giving up our gambling. He was serious. I was not. He landed a job as a bank teller. Paula, his new wife, put me on the payroll at her café. I worked after school and on Saturdays. That didn't leave much time for making friends—but then, the heart doesn't miss what it never knew. Which was another of Frank's sayings. I never told her or Frank that I earned less as a waitress and cleanup girl than I did playing poker every day during lunch hour at school.

Rosalie flipped the pancakes over. "Ever done any cooking?"

"No, ma'am."

"What do you intend to do as the new owner?"

I polished off the last bite of pancakes and carried my plate, silverware, and mug to the sink. This place was only about a quarter the size of my stepmother's café, and didn't have the dish pit or the commercial-size dishwasher that she had. "Whatever you tell me to do."

"Then you can take this food out to Miz Ada Lou and help Scarlett clean off all the tables from the bus run. She would have had it done, but I called her back here to meet you. And if you were serious about not selling this place, you can take down that sign from the window."

Chapter Two

"Miz Ada Lou, I want you to meet Carla Wilson, the new owner of the Tumbleweed," Scarlett said as they approached the table. Then Scarlett hurried off to the back to pick up an order.

Ada Lou drew down her well-plucked eyebrows and stared at my face for a few seconds, then scanned me all the way to my toes. "You don't look like you have enough money to buy a setting hen, much less enough to shovel out for this place. How old are you, anyway? I'd say mid-twenties, but your skin might have held up better than mine and you're in your forties."

"I'm thirty years old, and I won the place in a poker game up in Tucson yesterday."

Ada Lou pushed the red streak back behind her ear and grinned. "That's good enough for Larry. That sorry sucker was only interested in what was left in the safe every Monday afternoon. That's the only day he showed up here. If he used the deed to this place in a poker game, that means he's probably gone through everything that Matilda worked so hard to build up."

"Who is Matilda?" I asked as I cleaned off a nearby table. The food had given me enough energy to keep my eyes open, but I would have loved to curl up in a corner and sleep until sometime the next day.

"She was Larry's great-aunt. Since he was the only living relative she had, she left the Tumbleweed to him in hopes that it would give him some purpose in life—he never could hold his liquor, and he wasn't any good at poker," Miz Ada Lou answered.

"Order up!" Rosalie called from the service window.

"He walked away with a pretty good amount in Tucson," I said. "He had a half-decent poker face—but then again, he might have been slack-jawed from all the Knob Creek whiskey he kept drinking."

"You are right," Ada Lou said with a nod. "Reading him was like trying to figure out what a chicken was thinking. The only thing that lit up his eyes was a woman in a short skirt, or money."

I didn't say that I had read him very well and that was the reason I owned the place. I also didn't say that I was trying to figure out whether I was experiencing a waking nightmare.

"Nice to meet you, Miz Ada Lou." I picked up a bar rag and went back to my job. "I better get busy busing these tables, or Rosalie won't cook for me again."

"An owner that works like Matilda did," Ada Lou said with another nod. "You might find a home here."

*Maybe for six months, but not a single day longer than that. I'm a gambler, not a waitress or even a busboy—or is it bus*person *these days?* I loaded dirty dishes and glasses into a bin and wondered where Larry was today. Had he already gambled away everything he had won, including my last five hundred dollars, with that final hand? Or had he turned it into enough to get into a high-stakes game in Vegas?

"Well?" Miz Ada Lou barked.

"What?" I asked.

"Are you going to sell this place or gamble away every dime like Larry did? Gambling is an addiction and will ruin your life." Her voice had an edge to it.

"That's getting really personal, and I only just met you," I shot back as Scarlett brought her order and set it on the table.

"Decisions can be made in a second, and it's a long drive from Tucson to here. You've had a lot of time to think."

"Yes, I did, but I've only been here an hour. We never know what the future might hold. When I sat down at that poker table last night, my plan was to be checked into a hotel in Vegas by tonight, and look where I am."

Ada Lou took a sip of her coffee. "If anyone would have told me that I'd be living in an RV park in the middle of nowhere when I retired, I would have thought they had lost all their marbles, but here I am. Fate throws us some curveballs, doesn't it?"

So does Lady Luck.

"Yes, ma'am, it does. Enjoy your brunch."

Her whisper traveled across the room as I headed for the kitchen: "She won't be around long."

"At least she's willing to help while she's here. Larry never lifted a finger except to carry out the money Rosie and I made all week," Scarlett said. "Maybe you can work some of your magic on her like you did on me."

"Might be a waste of time," Ada Lou said. "But since she's helping y'all, I'll think about it."

"What else have you got to do?" Scarlett pressed.

"It takes time and patience for miracles or magic to get a hold on a person. You know that, so don't expect anything in a hurry," she said.

With a bin of dirty dishes in my hands, I changed my course and walked across the dining room to the window. I set the bin on a nearby table, picked up the For Sale sign, and tossed it into the trash can. Selling the place wasn't an option right then—not when there was less money in my pocket than the nickels, dimes, and quarters I'd won from Frank when I was just a kid.

I can always buy or make a new sign, and I need these women to trust me if we're going to work together until I can unload this place.

Rosalie didn't even look up when the swinging doors squeaked. She just kept peeling potatoes. "Rinse the dirty dishes and then load the dishwasher. We'll probably run it three times before the lunch run begins."

"Do you and Scarlett live in that town up north that you mentioned?"

"No, we live in the trailer out back of the Tumbleweed," she answered without glancing at me. "Larry didn't stay here very often, but when he did"—she nodded toward a door to the right of the sinks—"he slept in the storage room on a futon." She finally looked up at me. "The trailer has three bedrooms. Larry cleaned everything out of Matilda's old room, so you can use it. We share one bathroom and the living area."

"Is there a bed?"

"Nothing fancy. Just a regular-sized one, same as me and Scarlett have."

"That will do just fine." King-sized beds with soft sheets and big pillows were my favorite, but hey, when the sun came up that morning, I was planning to sleep in my car or on top of a table in an empty building. Suddenly, I had a job, a roof over my head, and all the good food I could put away. Maybe Lady Luck had felt sorry for me and thrown me a bone or two.

"That sounds great. What time do we close?"

"We get a breakfast rush when the first bus comes through from the west. Most of the folks on that one are coming from Vegas, where they've gone to gamble." She rolled her eyes toward the ceiling and muttered something.

Tears formed in my eyes at the thought of all the poker tables I had sat at in that city. It would be months before I could go back. Maybe even a whole year.

"Usually, both buses have gone on their way by two o'clock. We lock the door, clean up the place, and go out to the trailer until five o'clock the next morning, when it starts all over again."

"Do you ever get bored?" I finished loading the dishwasher.

Is this my life until I can sell this place?

You have no right to bitch, the voice in my head argued. *Your choices brought you here, and now you have to pay the piper.*

"Would you please show me how to start this thing?" I asked with a sigh. "I'm a fast learner and promise I won't ask again."

She crossed the room, turned a knob, and then pushed it in. "That's all there is to it. And to answer your question: No, I do not get bored. I'm just thankful to be alive and have a job."

That seemed like a strange answer, but if that was the way she felt, then I wasn't going to pressure her to say more. I carried an empty bin back out to the dining area, where Scarlett was sitting at Ada Lou's table. They were deep in conversation, so low I couldn't understand a word they were saying. It felt like those first days when I'd attended public school after Frank remarried. The popular girls had all huddled up and whispered. I had held my head high and ignored them, but it stung when they rolled their eyes and giggled. That was their choice. Mine was taking all their boyfriends' money so they couldn't go out with them over the weekend.

Rosalie had told me to help Scarlett, not to do the work while she visited with a customer. I owned the place and she was the help, so why was she having a mean-girl conversation with Ada Lou while I dealt with dirty dishes and nasty, cold leftovers?

Get off your high horse. Earlier today, you were flat broke.

I started to argue with the voice in my head. Then I remembered that if I'd listened to what it had to say before I checked into that seedy little motel in Tucson, I wouldn't be at this place anyway.

"Nice meeting you, Clara," Ada Lou said as she stood up and left a couple of dollars on the table for a tip.

"My pleasure—but it's Carla," I said, raising my voice.

"For my age, getting it close is good enough." She winked and went out the door.

A few seconds later, the sound of a motorcycle engine revving up filled the whole place. Expecting to see a biker, I looked out the window, and there was Ada Lou, sitting astride a big Harley with a helmet covering her gray hair. She threw up her hand and waved when she caught my eye.

"Surprised?" Scarlett asked.

"Yep."

"I was, too, the first time she rode up to the café on that thing. She has a pickup truck and brings it down here to fill up with gas when she goes to El Paso for supplies about once a month. But if the weather is nice, she rides the cycle," Scarlett explained.

I covered a yawn with my hand. Three o'clock couldn't come fast enough. "She looked like an old biker chick on that thing."

"She really is an old hippie. She even went to Woodstock back in the day. I've been to her trailer many times."

"For what?" I asked.

"To watch movies, play board games, and just to visit. She should have been a therapist."

"What kind of movies and board games?" Something about an old hippie woman who rode a Harley piqued my interest.

Scarlett shrugged. "All kinds of both. She doesn't like action movies but loves 'chick flicks,' as she calls them. When I first got here, she took me under her wing, and we watched lots of movies—especially on Sunday afternoons. Oh, and the bike's name is Hilda."

"Why did she name it that?"

"That's her story to tell," Scarlett answered.

I stopped what I was doing and sniffed the air. "What is Rosie cooking? It smells delicious."

"Don't you know? This is New Year's Day," Scarlett answered.

"What does that have to do with anything?"

"Well, what do you eat *then*?" she asked.

"Frank only had one tradition on New Year's. We never gambled until one minute past midnight."

"Why? And who is Frank?"

"Because superstition had it that whatever a person did on New Year's Day, they would do all year. He said if we lost, then we would be losers," I answered. "And he's the man who taught me to play poker."

"But what if you won?" Scarlett asked.

"He didn't allow us to tempt fate. I did when I played poker in Tucson. I should have walked away a few minutes before midnight."

She finished loading her bin and headed for the kitchen. "But what if you just *think* you lost? What if you really won?"

I cut my eyes around at the café, or diner, or bus stop—whatever it was called. Could she be right?

"Rosie is making ham, black-eyed peas, collard greens, cheesy potatoes, and lazy-daisy oatmeal cake," Scarlett answered. "That's the special lunch on New Year's Day. I never did like greens until I tasted how Rosie fixes them. She seasons them up real good with bacon. I just hope there's lots of leftovers."

"Why?"

"Because when we close up each day, we take them home for supper."

"Do you really think there will be that many customers on a holiday?" I asked.

"Always has been," she answered. "That second bus, the one on the way to El Paso, Vegas, and points west. They will be excited about maybe winning money or having already done so," she explained. "So, to answer your question, it will be a madhouse for a couple of hours. I'll be glad to have some help."

So, I am *the help, not the boss?*

"Did Martha ever hire more than just you and Rosalie?"

"Matilda, not Martha—and no, she didn't," she said. "Not in my day, but I understand there was a woman that worked here for a few years before I came to the Tumbleweed."

"I'm sorry that I called her by the wrong name, but I'm tired and sleepy. How old was Matilda, and what happened to the other woman?"

"She was eighty-eight when she passed away a year ago. Rosie and I are still in shock. She went to sleep and didn't wake up."

"In the room where I'll be sleeping?" I whispered.

"Do you believe in ghosts or something?" Scarlett asked.

"I don't know, but that sounds a little creepy." I thought about the futon in the storage room. My stuff didn't take up a lot of space.

"If you happen to see Matilda's ghost, call me. There are questions I want answers to," Scarlett said.

The futon was sounding better by the minute.

"Rosie said that the lady before me had moved somewhere on the East Coast," Scarlett continued, changing the subject. "I wouldn't ever want to live where it gets cold or where I'd have to shovel snow again."

My sixth sense shot into the red zone. With her big innocent eyes and love for conversation, Scarlett seemed like an open book, but there was something that had caused her to snap her mouth shut and abruptly talk about something else. That interested me even more than Ada Lou and her motorcycle.

"So, you come from a cold place?" I asked, glad not to have to think about sleeping where Larry the goat-man had—or in a bed where a woman had died, either one.

"Rosie and I don't talk much about the past," she answered. "We're just glad for the present and hope for the future."

That piqued my interest for sure, but there was plenty of time to go into stories of the past. "Rosalie or Rosie?"

"It's Rosalie until she gives you permission to call her Rosie. You have to earn her trust. It took six months for me to get to do that. Larry never did."

"How long have you been here?" I asked.

"Five years. Since I was nineteen. Matilda saved me," she answered, and then pointed at the window. "There's Jackson Armstrong pulling his truck up to the gas pumps."

The abrupt way she changed the subject again and the pain in her eyes told me not to ask any more questions. Figuring out this new lifestyle wasn't going to be easy, but on the flip side, I did have a room to sleep in at the end of the workday, even if Matilda had died there. And I could spend my time trying to figure out the mystery of why Scarlett and Rosalie didn't want to talk about their pasts.

Lord knows I sure don't want to, either.

"Hey, Scarlett!" a guy yelled as he came through the door. "Can you rustle me up a double bacon burger and some fries?"

"I sure can." She moved over to the service window and raised her voice: "Rosie, Jackson wants his usual."

"Coming right up," Rosie shouted back.

He removed his coat and hung it on the back of a barstool. The tattoo on his upper arm of a knife with the words *De Oppresso Liber* wrapped around it told me he had been in Special Forces. That little four-inch dark-brown ponytail said it had been a while since he was discharged. His eyes were the same color as the army-green T-shirt that stretched across his biceps and didn't leave any doubt about his strength.

"What can I get you to drink?" I asked.

"Sweet tea, and keep the pitcher handy," he answered. "How long have you been working here?"

"This is my first day."

"Have we met before? I never forget a pretty face, but names are a different matter." His green eyes twinkled. Was he flirting?

I set a glass of iced tea in front of him. "My name is Carla Wilson, and unless you've played poker, I don't think we've met."

"So, you were a gambler in your past life?"

"Who said it was past?"

He chuckled. "I can't imagine Rosie letting any backroom poker games go on here at the Tumbleweed."

"I'll keep that in mind." I wondered what he had done to earn her trust. If it took being in the military, then I would just call her Rosalie for as long as I owned the place. But . . . there was another tidbit to file about the people I would be working with until I squirreled away enough money for my next trip to Vegas. Or maybe I would bypass that place and go on out to Los Angeles.

"Where are you headed today?" Scarlett asked.

"Up close to New Mexico," he answered, "but I'll see y'all in a few days. Right now, my crew is staying in Carlsbad until we can get moved into the area. I can't survive without one of Rosie's burgers for very long."

A bell sounded and Scarlett hurried over to the window, picked up the red plastic basket, and set it before Jackson. "There you go. Enjoy."

"I always do," Jackson said and popped a french fry into his mouth.

I grabbed a bar rag and a spray bottle of cleaner and set about wiping down the tables and chairs. When I'd finished that, I swept the floor. Like folks say about riding a bicycle, even if a person doesn't get on one for years, it all comes back to them—the same with restaurant work. Other than cooking, I knew the business; Frank's new wife, Paula, had drilled that into my head. I could almost hear her growling at me to sweep the floor again because she found a single breadcrumb under a chair.

I set the broom and dustpan behind the bar and refilled Jackson's tea glass. "So, how do you like civilian life?"

"How did you know I was in the military?" he asked.

She pointed to the tat. "By that."

He smiled and nodded. "Guess it's a giveaway, isn't it? I don't like it as well as the military, but I promised my dad I would give it a try. His oil company has a place for me, so I don't have to make up my mind for a few months," he answered as he finished off his food. "Can I get a sweet tea to go?"

"Of course."

Scarlett came from the back, handed him the ticket, and turned to me. "You know how to run a register?"

"No, but I'm a fast learner."

I watched carefully as she hit a few keys and the drawer opened.

Jackson handed her a couple of bills and said, "Keep the change, but I do need a receipt."

"Here you go—and thanks." Scarlett closed the drawer with a smile.

"See y'all next week." He slipped on his light-tan suede jacket and picked up the to-go cup of tea. "Stay warm, and don't let the tumbleweeds cover up the diner."

"We'll do our best," Scarlett said.

"Nice meeting you, Miz Carla," he said.

"Glad to make your acquaintance. Come back to see us," I said, amazed that I sounded a little breathy.

He hunched his broad shoulders against the cold on the way out the door. I made my way over to the booth beside the window and caught a glance of his truck pulling out onto the highway.

"He fueled up before he came in," Scarlett teased.

"Not interested."

"Then you are cold as ice inside," she said.

The thing that warms me up is a good poker game.

I cut my eyes around at Scarlett. "Why don't *you* flirt with him?"

"One." She held up a finger. "I do not date pretty guys. Two." Another finger went up. "I have a boyfriend in Dell City. And three." Her ring finger shot up. "He's too old for me. I don't even flirt with a man that's more than two years older than I am. Jackson is thirty-eight and did twenty years in the military. Every time I look at his pretty green eyes and that sexy body, I remember that I was only four years old when he enlisted."

I thought back to where I was twenty years before. At the age of ten, I was traveling all over the country with Frank so he could gamble. He said he was homeschooling me, and I had the books and took the online tests to pass each grade. But dear old Frank did little to nothing to help me from the time I was eight and my mother died. At eighteen I took and passed my GED test. By that time, I had been using my phony ID and living on my own for two years.

We barely had time to sit down and have a quick bite of lunch before the rush hit us. Scarlett had not stretched the truth one iota. The Greyhound bus pulled into the parking lot a few minutes before noon, and people of all ages piled out of it. Some had the look of winners at the slot machines or card tables. Others had a hangdog expression that said they were going home broke. Still more were families, most likely going home to Dallas after visiting relatives over the holidays. I had seen both kinds on my travels with Frank, and then again when I went out on my own. Some of the new customers stopped long enough to read the day's special written on the blackboard inside the door, but most of them headed toward the bathrooms.

"I'll take care of the tables, and you do the bar and payouts." Scarlett handed me an order pad. "Write down the barstool number when you take their order and then pin it on the thing over there." She pointed at a carousel in the service window. "Rosie is really fast at turning out orders, and she'll set them on the shelf right there. It's going to be hectic for a little while. We'll have to keep on our toes to get the tables cleared before the next busload hits us. I'm always glad when they don't pull in at the same time."

I picked up an apron from a hook behind the bar, tied it around my waist, and slipped the order pad into my pocket. Six elderly ladies had each claimed a barstool with much grumbling as they settled, so I had a full house right off the bat.

"Good afternoon, what can I get you to drink?" I asked.

"We'll have sweet tea," the one at the far end answered. "Put it all on one ticket. I am treating."

I turned around and started filling six tall glasses with ice and tea—close enough that I could hear every word that was said.

The one sitting to her left gave her a sideways hug. "Thank you for this, Linda. That's so nice of you to pay for our dinner."

"You are welcome, Ellen Mae," she said. "I'm telling the assisted-care place that I only won twenty dollars more than what I took with me."

"Shame on you," the one next to her said.

"Don't judge me, Myra," Linda snapped. "You have more money than God, so you don't have to worry about whether you'll have enough to go on the next trip."

"As long as you go to confession on Sunday and do your penance, everything will be fine," Myra said.

I set a glass of tea in front of each of them. "Y'all ready to order?"

Myra brushed an imaginary bit of dust from her rhinestone-studded jacket. "I'll have the special, and Myra, I'll go with you on Sunday. I lusted after that sexy young waiter at the last place we ate."

"If we have to repent for that, then we'd best all go to confession," Ellen Mae chuckled. "The special for me, too."

"Well!" another lady huffed. "I would have done more than lust if I could remember what to do if I did sweet-talk him up to my room. And as far as Linda goes, she did win twenty more than she took with her, so she's not lying. They don't need to know about the two thousand above that. She's already offered to pick up the ticket for our meal, so she's putting the money to good use."

"Thank you for standing up for me, Gloria," Linda said. "Whatever I've got left over will go in my piggy bank for our next trip to Vegas. And I'll have the special also."

I bit back a smile when the rest of the ladies ordered the same thing. I wrote out the orders on tickets and hung them on the carousel. Miz Linda was smart for squirreling away her winnings. I knew that because I had learned to hide a portion of my own winnings rather than giving everything to ol' Frank. He was a decent player, but not great. After he'd bought my first fake ID, I won most of what we had to live on.

"I'm so glad y'all are serving the traditional New Year's meal today," Myra said. "Hopefully, eating our greens will bring us good luck next time we go to Vegas."

"That would be wonderful. What do you like to play? Slots, cards?" I could hear the wistfulness in my own voice.

"I hit the slots, but Linda is pretty good at blackjack," Ellen Mae said. "I came away with a fifty-dollar profit after my bus ticket and hotel was paid for, so it was a good trip."

"And we got to see the fireworks, didn't we, Stella?" Linda asked.

That was five of their names, but I didn't need to remember them any more than any of the folks who had sat around a poker table with me. In an hour or so, these sweet old gals would be gone and another group would sit on the barstools.

"It was beautiful," she answered. "I hate to go back to the center, but at least we all get to live in the same place, and we can talk about the fun we had until we start planning the next trip."

"Order up!" Rosalie called.

I shifted plates from the shelf to the bar. "Y'all been friends long?"

"Since we were in kindergarten," Ellen Mae answered. "We have done crazy things, all got married within two years, and even had a bra-burning one night."

Myra patted Linda on the shoulder. "We were all drunk, or we might not have thrown every single one that we owned into the bonfire."

"I was not drunk," Linda protested. "Maybe a little tipsy, but I had to be semi-sober to drive all y'all home."

"You were drunk as a skunk," Ellen Mae argued. "If you hadn't been, you wouldn't have gone to bed with that good-looking soldier."

"My sorry-ass husband cheated on me first," Linda declared.

I was almost green with envy. Friends were a luxury I had never had before in my life. Folks needed to put down roots to make lasting friends. From trailing along with Frank all those years and then striking out on my own, I had never stayed in one place more than a couple of days.

When the café was empty, Scarlett brought a fistful of bills to the bar and shoved them into a small wooden box under the counter. "We put all our tips in the box and split them three ways each evening."

Pulling my last ten-dollar tip out of my pocket and putting it in the box with all the rest of the day's tips was the hardest thing I had done in a very long time.

Chapter Three

When the day finally ended at three thirty, my butt was dragging so badly that we didn't really need to sweep the floor. I had been awake for more than thirty hours, and it would be a while longer before I could fall into a heap in my new bedroom.

Rosalie cleaned the kitchen. Scarlett set the chairs up onto the tables and swept. I came in behind her with a mop. When we'd finished, the whole place smelled like lemon cleaner, probably the same type of stuff that Paula used. At least Rosalie didn't grab a pair of disposable white cotton gloves and go over every surface and corner like Paula had done. I could handle Rosalie making the sign of the cross and looking up toward the ceiling to pray. But I would have drawn the line if she insisted that I drop down on my knees in front of a chair and listen while she thanked God—loudly—for giving her a good day at her café. After all, I was the owner of the Tumbleweed, even if Rosalie was the boss.

Scarlett took the tip box to the kitchen and dumped it on the table.

Rosalie counted the money, split it three ways, and then glanced at me. "You want to put your share in the safe each evening like I do, or keep it with you like Scarlett does?"

"I'd rather keep it with me," I answered.

She handed Scarlett and me our shares. I tucked my two hundred dollars and forty-two cents into a zippered side pocket on my purse and slung it over my shoulder.

Scarlett crammed her money into her small purse and picked up a paper sack from the table. "These are leftovers for our supper tonight. We only have time to grab a quick bite at noon, but Rosie always makes plenty so we can eat our big meal of the day in the evening."

Breakfast had always been my big meal, usually at one of those waffle places that stayed open twenty-four hours. Lunch was a burger or chicken strips on the road. Supper had been a bag of chips from a hotel vending machine and maybe a fistful of peanuts at the poker table. But I could adjust to this new schedule very well.

We went through a small room with a futon on one side and shelves loaded with supplies on the other. At the far end, I could see a bathroom with a tiny shower, a potty, and a wall-hung sink. They were all sage green, like the ones in the house where I'd lived with Mama.

Bright sunlight flowed into the building when Rosalie opened the next door. I shaded my eyes with my hand and blinked several times.

"Happens every time," Rosalie said.

"What?" I asked.

"How much we fight it when the darkness is replaced by light," she answered.

Was she telling me that my poker playing was dark and that I had walked into the light that morning when I'd arrived at the Tumbleweed? Or was she angling for me to ask questions so she could deliver a sermon to me? Frank used to tell me not to ask a question if I didn't want to know the answer. Something told me that if I swore out loud, Rosalie would preach at me, and I was too tired to do anything other than take a shower and fall into bed, so I didn't ask her what she meant.

Scarlett must have thought the look on my face was because of the older pickup truck and the compact car parked in the space between the store and café, because she said, "The truck belongs to Rosie. The car is mine."

"My SUV is in the parking lot," I said.

"I didn't think you rode in on a bus." Scarlett walked three steps up to the tiny porch in front of an aqua-colored trailer. I was so tired that I didn't even flinch when a lizard crawled across the porch.

Scarlett used the toe of her shoe to send the critter flying out into what passed for the front yard but was more like another small gravel parking lot. No picket fence or rosebushes—even though they would have been dead at that time of year—or a pet of any kind to greet us, unless that had been a pet lizard. Nothing to remind me of Paula's house, with all the flower beds and her two big yellow dogs that ran out to meet us when we came home in the evenings. So why did a vision of them flash across my mind?

Rosalie covered a yawn with her hand. "I'm ready for a nap, and when I wake up, I'll be starving. If either of you get up before I do, don't eat all the corn bread."

"No promises," Scarlett chuckled and opened the front door.

In all my thirty years, I could never remember being inside a trailer house, and I was surprised to see how cozy and compact it was. I was standing in an open area with a short bar separating the tiny kitchen from the living room. A sofa with a recliner on each end was to my right. To the left, past the kitchen, was a long hallway.

Rosalie removed her coat and hung it on one of the wall hooks. "We take turns at taking a shower after work each day. Since you look like a warmed-over sin on a Sunday morning, you can have the first shower. But even if you own all this, you'll have to be last tomorrow."

"Yes, ma'am, but you sure are bossy."

Scarlett laughed as she finished taking containers out of the paper bag and stacking them in the refrigerator. "She says that what she does is advising and she does it out of love."

"That's right, and don't either of you forget it." Rosalie shifted her stone-cold gaze from Scarlett to me. "Your bedroom is at the end of the hall. The bathroom is the last door on the right. You'll pass the washer and dryer on the way. We are all responsible for our own laundry and for ordering the detergent we like. There's some of those pod things that

Matilda used still on the shelf. They should last until Monday, when the supply guy comes by the café. You'll need to write down what you want, because you'll leave for Sierra Blanca right after the lunch run."

"Why am I going there?" I asked.

"To set up bank accounts for the business," Rosalie answered. "Matilda kept her money in Sierra Blanca, but when she died and the will was read, Larry moved it all to El Paso. And yes, Carla, I am bossy. Matilda left me in charge. She hoped that Larry would learn the business and I could help him straighten up his act. She would turn over in her grave if she knew what he had done this past year. Going through every dime she had saved, to the point that we are on the verge of bankruptcy. You are the owner of the place, so on Monday you will go to the bank, start an account, and then go file that deed at the courthouse so that everything is legal. You might even want to put a copy of it in a safe deposit box. It's fifty miles down there, and the bank closes at four. Leaving when the last bus pulls away will give you plenty of time to take care of everything."

Dealing with accounts was something else I would have to learn, but that would come on Monday. Frank and I dealt in prepaid credit cards that we could pick up at any bank. Those were only for hotel rooms. Everything else was cold, hard cash—until Paula came along, of course.

I suddenly felt a kinship with the place. Both of us needed some cash flow to keep doing what we wanted to do. "Why is the café in financial trouble?"

Rosalie yawned again. "Larry would come through on Monday and empty out the safe. If I hadn't hid enough money for paychecks and to pay for our deliveries, we would have folded months ago. He let the insurance lapse, so if a tornado ripped the roof off or we had a pipe burst, we would have to pay out of pocket. Only, there was no pocket."

"Then I guess the first week's profit will go to buy a new insurance policy, right?"

"That would be a great idea. We'll look into that after my nap," she answered.

"We'll give you our paychecks to put into our accounts while you are there," Scarlett said.

"Did you do that with Larry?"

"Oh, no! After he moved all of Matilda's affairs to El Paso, he never went back to Sierra Blanca. Besides, we didn't trust him. One of us drove down to Sierra Blanca every two or three weeks to make a deposit."

"Can I buy detergent or whatever I need at a Walmart there?"

"Nope," Scarlett answered. "We try to get whatever we need from the delivery truck that comes every week. If you want a Walmart, you go to El Paso. Sierra Blanca is about the same size as Dell City. The difference is that it's the county seat and has a bank."

"I'm really out in the boonies," I groaned.

Rosalie nodded and sank down into one of the recliners. "Yep, and it could be where you need to be if you give it a chance. I don't know you, but you seem like a good person. Go get your shower. I'm next in line, and I need my afternoon nap."

"Yes, ma'am."

A memory of something my granddad said once popped into my head when I opened the door into the tiny bathroom. I was seven and he was dying when we'd gone to the hospital to visit him. He winked at me and said that the room they had him in was so small that he couldn't cuss a cat without getting a hair in his mouth. He and my grandmother both died six months before my mama did. And then it was just me and Frank.

The trailer might have been as old as the café, because the bathroom was almost entirely pink. I wouldn't have cared if they were turtle-poop green that afternoon. Everything was spotless, and I didn't see a single roach or spider. On the trip from Tucson, I had hoped the utilities would be turned on so that I would have lights and water to wash up in the public bathroom. To have a place to live and plenty of food was pure luxury. I adjusted the water temperature and had one foot in the tub before I realized I wasn't naked.

I quickly pulled my foot back and stripped out of my stained jeans and T-shirt. "I don't care about supper. I'm sleeping until it's time to go to work in the morning."

Even though it was winter and cold outside, I'd sweated so much during the day that my silk panties were stuck to me like they'd been rolled in maple syrup. The warm water beating down on my aching muscles was downright glorious. I leaned against the wall, closed my eyes, and dozed off. The next thing I knew, I was sliding down the wall. In a knee-jerk reaction, I straightened up, knocking over two bottles of shampoo sitting on the edge of the tub. I washed my hair and hoped I wouldn't break any rules by using it. My own toiletries were still in my SUV, and there was no way I was going to get dressed back in my dirty clothing and go get them.

The towels stacked on a rack above the potty weren't as fluffy or as big as the fancy monogrammed ones in the hotels, but they were a helluva lot better than those in the cheap motels that Frank and I stayed in during slow weeks. With a towel wrapped turban-style around my blond hair and another around my body, I picked up my dirty clothing and headed down the hallway.

That was when it dawned on me that everything else was in my suitcases. I didn't have clean underwear or a nightshirt. I had two choices: sleep naked or put my dirty clothing back on.

Naked it is, I thought as I put everything I was holding into the washer, took a chance on what water temperature and cycle to use, and tossed in one of the pods.

"That all the clothing you have?" Rosalie asked.

"No, but I'm too tired to walk back outside to bring in my suitcases."

"Toss me your keys, and I'll drive your vehicle around here and bring in your stuff," Scarlett said.

"They are in my purse on the counter—and thank you. I owe you one."

"And I will collect," Scarlett said with a grin.

Hours seemed to pass, but in reality, she rolled my two suitcases into the trailer in only a few minutes. "I noticed your gas tank was setting on empty, so I filled it up before I drove it around. Is this all you have?"

"Yes, other than a small lockbox, but it's empty, so there's no need to go back outside." I rolled the suitcases down the narrow hallway and into a room even smaller than the cheap hotel I'd left behind less than twenty-four hours ago. How could my life have done a 180-degree turn so fast in such a short time?

Because you ignored Lady Luck, the pesky voice in my head whispered as I dropped the towels and dug through my larger suitcase to find a pair of underwear and a nightshirt. I pulled back the chenille bedspread and crawled beneath the cold sheets. There was no need to argue. Lady Luck was right: I should have listened.

Other than the light from a sliver of moon peeking through the slats of the window blinds, the room was dark when I opened my eyes. I'd lived in hotel rooms for more than a decade, so disorientation wasn't anything new. Footsteps right outside in the hallway made me sit up and throw back the covers. Then I remembered where I was and fell back on the pillows.

Rattling noises in the kitchen and the smell of coffee wafting under the bedroom door brought me out of bed. Yesterday was New Year's Day. I hoped the superstition Frank had taught me was wrong and that I wouldn't be working in a café for the whole year.

I dressed in a clean pair of jeans, a T-shirt printed with the title of one of my favorite songs, "Brenda Put Your Bra On," and my only pair of athletic shoes. Then I changed the shirt to one that had a happy face on it. I didn't want to suffer the stinging wrath of Rosalie if I came out wearing something with a red bra on the front.

I made a stop by the bathroom and then went on down the hall to find the front part of the trailer empty. I poured a cup of coffee and heated the last of the black-eyed peas and a piece of corn bread in the microwave.

"Good morning," Rosalie said as she came into the kitchen. "You must have been tired. You slept right through the afternoon and on through the night. Got to admit, you look a little better than you did yesterday. Your hair will have to be put up in a ponytail or twisted up like you had it yesterday. If an inspector dropped by, we would be in trouble. We've never had a complaint about a hair in the food, and we aren't starting now."

"Thank you. Sleep did me a world of good. Who made the coffee?" Five o'clock in the morning was the time that I usually went to my room and slept until I had to check out of the hotel.

Scarlett poured two mugs of coffee and handed one to Rosalie. "Rosie gets up every morning and makes coffee. We need it to wake up before we start the day. I truly believe that Matilda's spirit didn't go straight to heaven, but she left behind the bossy part for Rosie."

Rosalie took a sip of coffee. "Be grateful for that. She knew you would need someone like me in your life, and it looks like Carla might need some direction, too. God has put her in the middle of nowhere so she can kick her gambling addiction."

Addiction? I'm not addicted to anything—not drugs, liquor, sex, or even cigarettes. And who says I would want to give it up anyway if I was addicted? Dammit! I haven't even been here a whole day yet, so don't be preachin' at me or making plans for my life.

Rosie shook her finger at me. "Don't look at me that way. I know an obsession when I see it."

"My gambling is a job. I do not use drugs. I do not smoke. I only have a shot of whiskey to celebrate winning," I argued.

"That's good to know, but I smelled smoke on you when you got to the Tumbleweed yesterday morning," she fired back.

"Secondhand. Smoke hung in the air like fog at the place where I was playing poker the night before."

"You better be telling her the truth," Scarlett warned. "She will quit and move away if there's liquor, cigarettes, or drugs ever found on either of us. And she does not tolerate swearing, especially the f-bomb or using the Lord's name in vain."

"What about sex?" If I had to give up poker, I might resort to sex.

"What about it?" Scarlett asked.

"If I have a one-night stand or leave for a weekend romp, will she leave?"

I was halfway teasing but mostly serious. I was not a virgin, but my previous encounters had been one-night stands or, in a few cases, had lasted for a weekend.

"Those were Matilda's rules from the get-go, and I mean to keep them in force," Rosalie said. "Now, that's enough talk for one morning, especially about sex, which should be reserved for a man and woman behind locked bedroom doors after they are married. It's time to go to work. Maybe we'll do as well on tips today as we did yesterday."

I finished off the last bite of my leftovers and headed back to my room to get a hoodie from my suitcase. On the way, I noticed that what I had put in the washer the night before had been dried and was now lying on top of the dryer. I gathered it all up, tossed it on the bed, and took time to put my denim coat in the washing machine before I followed Scarlett out of the trailer.

"Thanks for helping with my laundry."

"That was Rosalie, not me," Scarlett said. "She's tough, but if you give her a chance, she can be the best friend you'll ever have."

"Are y'all related? What brought you to this godforsaken area?" I asked.

"We are not related by blood, but she is like a surrogate mother to me. And why we came here is a story that we don't tell unless we know you very, very well," she snapped. "And for your information, there is a Catholic church in Dell City where Rosalie goes to Mass at least twice a week, and a Baptist one that I attend for night services on Sunday with my boyfriend, Grady. So this place is not 'godforsaken.'"

She set her full mouth in a firm line and didn't even hold the door for me when she went inside the café's storage room.

"Lesson number one," I muttered. "Do not ask any more questions."

Rosalie slipped a bibbed apron over her head and tied the waist strings behind her back. "You can wait on the tables today, and Scarlett will do the bar and the register."

Anger shot through me like a fiery-hot poker. I had never cheated a single soul out of anything. What I had won had always been fair and square. "Do you think I'll skim money?" My voice had a razor-sharp edge to it.

"It's basically your money, and you'll have to answer to the tax people and God for whatever you do," Rosalie said.

"When I came to the Tumbleweed, I had even less experience than you," Scarlett said. "Matilda made me learn everything from the ground up. I started by cleaning up after the breakfast and lunch runs, then graduated to waiting tables, and finally to taking care of payments. Since you said you had experience and learned the cash register so quick . . ." She paused for a breath. "And looked like you were about to drop from exhaustion, I gave you the bar yesterday."

"She did the same for me in the kitchen. I had been a fry cook before. I learned from the previous cook, who was retiring." Rosalie's voice had softened. "'Baby steps' is what Matilda called it."

"I haven't worked in a café since I was sixteen. A refresher course will be good for me," I agreed. "I'll go get the chairs set up and make sure all the condiment containers are full."

"I'll help with that after I get the money from the safe and set up the register," Scarlett offered. "By the time we get everything in order, Rosie will have breakfast started. I usually have an omelet and biscuits. You need to put your order in now if you want something, or else you'll have to wait until after the rush."

Rosalie was already making biscuit dough in a huge bowl. "You had peas and corn bread at the trailer."

"I slept through last night's supper, so that counts as yesterday's food. I'll have whatever you are making for Scarlett for breakfast, and later, if you are making gravy, I'll have that and biscuits for my midmorning snack."

Rosalie focused on my eyes so intently that I felt like she was seeing right into my soul.

"What?" I asked.

"How do you eat so much and still look like you do?" she asked. "I can gain weight just watching a cooking show on television."

"I have no idea, but I love good food, so I hope I never have a problem." I was glad we were back on better terms. Having a friendly relationship with the two women would be a blessing in case I had to stay a long time.

We had barely finished getting things set up when Rosalie yelled, "Come and get it."

On our way to the kitchen, Scarlett flipped on the light that blinked Open and then went straight to the sink to wash her hands. I followed her example before I sat down in one of the chairs and picked up my fork.

"Grace," Scarlett whispered.

Rosalie had already bowed her head, so I quietly laid my fork down and tucked my chin to my chest. This was surely a whole new lifestyle I had fallen into.

She chanted a quick prayer and then, with a nod, gave us permission to begin. "God has been too good to me these past years for me not to give thanks every time I can. Now, let's eat before the first bus arrives."

"Mmmm," I muttered when I put the first bite in my mouth. "This is the best omelet I've ever eaten, and these biscuits are . . ."

"Heavenly?" Scarlett butted in.

"Yes. What is your secret, Rosalie?"

She slathered butter on the two biscuits lying on her plate. "I bake them with love, and that's all you need to know."

As I was finishing my second cup of coffee and third biscuit stuffed with strawberry jam, we heard the first bus arrive. In minutes, the dining room filled up and there was a line for both bathrooms. I had a soft heart for little kids who were hungry, so I hurried over to the first table, where a young couple and two little boys in their pajamas were sitting. I handed each of them a menu and rattled off the breakfast special.

"What can I get y'all to drink?"

"We'll have two cups of coffee and two glasses of milk," the mother said.

One of the little boys turned around and pointed toward the candy display next to the register. "I want candy and root beer."

"After you eat breakfast, you can have some to eat on the way home," his father said.

His lower lip poked out, and he dropped his chin down to his chest. "Granny let me have candy anytime I wanted it."

They were still arguing while I filled their drink order and headed back to the table. My grandmother had not been that lenient when I was a little girl. I got good, healthy food when Mama and I visited her and Grandpa. She said it would make me live a long life.

I took a tray with the drinks to the table in time to hear the father say, "I'm not arguing with you. The answer is no, so stop asking. This is why we live in Dallas, not in Arizona." He looked across the table at his wife. "Next time we are flying, no matter what the cost."

"If we do, then that will be our only vacation for the year. Do you want that?" she snapped, and then softened her tone when she realized the drinks had arrived. "Thank you for being so prompt. The boys will each have the kid's meal with pancakes and bacon. I want the Full Works breakfast."

"Make that two," the father said.

"How do you want your eggs?" I asked.

"Scrambled," she said.

"Same," he added.

The whiny one crossed his arms over his chest and glared at his father. "I want root beer and candy."

"What you want and what you get are two different things," his mother told him.

Amen to that, I thought as I hurried away to pin the order on the carousel and get their drinks.

Chapter Four

Staying in a new hotel, putting on my good-luck outfit, and sitting down with a new group of poker players was exciting and jacked up my adrenaline levels. And if a late checkout wasn't available, I left at the last-possible minute. Perhaps if Lady Luck had been good to me, I'd keep the room for one more day and play again the second night. Card players had their own set of superstitions, and one of mine was to never play in the same place three nights in a row. If we won two nights, you could bet bad luck would hit on the third. That was what Frank had always said, and I listened—just like I should have in Tucson.

On the third day at the Tumbleweed, my energy was completely shot. I awoke to the smell of coffee—again. I was in the same room in the same trailer—again. The time on my cell phone was the same as it had been the past two days—again. I groaned like Bill Murray did in that old movie *Groundhog Day*. I crammed the pillow over my head and silently screamed, but that didn't alter a blessed thing. The same day stretched out before me like the previous ones. I couldn't get away from the place until my lockbox had a lot more money in it, so it would be like those shampoo commercials—wash, rinse, repeat.

I could press the pillow down until I smothered myself to death, and nothing would change. Tomorrow would be the exact same. I finally got out of bed, dressed, and made it out of my room in time to follow Rosalie and Scarlett outside into the bitter cold wind sweeping tumbleweeds and leaves across the yard.

"Another day, another dollar," Rosalie said.

"Amen!" Scarlett opened the door into the place.

"Do y'all ever get bored with the same thing every single day?"

"No, of course not," Rosalie answered. "We are all lucky to be here. Hopefully, you will figure out that you are, too, in a few weeks."

Arguing wouldn't make a bit of a difference, so I kept my mouth shut. But I still yearned to have my former lifestyle back. I was already craving a poker game. But the voice—be it Lady Luck, Madam Fate, or the universe scolding me—didn't leave any doubt that the days were going to remain the same for a long time. At this rate, even with the tips, it would take a year for me to save enough money to start again. Even then, I would have to start small and work my way up to a high-stakes game. That would mean more cheap motels and no fancy restaurants.

"What do y'all want for breakfast?" Rosalie asked.

"Biscuits, an over-easy fried egg, and bacon," I answered, in hopes that by varying my breakfast, I would wake up tomorrow in a different place and the box would be so stuffed that the lid wouldn't close.

"My usual," Scarlett said.

Rosalie crossed the room, put on an apron, turned on the oven, and said, "I'll have it ready by the time y'all get the dining room put to rights."

"It's still Groundhog Day," I muttered.

"What?" Scarlett headed toward the safe to get money for the cash register.

"Nothing. I was talking to myself."

Rosalie set the big mixing bowl on the worktable and began making biscuit dough just like she had the day before. "Why are you talking about Groundhog Day? That doesn't come around for another month—and in my opinion, it's a useless holiday. No matter if the groundhog sees his shadow or not, there's still six more weeks of winter."

Two and a half months until spring officially arrives. Will I be able to leave this place by then, or will I still be kicking tumbleweeds out of the way to get to the trailer?

Tomorrow and every day after that, I planned to ask for a different breakfast in the hope that it would help break this boring cycle. I was finishing the last of my coffee when the bell above the door jingled. "I'll get it. Scarlett, you finish eating."

"Thanks," she said without looking up from her food.

"Well, good morning, beautiful," said a big, burly man with a sprinkling of gray shining in his close-cut brown hair. "What is your name, and where have you been all my life?"

"My name is Carla, and I've been lots of places," I answered with my best fake smile. "Have a seat anywhere you like."

He chose the barstool closest to the register. "No need to bring me a menu. Just tell Rosalie that Buddy is here, and she'll know what I want. Iced tea to drink, and if you're not busy, you could sit with me and tell me all about yourself."

The growl of an engine caught my attention. Saved by the bus. I nodded toward the window and hoped that Buddy didn't come in every day. "Sorry, but I don't have time. We'll be swamped in a few minutes."

I pushed through the doors into the kitchen. "Buddy is out there and said you'll know what he wants. Scarlett, you are working at the bar for the breakfast rush. He wants iced tea to drink."

"Spoken like a true boss who is running from a flirty man. Scarlett can handle him," Rosalie said. "But you should steer clear of Buddy. He's got a bad reputation."

"Oh, I know his kind. I'm avoiding him so I don't have to insult the man—or worse yet, do bodily harm to him," I said.

"If you do have to do the latter, we can always get Ada Lou to help us drag him out to the base of the mountain and let the coyotes fight over his carcass." Rosalie's tone didn't have a bit of humor in it.

"That would be one way to kill a whole pack of coyotes," Scarlett whispered.

"What?" I asked.

"A man like him would poison them for sure," she explained as she headed back out to the dining room.

A hard-looking woman with pink streaks in her bleached hair pushed open the door, scanned the whole room, and smiled at Buddy. She unzipped her black jacket to show off a red shirt that was at least three sizes too small and chose a barstool beside him.

"Well, hello, handsome," she said in a husky smoker's voice.

"Good mornin', darlin'." He grinned.

I glanced out the window, saw that the bus driver hadn't even opened the door. There were no other vehicles in the parking lot, which meant someone had dropped her off in front of the café. Maybe she saw the sign and thought she could buy a bus ticket.

"She's a truck bunny," Scarlett whispered.

I must have frowned, because she leaned closer and whispered, "She catches rides with whoever is willing to give her one."

"Oh!" I thought of what Rosalie had said about giving his cold dead body to the coyotes. Did she personally know someone like Miz Pink Hair? Or maybe she had known a man like Buddy in her past. Lord knew I had.

It seemed like we had more families than usual that morning, which gave me hope that things would move from the never-changing routine into something better. Maybe switching my breakfast that morning had helped things along. Baby steps—that was what Rosalie and Scarlett had called it.

But there are pros and cons to every situation in the world. The con that morning was that all the children were royal pains except for one little blond-haired girl sitting with her father. She stole my heart because she reminded me of myself at that age when I was traveling with Frank.

I handed them each a menu and asked, "What can I get y'all to drink?"

"Water for me," she said, "and Daddy will have a cup of coffee with sugar and cream."

"She knows me all too well," he said.

"Where are y'all headed to?"

"Wherever the wind takes us," the little girl answered. "We're on a road trip until my school starts back next week."

"I'll be right back with your drinks and get your order."

Scarlett came up behind me and whispered, "The woman at the bar ordered a cup of coffee and a stack of pancakes. Buddy is buying her breakfast, and I'm pretty sure she will leave with him. She is *definitely* a truck bunny."

A memory flashed into my mind. Frank and I were in a little roadside place like the Tumbleweed when he noticed a woman sitting in a back booth. I'd thought for sure he would leave me and go talk to her, but when a trucker came inside, she latched on to him. Frank had looked disappointed, but he didn't say anything. I never saw or met one of the women who left him smelling like booze and cheap perfume, but I knew at a young age that the women he stayed out with all night were not like my mother.

When the place was finally empty, Scarlett plopped down into a chair and wiped her forehead with a bar towel. "Whew! That was fast and furious."

I eased down in a chair across the table from her. "Having all those whiny kids made it seem worse than usual. I was too busy to even notice if the pink-haired lady left with Buddy."

"She did, and I don't know how she can stand him. He drives a semi and stops by every few weeks. Matilda could keep him in line, but since she's been gone . . ." She shrugged. "I keep my distance from him. You'd do well to do the same."

"Thanks for the warning, but I've seen men like him before at poker tables. If he ever pushes his luck and touches you, we will buy three shovels and bury him beside a big old yucca plant. We wouldn't want to make the coyotes sick." I stood up, picked up an eraser, and removed yesterday's special from the board. "I saw a sawed-off shotgun under the counter. I expect that would do the trick."

She gasped. "Are you serious?"

"Yes, I am."

"You are a lot tougher than I thought you would be," Scarlett said. "Got a question, though: You called them 'whiny kids.' Don't you like children?"

"Depends on whether they are whiny or not." I finished cleaning the board and turned around to face Scarlett. "What about you? Do you ever want to have a family?"

Her eyes lit up. "Yes, I do. I want a husband who treats me like a queen and a whole yardful of kids. Don't you?"

"My lifestyle has never had room for that," I told her.

"Then change it," she said. "You aren't too old to have children."

"Ouch," I said and moved over to the board where the specials were written. "What goes up here today?"

"This is Saturday. That means beef tips over noodles, green beans, a house salad, and a bowl of peach crisp, all for the price of . . ." She quoted the price with a grin. "Wait for it, wait for it . . . You get a free drink with the order, and there's no charge for a scoop of ice cream on top of the dessert."

"Every Saturday?"

"Yes, and Sunday is chicken and dressing. Monday is spaghetti and meatballs, and so on. The same thing on each day of the week—but I don't mind. I love every one of them."

I wrote SATURDAY'S LUNCH SPECIAL and then what Scarlett had told me. Evidently, in this part of the world, Groundhog Day lasted a week.

"I'm going for a jog," I said at the end of the day. Whether in a gym or a run around a parking lot in a motel, exercise had always cleared my mind after days of riding in a vehicle or sitting at a poker table.

"Are you crazy?" Scarlett asked. "It's cold out there, and the weatherman says we're in for some snow. A lot of it by the middle of next week."

"Maybe so, but I need some exercise."

"Don't you get enough by running from one table to another?" Rosalie asked.

I slipped on my hoodie and shook my head. "I'll be back in a couple of hours. Either of you want to join me?"

"I wouldn't make it to the end of the parking lot," Rosalie answered.

Scarlett waved away the idea with a flick of her wrist. "And I've got a date tonight, so I'm taking a short nap before I get ready. If your hands turn blue or if you fall over by the side of the road, call me. I'll come and get you. Which way are you going?"

"North, since there won't be as much traffic." I did a couple of stretches and then stepped outside. With every breath, I seemed to suck icicles into my lungs. I dug into my pocket, brought out a disposable mask, and covered my mouth and nose with it. That helped a little, but not much.

"See there? If I look deep enough, there's a solution to everything—even cold air." I fast-walked out to the road and then sped up.

My thoughts swirled as I ran along the side of the two-lane road. There was Larry tossing that deed out in the middle of the table. Looking back now, he probably had come to that poker game knowing he wasn't ever going back to the Tumbleweed. I hoped that someday he had to walk down a candy-and-chip aisle in a convenience store with no money in his pocket.

You never wish bad luck on a player when you leave a table, or it will be like a boomerang and come right back on you. Frank's words, not mine.

"Okay, okay! I hear you." I used up every bit of breath to scold myself when I came to a dead stop and put my hands on my knees.

I didn't even realize a vehicle was coming up behind me until it stopped, and the passenger door flew open. I hoped that it wasn't someone like Buddy. I wouldn't have the strength to fight him off. My pistol and Rosalie's shotgun were both back at the Tumbleweed.

Ada Lou yelled over the sound of the howling wind. "What in the hell are you running from? If you don't start moving or else get into this truck, the tumbleweeds will cover you up and we won't find your body until spring."

I panted between words. "I'm . . . out . . . for . . . exercise."

"Then do some of that Jane Fonda stuff in front of the television where this wind doesn't suck all the air out of you. This ain't no weather to be out jogging in," she said.

"I'm finding that out," I gasped.

"Get in here before you drop dead. You are going home with me for some hot chocolate and cookies. Once you get warm, I'll take you back to the Tumbleweed. You've run a mile. That's more than enough on a day like this."

I didn't argue and had started to shiver as I stretched the seat belt across my chest.

"Have you always been stupid, or did you just catch a dose of it when you came to this area?" she asked.

"I believe . . ." I had to stop talking and catch my breath. "It all started in Tucson."

"You should stay away from there from now on."

"I won't be going back again, for sure," I said.

"Like Kenny Rogers says in one of his songs, it might be time to fold the cards and leave the game." She turned into a driveway leading back to half a dozen travel trailers of all sizes.

"I don't think so," I argued. "I've always been happy with my lifestyle."

"Honey, happy is a state of mind. I get up every morning, look in the mirror, and say to myself, 'Ada Lou, today you will be content with your lot.' Some days I fight with myself a little, but I don't let the enemy of my joy win the battle. Now, I haven't saved your life for nothing . . ." She parked in front of the first of the trailers. "You can help me carry in the groceries I bought in El Paso. I hate having to drive so far to get necessities, but the pros outweigh the cons."

"How can you be happy in this place?" I looked across acres and acres of nothing but dead grass all the way to a mountain range out there in the distance.

She opened the back door to her truck and pointed to a case of water. "You take that, and I'll bring the bags. When we get settled into the warm house, I'll tell you a little about why I like living here. Maybe if you stick around long enough, you'll find the beauty in the spring, or even how pretty everything can be when it's covered with snow."

Had she asked me to pick up that water before I had time to catch my breath, I would have had to lie down on the side of the road and let the coyotes and buzzards get me. Even after the short ride in the warm truck, my legs were a little wobbly when I reached the last step leading up to her small trailer, but I made it without falling on my face.

"Set that on the bar. Then take off your jacket and have a seat in one of the recliners. Do you make a habit of running when it's this cold?"

I did what she told me without a word and slumped down in a soft leather chair that molded to my body. "No, I usually work out in a hotel gym, but a few times I have jogged around a motel parking lot to get in a little exercise."

Ada Lou set a pan on the stove and filled it with milk. "Well, running when there ain't nothing but a few barbed wire fences to break the wind is a different thing. A little hot chocolate and a couple of pecan sandies should warm up your insides."

Tears welled up in my eyes, but I kept them from streaming down my cheeks. I had only a few good memories of my mother. Her life had been snuffed out in the blink of an eye. The doctor had said that she slipped and fell and hit her head so hard on the edge of the kitchen cabinet that she died before she hit the floor.

My favorite memory was coming home after school to the aroma of baked cookies and real hot chocolate—not that packaged kind made in a microwave. Mom would ask me all about my day and tell me about hers while we had our after-school snack.

Ada Lou opened a package of cookies and laid half a dozen out on a small plate. She brought those to the living area and set them on a narrow table between the two chairs. Then she went back to the tiny galley kitchen to pour two big mugs of hot chocolate. After she'd added marshmallows, she crossed the short distance and handed one to me.

"What are you waiting for?" she asked. "If you don't put something in your stomach to heat you up from the inside, you won't ever stop shivering."

I picked up a cookie, bit off a chunk, and then sipped the cocoa.

"In a few minutes you'll be able to take off that sweatshirt," she said.

She was right on both counts. When my mug was half full and I had devoured two cookies, I removed my hoodie.

"Now that you are warmed up, we can visit about how long you plan to stick around these parts," she said.

"I've only been here a few days. If I had to decide today and if I had enough money, I would be gone by nightfall—but since I don't, I will stay until I do," I answered with a long sigh, and wished I could get in my vehicle and drive to the nearest poker game. "How long do *you* intend to live out here in this desolate place?"

"Until they carry me off to be cremated, and then Rosalie will scatter my ashes at the base of the mountain," she answered without a moment's hesitation. "She will inherit this trailer and can do whatever she wants with my estate. That's what the lawyer called it, and I laughed at him. She can sell it, burn it to the ground, or move it behind the Tumbleweed. I'll be dead, so it won't matter to me what happens to it."

A cold chill that had nothing to do with the wind slamming against the trailer chased down my spine. My mother had died when she was only a year older than I was, but I had never even thought about my expiration date. Frank had told me that she'd always wanted to go to Florida for a vacation. She'd wanted to smell the salt air and feel the sand beneath her feet. She had never told me anything like that—but then, I was just a little girl. We took the box her ashes were in to a pretty beach and scattered them into the ocean.

It wouldn't be kosher for mine to be poured out in the middle of a poker table, would it?

Mama's death had ended my days in public school—at least for the next eight years. But good ol' Frank cleaned out the house, put it up for sale, and I left all my little friends behind. Frank and I had good times traveling all over the country, though, staying in hotels and eating at small cafés. He took me to Disney World and Disneyland, to Dollywood and Six Flags Over Texas. We saw all the famous spots, like the Grand Canyon and Niagara Falls.

At the age of thirty, I would have traded all that for a bunch of friends I could call when I was lonely or scared or had fallen on hard times—like now.

"I haven't had roots since I was eight years old. I'm not sure I would ever be able to be anything but a poker-playing nomad."

"Whether you stay or go is immaterial to me," Ada Lou said. "As long as Rosie and Scarlett are here, it doesn't matter who owns the Tumbleweed. Matilda made a small fortune at that little bus stop and café. Then Larry went through it all in a year, from what I heard. But the Tumbleweed is still standing. A man I knew long ago once penned a poem for me and it ended with, 'So, you can stay or go away. It's all the same to me.'" She laughed and then finished off her hot chocolate. "Now," she said, "let me tell you a story about myself."

"Is it why your bike is named Hilda?" I asked.

"Nope, that's a different story, but I'll tell you that one right now. Hilda was my wild aunt—my mother's sister—that I adored. She rode a cycle in her day, and my mama said she was an abomination unto the Lord. Now, back to my real story."

For some reason, when she said *story*, a memory of my mother reading *Harry Potter* surfaced and made me feel all warm and fuzzy inside, so I nodded and settled in to listen.

"I was an addict," she said. "Not to drugs, alcohol, or gambling—or even sex—but what I suffered was an addiction as real as if it had been any one or a combination of all three."

"I am not an addict," I declared.

"Not saying you are, or was, or will be, but I was, and a rather unusual one. I am eighty years old. I came up through the era when we fought for women's rights, burned our bras, and openly believed in free love. I was in my early twenties when Woodstock happened, and I was there. I heard Creedence Clearwater Revival sing. I brought home a severe hangover and a daughter that was born nine months later. I didn't even know her father's name, but I loved my Robin from the moment they laid her in my arms. And I raised her as a single mother in a time when doing that kind of thing was not socially acceptable."

What has all this got to do with addiction? I wondered.

"It was a time of transition, of morals and values changing, and it was hard for older folks to accept. My parents told me if I went to that place 'where the devil would roam free' that they would disown me. I went, and they did." She paused and took a long breath. "I had my own apartment, so it wasn't a big deal to a rebellious woman like me, but when they didn't want anything to do with me or my bastard child, it really hurt." Her voice trembled, but she went on. "I was a kindergarten teacher and was not rehired. Small towns in the Puritan East did not take to unmarried pregnant women around their children. I liked to cook, so I started selling baked goods out of my apartment. That way I could keep Robin with me. The business grew, so I rented a building in town and hired a couple of women to help me."

Were you addicted to doughnuts or cookies?

"I see questions in your face," she said with a smile. "My addiction was my daughter. I made sure that she knew she was loved beyond what words can describe. She graduated high school, went to college a hundred miles away, and I was completely lost. That first semester, we talked every day—more than once, most of the time—and then she was gone."

"What do you mean, 'gone'?" I asked.

Ada Lou wiped tears from her cheeks with her shirtsleeve. "She was coming home for the Christmas holidays, and a drunk driver T-boned her car. She died instantly."

The same feeling I'd had when Frank told me that my mother was dead swept over me like an icy cold wind.

"I'm so sorry," I said past the lump in my throat.

"Thank you," she said with half a smile. "A few of her high school and college friends came for the service. That was comforting, but the next two years were horrible. I didn't turn to drugs or alcohol or even work. I visited her grave at least twice a day and got it in my head that I had to go talk to her so she wouldn't think I had forgotten her. It became a deep-seated obsession."

"What did you finally do?" I thought of my need to shuffle my lucky deck of cards every evening before I went to bed. Frank had declared that was his lucky charm for the next poker game, so I guess I was following his example.

"I had a dream one night. Robin came to me and said, 'Mama, you have to let me go so I can find rest and peace.'"

Is this a made-up story or a real one? If it was a lie, she was an expert at controlling her expressions, and I damn sure didn't want to play cards with her.

"Is she buried in Dell City?"

"No, she's in a little town in southern Virginia. After she spoke to me in the dream, I tried to move on, but her tombstone kept calling to me. If I didn't go visit her, I couldn't sleep. I even stopped eating. The only thing that held meaning to me had disappeared. So I sold the business, bought this trailer and a truck to pull it, and set off on a journey. When I arrived in this desolate place, I decided to stay a week to rest up before I went on any farther."

"How long ago was that?" I asked.

"Way more than a decade, and the first friend I made was Matilda. She helped me to see that what I was doing was an obsession. I had to be far enough away from the addiction that it couldn't call me back into it. That's where you are, Carla. There is enough distance between you and your poker tables, and from what Scarlett tells me, you are so broke right now, you can't even think about going back to that lifestyle. You don't have to decide today, but there will come a time when you have to give some serious thought to what is most important to you. Until then, just think of this place as a dose of medicine."

"What if I don't want to be cured?"

"Then you won't be, and when you have enough money, you can move on," Ada Lou answered. "Before you drive away, be sure to enjoy the time you have here."

I shook my head. "Where's the joy in this place?"

"All around you. You won't find any better friends than Rosie and Scarlett, and there's always folks coming and going in the Tumbleweed, so it's never boring. All that can bring happiness, but that will be your decision to make . . . and yours alone. Now, it's getting up toward my nap time. So put your jacket on, and I'll take you home."

I had not had a *home* in more years than Ada Lou had lived in her tiny RV. Could she be right about me making real friends in this place? And if I did, would it be more painful to leave them or to give up the excitement of the next card game?

I slipped my arms back into my hoodie and followed her out to her vehicle. "Have you been back to Virginia?"

"Nope, and don't intend to ever go back. Peace is a hard commodity to come by, and I'm afraid if I ever visit my daughter's grave again, I will fall into the same obsession I had before," she said as she slid in behind the steering wheel. "I have made friends with the other folks that live out here, as well as some in Dell City. I have my daily brunch with Rosie and Scarlett, and my good friend Nancy, who lives in the last trailer in the row, and I play board games a few times a week. The next time I see Robin, it will be on the other side."

The thought of seeing my mother again put tears in my eyes and fear into my heart. She hated gambling, and I didn't want her to be disappointed in me.

Chapter Five

After we closed on Sunday afternoon, I tried to take a nap. I closed my eyes and curled up on one side. The tinkling of the wind chimes hanging to the left of the front door, a chirping cricket that had managed to find a corner under the trailer, and my own breathing blended into one loud noise that wouldn't let me sleep. I slammed a pillow over my head, leaving only my nose and chin out from under it. That didn't work. I tried playing blackjack in my head. That didn't work, either. Finally, I got up and wandered over to the living area and turned on the television.

A Charlie Brown Christmas was playing. I sure didn't want to watch that, but there was something about that silly tree that reminded me of my mother's laughter. She used to say that we had a family stick instead of a family tree when I asked her why we didn't have a big Christmas gathering like Frank did.

"I'm sorry, kiddo," she'd said. "I always wanted to have one holiday with lots of kids gathered around a huge tree on Christmas morning, too, but we are doomed. We both come from a long line of only children going back for centuries."

"What do you mean, 'doomed'?" I'd asked her.

She'd wiped her hands on a tea towel and hugged me. "*Doomed* is when you don't get brothers and sisters. I'm hoping that when you grow up, you break the record and have a dozen kids."

So far, she had not gotten her wish, but I did the DNA thing a few years ago just to see if she was right. I have never even gotten a report about a tenth cousin who has been dead for decades.

Because I'd always asked for a tree, Frank set one up in each of our hotel rooms during the month of December. They had usually only been a foot tall and had come with a few tiny little bulbs glued to it. He'd told me that the big tree in the lobby had been decorated just for me. I believed him for years.

Evidently, it was commercial time, because the next three channels I surfed through were all advertising either wine, beer, or liquor. A visual of my mother with a drink in her hand after one of Frank's horrible family reunions appeared as clear as if it were real. Mama and I had dreaded those events that happened four times a year—Easter, the Fourth of July, Thanksgiving, and Christmas Eve. He loved all his loud relatives, and the liquor and beer had flowed freely when they were all together. Mama and I had tolerated them—barely. I did not want to be related to any of those people.

Independence Day was the worst holiday. I still shiver to this day when I think of Frank's Aunt Minnie. She would always be the first to greet us. She would bury my face in her big boobs so tightly, and when I finally wiggled free, she would bend down and kiss me on the cheek. Her mustache was like being scraped by a porcupine. Before I could get to my hiding place, one of the many drunk great-uncles would hug me and fog up my eyeballs with his breath. Had Mama lived and I had gotten married and had kids by now, I would have refused to take them to those gatherings.

I remember hiding behind a big oak tree every time the event was held outside. Two big roots that ran on top of the ground made a lovely little nest for me. The Christmas party was held at Aunt Minnie's big old two-story house, and after dinner I escaped to the attic. That place was like going on a treasure hunt for a kid. In both of my hiding places, I usually sat alone and practiced shuffling my old maid cards like Frank did with his lucky deck every night. If I'd had relatives my age, I might have been a different person—but then, probably not.

Frank would always come home drunk after spending time with his relatives, and Mama always had a migraine that put her to bed for at least two days. When I fussed about not wanting to go, she would tell me that she'd promised Frank she would become part of his family, and he vowed that he would never forsake us, and that he would not gamble again. He'd kept both promises: He didn't put me in a foster home, and he didn't gamble until she passed away.

Those big family occasions were in Kentucky. The summer before my sixteenth birthday, we made the trip from West Virginia, where I had won a lot of money in an illegal game. Frank spent so much on fireworks and booze that he was the big man on campus that year. Aunt Minnie's mustache was still as prickly as it had always been, but I was tall enough that I didn't get smothered by her big boobs. I just wanted the day to be over, but the universe had other plans. On our way out of town, Frank and I went into a café for breakfast. He met Paula, the owner, and decided that since we were flush, we would stay in Kentucky for a while longer. He married the woman a month later in a fancy ceremony at Aunt Minnie's house.

"Go live a normal life. Make friends," he'd said the day after he and Paula got married at the Harlan County Courthouse in Kentucky. That fall, he enrolled me in Harlan County High School. *"Go Black Bears."*

"What about our next poker game?" I'd asked Frank when we left the courthouse.

"There will be *no* more gambling," Paula had said. "Frank loves me enough that he promised he would give up poker."

Yeah, right! He promised Mama the same thing, and look what happened.

All I had known for almost eight years was going from one place to the next, studying in whatever hotel or motel room Frank had left me in until he bought me a phony ID. Then I was able to go to the poker games with him, and often won more money than he did. Friends were not part of the equation.

Until I came to the Tumbleweed.

I'd been at this place for four days and now had $503 and some change in my lockbox. I had been excited to see Scarlett and Rosalie leave that afternoon so that I could have some alone time in the trailer, but now I wished they were still there.

"Here I am without Rosalie singing hymns under her breath or Scarlett watching television," I whispered and closed my eyes, shutting off the visions, "and I miss them."

Did friendship mean dependency on another person? If so, I wasn't sure I liked the feeling at all.

I turned off the television and stood up. I rounded the short bar, opened the refrigerator door, and stared into it like it were an abyss. "This place is as quiet as a tomb."

What do you know about a tomb? Mama's voice popped into my head.

"It's just a saying." I shivered at the thought of Mama being forever in a tomb.

I was glad that I could envision her laughing and having a good time on the beach and in the cool ocean water, rather than imagining how I would feel if I visited a cold tombstone in a cemetery.

Everyone needs friends, she said.

"Why? And what has that got to do with us pouring you out in all that water?"

A hard knock on the door startled me. I whipped around so fast that it made me dizzy. I figured Rosalie or Scarlett had their arms full and couldn't open the door, so I hurried across the floor to find Ada Lou standing on the porch.

"Put your coat on. I'm going to give you a tour of Dell City," she said. "And then we're stopping by my place for a movie and popcorn."

I was glad for anything that would take my mind off the past, but something about being told what to do set me on edge. "You've been around Rosalie too much."

"What makes you say that?" Ada Lou asked.

I reached for my coat. "You are almost as bossy as she is."

"I've been accused of worse," she said with a grin, and led the way to her truck.

She could barely see over the steering wheel, and she had to stretch her leg to get her foot to the gas pedal. But that didn't stop her from driving several miles an hour over the speed limit.

"Why are you doing this?" I asked.

"When is your birthday?" she fired right back at me.

"December 24. Mama told me that Santa Claus left me under the tree."

"I like that better than a stork flying through the air with you, or some stranger leaving you under a cabbage plant in the garden. When I realized how old my Robin would be today, it made me think that any child she could have had would be about your age. You could be my granddaughter."

"I don't think so," I said and told her the story of what my mama had said about the family on her side only having a stick instead of a tree.

She laughed out loud. "I would have liked your mama. And, honey, family doesn't always mean that you share blood or that DNA crap. It can mean that you share heartfelt love. Look, I never got to be a grandmother, so I'm going to give you some advice. The family you are born into is just a starter one. The people in that one care for you the best they know how. They love you, feed you, clothe you, and all that until you are old enough to go out into the world and find your own family. I found mine right here in this place, and you could, too, if you just open your eyes."

"Why do you care?" No one else had ever—more or less—adopted me on the spot. Hell's bells, I didn't come from a dysfunctional family. I came from a nonexistent one. Frank was more like a friend than a father figure.

"Because in another world and another time, you might be my granddaughter, and grandmothers are supposed to be bossy and give advice," she answered. "Besides, Rosalie says that you are the best help she's ever had, and she is my friend. If I can do this for her, then I'm happy."

"And if you fail?"

"Then I tried, and that's all any person can ever do." She shrugged.

We sat in silence for a full minute before she spoke again. "Do you know why I named my daughter Robin?"

"No. Is it a family name? I'm named Carla after my grandfather. My middle name is Penelope, after my grandmother. Her nickname was Nellie." I stared out the window at nothing but dead grass between the road and the mountains.

"Oh, hell no!" Ada Lou declared. "Remember how I told you I went to Woodstock? Well, I made a vow to myself that I would name the baby the first thing I saw after she was born. And when I heard her first cries, a robin landed on the windowsill right outside my hospital room."

"Thank God it wasn't a buzzard."

Ada Lou threw back her head and laughed like a big, burly trucker. I would have never guessed that so much volume could come out of such a skinny little body.

"You got that right," she finally agreed when the echoes died down.

"I thought you didn't like me," I said. "I overheard you tell Scarlett not to get too close to me because I wouldn't stay around any longer than it took for me to sell the café."

"I meant for you to hear that so you would begin to think about what you have here, as opposed to what you had before you landed here broke and without so much as a dollar bill in your pocket."

I cut my eyes around at her and frowned. "You'd only just met me."

"I have no idea what kind of poker player you are, girl, but I saw fear in your eyes that morning."

"I was treading water in new territory, and it *was* scary," I admitted.

I didn't tell her that the only other time I'd been that terrified was the day I came inside from playing in the backyard and the house was filled with smoke and the smell of something burning. Mama was lying on the kitchen floor, and I couldn't wake her. I called 911. The lady on the phone told me to turn off the oven but not to open the door. Then I heard sirens. The policemen opened windows and the oven door to let the smoke out of the house. They told me to go sit on the porch, and I did. Then the ambulance came, and two men pushed a gurney across the yard and inside. To me, it was hours before Frank got home, but he was really there before they brought my mother's body out of the house. He tried to hold me back, but I got away from him and jumped up on the gurney with Mama.

"She can't breathe," I'd sobbed as I unzipped the black bag.

Ada Lou reached across the console and laid a hand on my shoulder. "Are you all right?"

"I'm fine." I took a couple of deep breaths and wished again that I'd never gone to Tucson. All these people around me seemed to be smothering me with painful memories.

We whizzed by a green sign that said Dell City, Population: 413.

"You looked like you were about to cry," Ada Lou said. "Was it the sign reminding you how small this place is?"

"It's not about the sign or how desolate this area is. I didn't want her to smother," I said around the lump in my throat, then told her about the memory of watching them take my mother away.

She patted my shoulder. "Bless your heart. No wonder you are a nomad. You're afraid to get close to someone for fear you'll lose them. But I'm not going anywhere, and neither are Rosie and Scarlett."

"Thank you."

She pointed to a water tower and then put her hand on the steering wheel again. "The internet lists several towns or communities in this county, but most of them are like salt flats—just a place where a town used to be. Fort Hancock can boast the biggest population with a little over a thousand folks living there. Dell City and Sierra Blanca are behind that, with four to five hundred. Over there is a great Mexican restaurant. I eat there at least once a week," she said and gestured as she drove. "And there's where the folks here can buy fuel and auto parts.

And there's the church where Scarlett goes, and the school. And on down here is the San Isidore Catholic Church."

Rosalie's truck was the only vehicle parked outside the building with crosses on the doors and a bell at the top of the false front. The wooden sign out front looked like it had been stenciled by an amateur.

"What kind of name is that?"

"Saint Isidore is the patron saint of farmers," Ada Lou answered.

"Why would they give a church that name out here in the middle of nothing but weeds and yucca plants? They should have named it after the patron saint of yucca plants."

She shrugged and chuckled. "I agree with you, but I doubt that yucca plants have a patron saint. That is the whole of Dell City. If you don't blink, you'll see it again as we drive through town on our way back to the trailer park."

"Why would anyone want to live here?" I asked, and then wished I could hit a button and take the words back. "I'm sorry. I didn't mean to insult you or any of the folks who make their home here."

"Home can be anywhere from this place to New York City, or Los Angeles, or the Sahara Desert. The size of the place or the land where it's located has no bearing on where your family lives," she answered.

"Why—"

As if she knew what I was about to say, she cut me off with a flick of her wrist. "I can read your mind—at one time, I had the same question. Why does your family have to be in a place like this? Truth is that I have no idea, but I listen to my heart, Carla. When I don't, I have regrets."

Amen to that, I thought when I remembered Lady Luck telling me not to go to that poker game in Tucson.

"Have you always paid attention to your heart?"

"I don't like the feeling I get when I am stubborn and insist on doing something different. My heart told me that you need an honest friend. So here I am." Her tone seemed to scold me.

"Okay," I whispered.

"We're going back to my place to watch *Sweet Home Alabama* and eat popcorn."

"Why—"

Another wave of her hand. "Because the underlying lesson in the movie is that we don't need to be looking at the grass on the other side of the fence, but rather listening to our hearts. I know I've repeated that phrase a lot, but sometimes we have to be taught a lesson many times before it begins to sink in."

"No regrets," I said.

"That's right," she said as she drove back through the small town and to the trailer park. "I believe the tree of life, like that one in the Garden of Eden, produces lemons as well as apples. Eve got an apple, but sometimes we pick a lemon. What we make with it is up to us."

Chapter Six

If my poor little SUV had a mind, it would probably think that it had been abandoned. Not once since I'd bought it and driven it off the lot had it been parked for five whole days without being moved. It also had never looked as pitiful as it did that Monday afternoon, either. Dust had mixed with the spitting snow we'd had the day before, leaving splotches all over the vehicle.

"If I can find one in Sierra Blanca, I'll run you through a car wash," I promised as I started the engine.

Frank and I had driven from Kentucky to Florida and then to California after my mother passed away. I wasn't impressed with the flat desert then any more than I was that morning. Miles and miles of monotonous land that all looked the same until I got into the area between the Guadeloupe Mountains and found a few hills and curves to drive through. Ada Lou had said that the place was pretty in the spring, but it looked awfully barren in January.

Kind of like your life right now, the annoying little imaginary creature on my shoulder said. *But perhaps, like the land around you, everything will be better come spring.*

To keep from arguing with the critter, I touched the button on the dash screen to turn on the music from my playlist. Ashley McBryde singing "Bonfire at Tina's" filled the whole vehicle. I sang along with her even though I couldn't carry a tune in a bucket. The song was about women who might not always see eye to eye, but if anybody—especially a man—wronged one of them, they banded together.

I played the video in my mind as I listened to the words and laughed a few times when all those women gathered around the bonfire. "Would Rosalie and Scarlett help me like that?" I muttered when the song ended.

Yep, they would. They didn't have to warn me about men like Buddy, or trust me, but they did. And Scarlett even said that she and Ada Lou would help me bury that fool.

Are you going to take the money in the bank bag and run with it? the critter still on my shoulder asked.

I didn't even bother to answer the ridiculous question, but the next song, "Keep It Between the Lines," brought back memories of when Frank had taught me to drive on the straight, flat roads of the Texas Panhandle. I had to sit on a pillow to see over the steering wheel of the old Astro van we drove back then. When I got the hang of keeping the vehicle in the correct lane, he let me take a turn every day for a few hours. I loved it when he went to sleep, because I had control of the radio, and I didn't have to pay attention to the speed limit sign.

Evidently, Miz Random on my playlist got stuck on Ashley McBryde, because the next song was "Martha Divine." I smiled at the lyrics because the song always reminded me of Paula, especially when the words called her a jezebel from hell. Looking back, I could truly say that the devil had made me do it when I packed up my car and drove away from Kentucky.

Her next song was "Girl Goin' Nowhere." I felt the lyrics just like I did back when I'd first heard her sing. I remembered when the tall, skinny teacher in my English class handed back my test paper and asked me exactly what I intended to do with my life.

Not caring what she or the kids around me thought, I'd answered, "I will be a professional poker player."

A few of the students snickered, but the boys who had been losing to me during the lunch break didn't make a sound.

Miss Robbins, with her sharp nose and squinty eyes, gave me a short lecture about needing to get a high school diploma, or I wouldn't go anywhere. I wanted to tell her that I had been doing very well without a piece of paper saying I had a formal education, and that I'd been to every one of the states except Hawaii. But I didn't want to suffer the wrath of Paula if she got called to the school because the teacher had sent me to the office.

The lady with the tinny voice on GPS overrode the songs, so I turned off the music and followed her directions. The town didn't seem to be all that different from Dell City, except it had a nice courthouse and a bank. I passed by two churches—a Catholic one, which would have made Rosalie happy, and a community church with a name I couldn't pronounce.

My first stop was at the courthouse to file the deed. Viola, the lady who helped with the paperwork, sure was a talker and had no kind words for Larry, or else I would have been out of there in less than the thirty minutes that it took. The guy who set up accounts for the business at the bank and a personal one for me went on and on about how much he missed Matilda. I signed my weekly paycheck for five days' work and groaned at how much had been deducted for taxes. Living off the grid all those years had not conditioned me for the real world. Staring at the piece of paper definitely did not make me feel much like a lucky wild card.

After all the transactions were done, I held my first-ever debit card in my hand. "As if I need it," I said as I stared at the little rectangle of plastic on the way to my SUV. "I don't have a thing to spend money on right now."

I had settled into the driver's seat and was about to start the engine when someone tapped on the window and startled me so badly that my soul left my body and floated around for a few seconds before it came back to me. I jerked my head to the side and saw Jackson Armstrong smiling at me and making a motion with his hand to roll the window down.

"What are you doing here?" I asked.

"Same thing you are, probably. We keep our business local," he answered. "There's a small café not far from here. Can I buy you a cup of coffee or a glass of sweet tea?"

"No, but I would love a Diet Coke. I don't know where it is. Shall I follow you?"

"Why don't we just walk? The sun is shining, and the wind isn't too bad. The café is nearby," he suggested, and opened the door for me.

I hadn't realized how tall he was until I walked beside him. I barely came up to his shoulder, and his legs were so long that he had to shorten his stride for me to keep up with him. Even then, I was almost out of breath when we arrived. He opened the café door for me and ushered me to a table with his hand on my back. Heat swept through the thickness of my jacket and shirt. I attributed it to the fact that I had not even had a one-night stand in several months. Plus, all that talk about families that Ada Lou had put out there had confused the hell out of me.

"Why do *you* come all the way out here to do your banking?" I asked on the way back to a table.

He pulled out a chair for me and helped me remove my jacket. "The headquarters for my folks' oil business is in Dallas. In that area, one town runs into another. I was born and raised in McKinney, which is a few miles north of the actual city limits."

"I am not fond of driving in Dallas. However, it beats New York City," I said. "But I still don't understand why you would be conducting business so far away."

"I kind of wondered the same thing myself, believe me. My father is putting me in charge of the new oil business in this part of the state. He's hoping that I don't go back into the service, but I'm on the fence about that. I have moved my travel trailer into that little RV park between the Tumbleweed and Dell City. I'll live in it for a year."

My mind spun around in warp-speed circles. I planned to be long gone before a year passed, and yet, looking at him, I had the strangest desire to stay.

"Why a year? Will your business move after a year?"

"No, it could even expand. It's just that I promised my dad I wouldn't go back into the military for a year," he answered.

"Does that mean we'll be seeing more of you at the Tumbleweed?"

"Probably not in the café. I'll be on the job from daylight to dark—but I will need a friend, so after I finish the day, we might get some time to talk. If you would be willing," he said.

A waitress brought over a menu and silverware for each of us and took our drink order. I hadn't planned on eating, but I had enough money in the bank now to buy a meal.

"Hungry?" Jackson asked.

"I didn't think I was, but the tacos look good." For the first time in years, I didn't have to check the price of the food to see if I could afford to order.

"Well, I'm starving. I was so busy setting up the trailer that I didn't have time for lunch. I could go for a double order of enchiladas."

Was this a date, or just a chance happenstance? The question made me think about living in the present no matter where I was. Having female friends was . . . I wasn't sure how to finish that sentence—but I wondered what it would be like to have a guy friend.

"Tell me about yourself," Jackson said.

"Well, I'm thirty years old, and I've been a professional gambler under the name Clara Williams for more than half of my life. I'm Carla Wilson the other half of the time. That's about it. Your turn."

"You know my name, though I only have the one. I'm thirty-eight years old. I spent twenty years in the military, and that's the basics. I don't tell anyone any more than that on a first date."

"This . . . is . . . not . . . a date!" I protested.

"Then that's all the information about me that you get the first time we break bread together."

I made a dramatic show of looking around the table. "I don't see any bread."

The words were barely out of my mouth when the waitress brought our drinks and a basket full of corn bread muffins.

He grinned. "What were you saying about bread?"

"I stand corrected."

"Y'all ready to order?" the waitress asked.

"I'll have the taco plate," I said.

"I want the big platter of beef enchiladas with cheese sauce on top," Jackson answered and handed both menus to her.

"Those come with beans and rice. That okay?" she asked.

We both nodded at the same time.

"Have it out in a few minutes. Enjoy the corn bread and honey." She pointed to a container on the condiment tray at the far end of the table and then rushed off to wait on more new customers.

Our hands brushed against each other when we reached for a hot muffin at the same time. I didn't know how it affected him, but I felt another rush of heat. Hoping it was only the warm bread and not hormones, I tried to ignore it. This was not the time to get romantically involved with anyone—not when I was still figuring out whether I wanted to stay or go.

"So, your family is in the oil business?" I asked.

He slathered a muffin with butter. "Yes, and the land where we have started setting up to drill is right up next to the New Mexico border. I'll be going to work early and leaving my office after the café is closed . . ." He shrugged. "But I'll be free in the evenings. Maybe we can meet up for coffee sometimes?"

"I'd like that. Give me your phone, and I'll put my number in it."

He wiped his hands on a napkin before he removed his cell from his pocket. I added my number and handed it back to him.

"I've never had friends before now," I said.

"For real? How is that possible?"

"I told you, I am a professional poker player—we like to move around."

His expression said that he doubted me.

"Are you also an exotic dancer named Sweet Clara in between card games?" he asked.

"I'm serious!" I snapped. "I was eight when my mother died. Frank and I went on the road. He taught me to play, and I am very good at it. I was never in one spot long enough to make friends."

"What about school?" he asked.

"I finished third grade before my mama passed away. The rest I did with homeschooling until I was a sophomore. Then Frank remarried and gave up gambling, but I didn't. I played at the high school where I went for one semester and won enough money during lunch to strike out on my own. That was fourteen years ago."

His eyes said that he was doing math in his head. "How did you get into games at sixteen? Don't they require an ID? Who is Frank?"

"How old were you when you got your fake ID?" I shot back, not wanting to get into a discussion about ol' Frank.

"Sixteen, but—"

I held up a palm to shush him. "Frank bought mine when I was fourteen—at that point, I could pass for twenty-one with the right clothes and makeup. I took home so much money the first night I sat in on a game that I played every time he did from then on. And so we had twice as much money to blow through until the next game. By the time he remarried, I knew how to read people, how to bluff, and that I had a good memory for cards. I also knew how to live off the grid and all that. Clara Williams is well respected in poker circles."

"You are serious, aren't you? You aren't teasing me."

"Do you still want to be my friend?" I asked.

"Of course. What about family? Like cousins or siblings?"

"I come from a long line of only children on my mother's side of the family tree. Frank and his wife, Paula, have two boys, but I have never met them."

"Why?"

I shrugged and took a big bite of my muffin. I had already shared more with him than I had with any other person. Not even Scarlett and Rosalie knew my gambling name. When I swallowed and sipped my tea, I figured *In for a lamb, might as well go for the sheep*, as the old saying goes.

"I didn't leave on good terms. Paula found my stash of poker winnings in my room and pitched a fit. She said that to live in her house and work in her café, I had to promise to never play again—not at school, where I could get suspended if the principal found out, and certainly not in the backroom games in the seedy part of town that I had been sneaking out at night to go to. I chose not to live in her house, packed up my things into the used car I had bought with my money, and left."

"Didn't Frank put up a fight to keep you from leaving? Y'all had been traveling together for a long time, right?"

"We had, and he did not. I believe he was relieved. Paula was pregnant by then, and they would have a family that I wouldn't fit into. My leaving made life easier for everyone." I washed the lump in my throat down with a sip of tea. Sure, it hadn't been difficult to drive away, but the idea that he hadn't even stood up for me still stung.

"That you have been taking care of yourself for so long is incredible," he whispered.

I didn't want to talk about my past anymore, so I forced a smile. "Thank you. Now, tell me about your friends."

He smiled. "You intrigue me, Carla. I bet you have lots more stories to tell."

"Your friends?" I asked again.

"I had, and still have, a few buddies from high school, but most of them are married with kids. One even has a son who is a senior in high school. Seems surreal to me that that is even possible, but we all choose our own path. I guess you could call my Special Forces team my long-term friends and family."

I remembered what Ada Lou had said about having a family. "Do you keep in touch with them?"

"Yes, I do. Since their base is in the States, we have planned get-togethers at least twice a year."

The waitress brought our food and refilled our drinks. "Can I get you anything else?"

"Looks like we're good," Jackson told her.

"If this is as good as it smells, I'll be coming back here every Monday." I took my first bite and gave it a thumbs-up.

"I'll have to make a trip to the bank every few weeks. We could ride together, have a midafternoon meal, and catch up," he suggested.

"Sounds good to me—and you better get after that food because I might steal some of it if you don't."

He chuckled and took a bite of enchilada. "You are right. It is good enough to be a tradition."

The waitress refilled our glasses once more as we ate and laid the bill on the table. We grabbed for it at the same time, but after a brief tug-of-war, he wound up with it.

I crossed my arms over my chest and shot an evil look across the table. "This is not a date. I will pay for my own food."

"My mother would make me cut a switch and then beat me with it if I let a lady pay for dinner, especially when I invited her to join me," he said. "You wouldn't want to see me come into the Tumbleweed carrying a pillow for me to sit on, would you?"

I laughed at the visual of him toting around one of those inflatable doughnut pillows. "I guess I wouldn't—but next time is on me."

"My mama is like God. She knows everything, and I don't cross her, especially when it comes to what she taught me. No, ma'am!" he said with a fake shudder.

I couldn't imagine someone as big as Jackson being afraid of the devil himself, much less his own mother.

"Are we ready to go?" he asked.

I took one more drink of my tea and nodded. "I suppose we had better be, if I'm going to get back before Rosalie and Scarlett send out the Texas Rangers to find me."

"Why would they do that?" he asked. "You are a grown woman who has been making her own way for years."

"They gave me their paychecks to deposit, and they don't trust me enough to really believe that I wouldn't cash them and leave this area to go to another poker game," I answered.

"They must have felt like you were honest, or they wouldn't have given their checks to you in the first place."

I pushed my chair back and stood up. "Everything is a test. Someday I might even pass enough of them to be able to call Rosalie *Rosie.*"

"I have faith in you." He paid the bill, and we walked out.

"When did you get to call her Rosie?" I asked.

"A while back, when I broke up a fight between a couple of guys in the café," he answered. "But don't worry. You'll pass whatever she throws at you."

No one had ever said that they had faith in me, though Frank and I had used to do our lucky handshake before we went into a game. In retrospect, he shouldn't have passed me off as twenty-one so I could join the others at the poker table when I was fourteen. But in his defense, I'd always looked older than my years.

A whole rash of tumbleweeds danced across the road and got hung in everything along their way—doors, windows, vehicles, and even the legs of my jeans.

"'Tis the season," Jackson chuckled and kicked them away with the toe of his cowboy boot. "Instead of snowball fights, we could have tumbleweed battles. Course, they are a nuisance when we are drilling for oil."

"They are trouble anywhere." I told him about thinking that I had run over a person when it was only the granddaddy of all tumbleweeds.

He laughed out loud at the story, but I must admit that I did embellish it a little.

"We don't see so many in the Dallas area, but Dad warned me about them, especially this time of year. If things are dry, they can be a fire hazard, and that's bad around oil wells."

"They are a nuisance at the café, too, but I didn't think about them being a fire hazard." I stopped at my SUV and opened the door.

What you thought of as troublesome *brought you to the place you are, so they can't be all bad.* My mother's voice was back in my head.

The whistling at the beginning of an old song I had heard in first grade, "Don't Worry Be Happy," came to mind. I shook it out of my thoughts and said, "Thanks for supper and the conversation."

"Right back at you. Do you think you'll still be around these parts after a year goes by?"

"Do you?" I shot back.

"It looks to me like we both have some things to figure out in the coming months, don't we?"

"Yep." I slid in behind the steering wheel. "Thanks again for everything."

"You are welcome." He closed my door and walked over to his big white truck.

Knight in shining white truck, I thought as I started the engine and headed back north. "But I am not a damsel in distress who needs saving. Never have been. Never will be."

Before I'd driven five miles, clouds began to roll in from the south, giving everything a gloomy feeling, and that silly song came back to my mind. One of the lyrics talked about not having a place to put your head because someone came along and took your bed. I laughed at how true that was.

Listen to the words, and don't worry about a year from now or next week. Be happy where you are right now. Ada Lou was in my head now.

"Yes, ma'am. I will try to do that," I promised with a smile on my face.

The first big drops of rain fell as I cleared the mountains and got back on flat land. The temperature on the dashboard said that it was forty-five degrees, so I didn't have to worry about the roads icing over. However, the roads *were* wet, which meant I couldn't use the cruise control. Since I tended toward a lead foot, I had to keep watch on the speedometer the whole way back to the trailer.

Rosie's truck was parked close to the porch. Scarlett's vehicle was beside hers, leaving me to have to dash quite a way to the trailer in the pouring-down rain. I tucked the bank bag under my coat, made sure my purse was zipped up tight, and ran from my SUV to the trailer. I was still soaking wet when I got inside. I shed my boots and jacket at the door, threw the bank bag on the counter, and headed back to my bedroom to change into dry clothes. I heard two doors open while I was putting on a pair of flannel pajamas and a dry T-shirt.

"Bag with all the deposit slips is on the counter," I yelled down the hallway.

"We found it, and thank you," Rosalie hollered back. "Are you coming out?"

"On my way." I smelled Italian food the minute I stepped back out into the hallway.

After feeling like I would starve to death on the trip from Tucson to the Tumbleweed, I'd vowed I would never pass up food when it was offered. Not even when I had eaten two hours before.

"Want us to heat up some food for you?" Rosalie asked. "You didn't have time to eat before you had to go to the bank."

"Yes, please," I answered, but I didn't tell them about dinner with Jackson, or that we were going to drive down together when he needed to go to the bank again. I wanted to hold that nice moment close to my heart.

"We've been talking about it, and we decided since we take turns with the shower, then we should do the same with that boring drive to Sierra Blanca," Rosalie said as she filled a bowl with spaghetti and meatballs. "So after next week, you will only have to go every third time."

"Why after next week?" I asked.

"I have plans on Monday afternoon with Grady. But if you don't want to go, I can change them," Scarlett answered.

"And I promised Father Luis that I would help with the books since his secretary is out on maternity leave for a couple of weeks." Rosalie slid the bowl of pasta into the microwave.

"No problem. I'll be glad to go next week, and any other time that y'all need a day off."

"You are a good friend," Scarlett said.

When she said that, I remembered a greeting card I saw in a shop a few years before. What had caught my eye was the picture of an old couple on the outside. The sentiment on the inside read *"It was only me, until it wasn't."*

Chapter Seven

Talk about a role reversal.

That saying about being the statue one day and the pigeon the next came to mind as I picked up two menus and carried them to the elderly couple at the corner table. The day before, I'd been the important statue, having dinner with Jackson. Today I was just a waitress with a stained apron tied around my waist. But like a wise woman once said, "Life is not all rainbows and unicorns. On bad days, laugh about them, remember the good ones, and move on."

"What can I get you folks to drink?" I asked.

"We'll have coffee," the woman answered. "I'm so glad that the Tumbleweed is still here."

"Me too," I said under my breath and hurried off to the next table to deliver menus and see what the pair wanted to drink.

"Do you have herbal tea?" the lady asked without looking up from her phone's screen.

"Yes, we do. I'll bring an assortment and hot water, if that's what you want."

"Make that two," the guy said, his eyes on his own phone.

Once everyone had their drinks and their orders were turned in, I picked up the coffeepot to do refills. The elderly couple were holding hands across the table, and their mugs were still full.

The young couple with the herbal teas were still scrolling through their phones. "Want a refill? I can get you more hot water."

"No, thank you. I just want to eat and get out of this place," the woman answered with half a shrug.

"Bad day?" I asked.

"Not only a day. It's been a bad long weekend," the man answered.

"It didn't have to be. I offered to buy plane tickets," the lady said.

"I'm tired of you paying for everything, and I thought a bus trip would be romantic," he said through clenched teeth.

"Just because you are poor and planned a shoestring trip—"

He cut her off with a glare and finally glanced up at me. "We got drunk and married in Vegas."

"And now," she sighed, "we are going home to pay for an expensive divorce, since I didn't have a prenup. My daddy is furious with me."

"God forbid if *Daddy*"—he dragged that last word out—"is upset with the princess. I don't want your money."

She shot a dirty look across the table. "You say that now, but I know you. When he offers you a settlement to leave and never come back, you'll take it."

Yikes. Of course, not the first Vegas wedding I'd seen. I left them hissing at each other and went back to see if the elderly couple needed a warm-up for their coffee. "Your food should be out in a few minutes. Can I get you anything else?"

"No, we're good," the woman said. "Fifty years ago, when this place was kind of new, we also went to Vegas on a bus and got married there. So we are celebrating our anniversary with a redo of those days. That's why we are so glad that the Tumbleweed is still here. We had breakfast right here at this table on our way back home. It's been a wonderful trip full of great memories."

The man reached across the table and took his wife's hands in his. "Patsy has stood beside me through thick and thin. But this is our last trip. We have made the full circle, and now we are on the final leg of life's journey."

"Hey, now." I smiled down at them. "You might celebrate another anniversary by repeating this same trip next year."

He patted Patsy's hand, and his eyes filled with tears. "Several weeks ago, the doctors gave me three months. My expiration date is as soon as next week, but we are not complaining. We had fifty wonderful years together, and we got to have this last trip. Patsy knows that I'll be waiting on the other side for her."

"Can I grow up and be like y'all?" I asked around the lump in my throat.

"Of course you can," Patsy answered. "Just be sure your glass is always half full and never half empty."

"Yes, ma'am, I will try to do that," I promised, and hurried away so they wouldn't see me cry.

Today I had seen a half-full cup—no, that wasn't right. I had experienced an overflowing glass and a totally empty one in the same room. Like Patsy said, how full my proverbial glass was each day would be up to me. If I could have remembered the opening music to *Groundhog Day*, I would have hummed it in victory, because I had finally gotten past the feeling that every day was the same at the Tumbleweed.

"Well, good morning to everyone," Ada Lou's voice echoed through the empty dining room that morning. She hung her coat on the back of a chair and sat down at the table she seemed to favor.

I had just finished busing the last table from the morning rush. "Right back at you. You want the same as always?"

"Nope, I'm changing it up today," she said. "I need something that will stick to my skinny bones in this cold weather. From what I heard on the radio on the way down here, there's a blizzard coming our way that will hit us in the middle of next week."

Tumbleweeds and now snow. What had I fallen into?

I picked up a menu and poured a cup of hot coffee, and dropped both off at her table. "What's the difference between a blizzard and a snowstorm?"

She took a sip of coffee and pointed to the Supreme Platter on the menu. "I'll have that. Just leave the coffeepot. To answer your question, compared to a blizzard, a snowstorm is a baby, or maybe a toddler, and it won't keep us cooped up in the house. Did you ever hear the Bible story of David and Goliath?"

"Yes." I remembered a few stories from Sunday school class at the church where my grandparents and mother went when I was a little girl. "Wasn't he the big giant that everyone was afraid of? I pictured him like the Hulk, only maybe not green."

"That's a blizzard," Ada Lou said with a nod. "A person better have what they need in their houses, because they will be stuck in their trailers or homes or wherever they can find warmth and food until it blows on through the place. Now, tell me: What put a smile on your face and that sparkle in your eyes?"

"My glass is more than half full."

"What does that mean in English?" she asked. "I don't speak all that metaphorical stuff."

I told her to wait just one minute so I could put her order in. I crossed the room, stuck my head in the service window, and told Rosalie what Ada Lou wanted. Then I went back and sat down across from her. "You aren't so old that you don't know what it means. You don't fool me one bit, Ada Lou."

The wrinkles in her cheeks deepened when she smiled. "Okay, then I'll rephrase: What is in your glass?"

"Peace," I answered.

"Where did you get it?"

I told her the story of the two couples who had gotten off the bus that morning. "I'm not sure where the peace came from, but I'm glad it's there."

"That's a good thing," she said. "Don't ever let anyone or anything take it away from you. Treat it like fine gold."

"Yes, ma'am."

"We have a new tenant at the RV park," she said. "His name is Jackson Armstrong, and he took the last available spot. He comes from the Armstrong family, who has their hands in a lot of Texas pies, but mostly in oil. I looked them up on the internet."

I played dumb. "How about that?"

"Good-lookin' and rich. You should meet him," Ada Lou said.

"Does he play poker?" I asked in an innocent voice.

"I wouldn't know, but tell me this: How much peace was in your glass when you were playing every night?"

"I never measured," I answered. "What does my glass have to do with your new tenant?"

"You got to look at life itself being at least half full. I've got this sexy-as-hell guy living only a few miles from you. If you meet him . . . who knows. He might fill up your glass to overflowing."

"Then I'd have a mess to clean up," I said.

"You!" Ada Lou threw up her hands in exasperation.

"You didn't tell me that you owned the RV park."

She pointed a long, bony finger at me. "No, I didn't. I bought it several years ago, and it's been a very good investment, but don't try to change the subject. I was talking about Jackson, who appears to be a nice guy. He's right handsome and built like a weight lifter, and he's got kind eyes and a gorgeous smile."

To me, his green eyes were downright sexy. *Kind* had never entered my mind—but then, there were fifty years between me and Ada Lou. Maybe when I was eighty and looking at a man like Jackson, I would think he had kind eyes. Thinking back to the day before, it could very well be that he was part of the reason I had a half-full glass.

But is it peace or just friendship that makes you happy? the voice in my head asked.

"Jerry Clower, one of my favorite comedians—may he rest in peace." Ada Lou rolled her eyes toward the ceiling and blinked several times before she stared right into my eyes. "He used to say that when you are arguing with yourself, you are about to mess up. I see you fighting with someone in your head. Who is it?"

"Myself," I answered.

"Then you *are* about to mess up," she said.

Rosalie brought the platter out herself and placed it in front of Ada Lou. "Things are caught up fairly well, so I'll take a break," she said as she sat down.

Scarlett came from the back and brought a platter of biscuits and three mugs to the table. "We can have these leftover biscuits for a midmorning snack with our coffee."

"I was telling Carla that I rented out the last spot in the RV park. My new tenant paid six months in advance with cash money," Ada Lou said between bites.

Scarlett squirted honey onto a plate and dipped a biscuit in it. "Who got it?"

"Jackson Armstrong. He's in charge of the Armstrong Oil Company that's drilling up north of Dell City. That'll provide jobs for a lot of people in this area. Who knows? It could even raise the population enough that the sign at the city limits will be telling the truth."

"He's stopped by here several times, but we didn't know he was actually moving to these parts," Scarlett said.

Ada Lou gave me a look that was meant to make me cringe in horror. "I was going on and on about him, and you didn't say a word."

I grinned at her. "You didn't ask."

Ada Lou shook a finger at me. "You are a sneaky one. You will bear watching, for sure. Okay, now, moving on: What are y'all going to do if the blizzard materializes?"

Rosalie buttered a biscuit and added strawberry jam from one of the individual packets on the condiment tray. "We will hunker down and get through it. I just hope we don't lose power."

Ada Lou refilled all our coffee mugs and nodded. "I intend to knit more baby hats if the snow puts me in the house."

"Baby hats?" I asked.

"I don't give out all my secrets at once, either, little lady," she said.

"She makes them for the little babies that are born in the hospital at El Paso," Scarlett explained.

"Hundreds of precious little bundles have gone home with one of my hats on. Knitting helps me keep my sanity when I'm stuck at home or bored."

"That's a good thing you do. If we can't open the Tumbleweed, I might get these two to play poker with me," I answered.

"No!" Rosalie declared. She made the sign of the cross and then dropped her chin to pray before she gave me a dose of the old stink eye. "I will not play poker, and neither will you."

"But I don't know how to knit," I protested and winked at Scarlett.

"Don't tease her about gambling, drinking, or swearing," Scarlett warned. "And once she has prayed, that's it. She says that God has hung up, and she's not calling Him right back because He has lots of other matters to take care of."

Rosalie nodded in agreement and pushed back her chair. "If it snows so bad that we have no customers, we will give the whole place a thorough cleaning."

Scarlett groaned and looked up at the ceiling. I got the feeling that she wasn't dialing up the hotline to heaven. "Then I hope that the weatherman is wrong this time."

I fought against the urge to take what money I had and run when I remembered the days that Paula had punished me for some infraction—sassing her was my number one problem—and made me clean her café. She always made me redo everything at least twice. Then she would get out her white cotton gloves and go over every inch of the place. If there was a hint of dirt on her fingertips, I would have to start all over again.

"If he's right, can we at least sleep late?" I asked.

"Only if we lose power," Rosalie answered. "In that case, we won't have lights to see how to clean."

"How often does that happen?"

Ada Lou polished off the last bite of food on the platter. "Four times since I've lived at the trailer park, and the weatherman was right every time. They've got all this fancy equipment now and can tell us when a hurricane is hitting down in Florida or wherever the hell—*heck*—those things make landfall. Or when a snowstorm or rain or a blizzard is on the way. If it is going to keep me inside, I always buy extra supplies and be sure I have stuff to make food that doesn't require the stove or microwave."

"Such as?" I asked.

"Sandwich makings, packages of junk food, and cereal. I freeze an extra gallon of milk and whine because I can't have coffee or hot chocolate until the utility guys come out and fix the lines," Ada Lou said.

I focused on Rosalie. "Do we have all that ready?"

She added a packet of sugar to her coffee. "Of course we do, *boss lady*."

"I might be a boss in a few months, but right now I'm just learning," I smarted off.

Ada Lou pushed back her chair. "I'm on my way to El Paso to pick up all those things I forgot—like honey buns and potato chips. A woman cannot live on bread alone. Will y'all be able to get everything you might need from your supply guy?"

"We could use some sandwich meat," Rosalie said. "Maybe three or four kinds. I'm planning on baking and freezing homemade cookies every day—just in case. I'll save you back some of each kind."

"Please make oatmeal with butterscotch chips, and snickerdoodles. They are my favorite," Ada Lou said as she put her coat on and headed outside.

"I'll start with those," Rosalie promised.

"Ada Lou won't let us pay for the stuff she picks up, so Rosalie gives her cookies or muffins," Scarlett explained when Ada Lou had paid for her meal and left.

Rosalie stood and picked up her half-full coffee mug. "Friendship makes for happiness."

"Do you really believe that?" I asked.

"There's nothing better than friends and family." She didn't look back at me, but I thought I heard a sniff.

"Maybe someday we'll have a confession night," Scarlett said with a smile, as if to distract me.

I really wanted to know what on earth either of them—especially Rosalie—had to confess about. In the short time I had been at the Tumbleweed, I already liked them better than I had anyone since my mother passed away.

Are you willing to spill all of your deeply hidden secrets that you've never shared with anyone in return? the voice in my head asked.

I didn't even try to answer that question.

Chapter Eight

I wasn't sure whether Ada Lou had taken me under her wing because she was lonely or because she wanted to broaden my list of friends so it would be difficult for me to leave when there was enough money in the bank for me to go back to my old ways. Whatever the reason, it was a little spooky, but I still found myself driving up the road toward the RV park. When she came into the café that morning for her daily brunch, she had asked—no, she *told* me—to be at her house for an afternoon game of Scrabble as soon as we closed and got the cleanup done. I didn't even know what that was, but I didn't like to be alone in the empty trailer, so I didn't argue with her. I asked Rosalie about it when she was walking out the door to do something at her church again. She turned around just long enough to tell me that it was Ada Lou's favorite board game.

"It has nothing to do with poker, so don't be disappointed when you get there," she said.

If it didn't involve a deck of cards, neither Frank nor I was interested. By some standards, that would most likely constitute a dysfunctional family dynamic. In my previous world it simply meant a different lifestyle. I'd seen and even played a few internet games, but they usually bored me after five minutes. If it didn't involve practicing for my next round of poker, it wasn't worth wasting my time on.

You are never too old to learn new tricks, the voice in my head whispered.

"Are you calling me old?" I growled as I parked beside Ada Lou's truck.

Ada Lou must have heard my vehicle on the gravel driveway, because she opened the door before I even knocked. "Come on in out of the cold. The hot chocolate is ready."

I stepped inside and removed my jacket. "I've never played board games before, so I'll require some teaching." That's when I noticed another woman sitting at the table.

"You'll catch on quick," Ada Lou said. "The game is more fun with more than two players, so I invited Nancy to come over."

"Pleased to meet you, Carla," Nancy said with a smile that deepened the wrinkles around her crystal clear blue eyes. "I'm the one that's too sentimental to leave during the winter months. The rest of the folks—other than the new guy who moved into space number two—are only here during the spring and summer months. I hear he's planning to stay for a while."

"She and her husband parked here the same year I did and planned to spend only a few days," Ada Lou explained as she poured a mug full of hot chocolate and set it down on the card table. "We play games when it's too cold to take long walks. That keeps our minds from going stale. Sit down and we'll explain the game as we go."

"My husband, Lonnie, died last year," Nancy said with a sigh. "All my favorite memories are right here in this place with him. After he retired, we bought a trailer and took off on a road trip."

"Just like me," Ada Lou added. "And just like me, they put down roots right here."

"Exactly. And besides, all the friends I had back home in Tennessee have either passed on or else they are in nursing homes. When Lonnie died, I had the mortuary put his ashes in a companion vase, so they're sitting on a shelf in my bedroom closet. When I die, I've instructed my son to cremate me, put my ashes with his dad's, and then scatter them out at the base of the mountain. This is where we spent our happiest years."

That was a lot of information to tell a total stranger—but then, maybe board game players shared more than poker players did.

"I'm so sorry," I said.

"Thank you." Nancy tucked both sides of her short, gray hair behind her ears. "Now, let's get serious about this game. While we play, you can tell me a little about yourself. Ada Lou is stingy with her information. She won't even tell me what she knows about our new sexy neighbor. I see him leave early in the morning and come home sometime after five."

I knew exactly who Nancy meant, and agreed that their new neighbor was indeed sexy.

Ada Lou sat down in the only other empty chair and cut her eyes over at Nancy. "How can you see that from your trailer?"

Nancy tilted her chin up in a defiant gesture. "I stand on a step stool under the window in my bedroom and get on tiptoe, because I'm too short to drool over all that testosterone without a little help."

"You might be nosy enough to know all the gossip around these parts, but you would never do that. We've both forgotten so much about what to do with men in the bedroom that we would have to buy a how-to book," Ada Lou argued.

"Speak for yourself. I figure that sex is like riding a bike. You don't forget something that important. And"—she shook her finger at Ada Lou—"don't underestimate *me*, Ada Louise."

I wasn't naive, and I wasn't a virgin. But I sure felt like I should make the sign of the cross over my chest. Old women shouldn't be talking about sex—should they?

Ada Lou slapped Nancy's finger away. "Don't call me that. I might be named for my Aunt Louise, but I despised that woman. I'm plain old Ada Lou, and don't you forget it."

"Then don't question my ability to spy on the neighbors." Nancy winked at me. "I'm up early to listen to the birds while I have my coffee in the mornings, and I hear him driving away. And I walk down to the mailboxes to get my mail at the same time he comes home each evening," she said. "But don't you doubt for one minute that I haven't stood on a stool to figure out what I want to know. I have ways of finding out things. Tomorrow, I plan to welcome him to the neighborhood with a plate of cookies. And don't even ask me to bring any of them to you. If you don't share your information, then I don't share my cookies."

"Downright bitchy today, are we?" Ada Lou said.

While they argued, I studied the board in front of me. This was a word game that used tiles, which were scattered off to one side of the table, and the game was scored according to how they were placed on the tiny squares.

"If you are through pitching a hissy fit, we should start this game. I need to be out of here by five so I can wave at the new resident when he gets home," Nancy said in a teasing tone.

"I was not having a fit," Ada Lou countered. "You know how much I love your cookies, especially those snickerdoodles."

"That's exactly what I'm making," Nancy said.

"You were a baker. Why don't you make your own cookies?" I asked Ada Lou.

If looks could freeze, I would have turned into a Popsicle.

"I have not baked since my daughter died."

"Sorry I asked," I said.

Ada Lou's chin trembled, but she soon got control. "Now you know. We'll take turns drawing tiles, and Nancy will start the game." Secrets all around these parts, it seemed.

By the time it was my turn to make a word, I had a pretty good idea of what was happening. I created *forever* by playing three of my tiles on the word *ever*, which Nancy had made. I didn't get any extra points like Nancy did with the letter *V*, but I was proud of myself for catching on so quickly.

I won the first game by three points. Nancy declared that it was beginner's luck, and maybe it was, because Ada Lou flat-out beat the socks off us in the second one. It was hard to believe that two hours had passed when Nancy pushed back her chair.

"I've got about enough time to get to the mailbox in time to wave at Jackson. I'll bet you a plate of snickerdoodles that I know more about him than either of you by next Thursday, when we meet again for a rematch. And if I win, you will have to bake me a red velvet cake."

Red velvet was not my favorite, but maybe she would make me a plain old chocolate one if I won the bet.

Ada Lou shook Nancy's hand. "Deal."

"I can't believe that you want to win so badly, you would turn on the oven," Nancy said.

"I won't lose," Ada Lou said with conviction.

"What if I win?" I asked.

They both looked at me like I had a horn growing out of my forehead.

"You don't even know how to spy on people," Ada Lou said.

"From what little you told us about your past, you are a drifter," Nancy added. "Watch us and learn if you want some pointers. But for now, all is fair in love and war."

I bit back a smile. Poker players are professional spies. We read people in brief moments, and we listen when they talk. To make two old ladies happy, I would let them teach me what they knew. But I was the one who'd had a late dinner with Jackson and had planned another one sometime in the future. Like Nancy said, *All's fair in love and war*, and I did not like to lose any more than Ada Lou did.

I stuck around long enough to help put the game away, fold the chairs and table and stash them in the hall closet, and have a second cup of hot chocolate.

"I'm going to take a late nap. You run along now," Ada Lou said with a glimmer in her eyes. "If you are lucky, you'll get to wave at Jackson, too, as you pass by the mailboxes."

"I thought Nancy was going to do that," I said.

"When she wasn't looking, I set the clock on the microwave up twenty minutes," Ada Lou whispered. "I'll teach her to bake my favorite cookies and not share with me."

"Shame on you!" I scolded. "Y'all are both old enough to be Jackson's grandmothers."

Ada Lou handed me my jacket and opened the door. "Don't call us *old*. Neither of us even need glasses. And like I told you, when the weather is fit, we hike every day."

I took a step outside. "And even if you would have to have a book to remember how to have sex, you still like to look at a sexy man, right?"

"Now you are learning—but, darlin', I would not need a book if I wanted to jump a man's bones. I was very good at that business at one time, and I'm sure I would be again." She closed the door before I could say another word.

I had just opened the door to my SUV when a white truck braked and pulled up beside me, and Jackson rolled down the passenger window. "Hey, what are you doing here?"

"Playing Scrabble with a couple of sneaky old gals," I answered.

"I forgot my backpack at the office, so I have to go back," he said. "Want to go with me?"

"I would love to." I grabbed my purse and got out of the SUV.

That was way too eager, the voice in my head seemed to shout.

I don't care. I don't want to go home to an empty trailer.

You never minded being alone in a hotel room, it argued.

I didn't have friends then. I do now.

I caught a movement in my peripheral vision and glanced back toward the trailer. Ada Lou was giving me a thumbs-up from the porch.

"Now, what's this about my new landlady being sneaky?" he asked as he turned around and drove back toward Dell City.

"She and Nancy—that's the elderly woman who lives in the last trailer—have a bet going about who can find out the most about you." Just thinking of those two old gals talking about sex put a big grin on my face.

His smile put extra sparkles in his eyes. "Why?"

"Because they're bored, and they like to bicker about everything."

"Then I hope I bring a little excitement into their lives," he chuckled. "I'm sorry I haven't called. This job is bigger than I thought it would be. I work nine hours a day and bring home paperwork to do after that. That said, I'm glad I caught you today. I really enjoyed spending time with you in Sierra Blanca."

"Me too." I held up my hand and splayed my fingers out. "Five."

"Okay. Congratulations. You have four fingers and a thumb."

"I now have five people that I can loosely call *friends*," I said.

"Are they lined up according to importance or how long they've been your friends?" Jackson asked.

"Why?"

"I'm competitive, so I want to know where I stand."

"You are right in the middle for both."

"Fair enough. Being number three gives me a starting point. I'll try harder to move up the ladder to number one before winter ends," he said.

"Why would you want to be at the top of the list?" I wasn't sure how to feel about someone actually wanting to be number one in my life—a little nervous, a whole lot excited, or maybe just perplexed.

"Because I want to get to know you, and I don't want to compete with the other four, plus whoever else you add to the list along the way," he answered, and changed the subject. "Have you had time to drive through Dell City?"

"Ada Lou gave me the grand tour," I said as we passed the city limits sign.

My thoughts circled back to Jackson wanting to move to the top of my new list. Did I even want to get involved—friendship or more—with a guy at this point in my life?

"I bet after traveling all over the place, Dell City seems pretty small to you, doesn't it?" he asked.

Rosalie's truck was parked in front of the Catholic church again. She must have done something terrible in her past to need to go to confession that often.

"Well?" Jackson asked.

"I'm sorry. I saw Rosalie's truck, and my mind went in circles," I replied. "I only lived in a house for a little while after my mama died, and then less than six months after Frank remarried. And yes, this place does seem small. If you gathered up all the people in town, you wouldn't have a third of what I've seen in a Vegas casino. Have *you* ever lived in a town this small?"

"Not really, but I've been in lots of communities in other countries that had fewer houses than this place," he answered.

We'd gone a couple of miles when I saw lights up ahead of us. "Is that the site?"

"Yes, it is, and the first place we plan to drill," he told me. "There will be others if this one turns out to be as profitable as Henry thinks it will be."

"Do you really think you'll be happy here?" I asked.

He hesitated while he parked in front of one of several mobile trailers. "Let's go inside where it's warm. I've got beer and sweet tea in the fridge, and I can make hot tea or coffee."

I opened the truck door, still without an answer to my question, and headed for a boxy-looking mobile trailer with no lights shining out the windows. "Why do you have so many of these homes out here?" *Maybe that could get him talking.*

Jackson used his long stride to get ahead so he could open the door for me. "The major crew members share four of them. They have all been working for the company for years and are pretty senior in the business. They each have different days off so that they aren't all gone at the same time. The head honcho out here is Henry, our oil engineer, and he has a trailer of his own. He's been with Dad's company since I was a toddler. Aside from that, we need extra people on the site to prevent vandalism."

I thought about some of the places ol' Frank and I had stayed in the days when we weren't flush. We always took everything in from the van on those nights and hoped that it hadn't been stripped of its tires the next morning. I didn't like to remember those times, but the life of a poker player was not all rainbows and unicorn farts—another of ol' Frank's sayings.

"And I'm not sure about being happy, but I'm going to give it a try," he went on to say. "The Good Book says something about being content with our lot. I didn't ever realize what a big order that was until recently."

Amen to that, I thought.

The place was even smaller than Ada Lou's travel trailer. A makeshift desk with two folding chairs were to my right. A sofa took up most of the room at the other end.

"Take off your coat and have a seat. The sofa is a lot more comfortable than one of those hard chairs. Want a beer or—"

"I would love one." I made a mental note to use a breath mint before I went home. It wouldn't do for Rosalie to smell any kind of alcohol on me. The very idea of her getting so mad that she walked away from the Tumbleweed came close to stopping my heart. I didn't cook, and Rosalie seemed to be the core of the whole café.

He removed two bottles of beer from the tiny dorm-sized fridge and twisted the tops off each of them. Then he took a couple of steps, handed one to me, and sat down on the other end of the sofa.

I took a long drink of beer. "If you are thirty-eight and Henry has been around since you were a toddler, isn't he about ready for retirement?"

"He doesn't have family other than me and says he would die of boredom if he didn't have new wells to drill."

"Did he teach you all this stuff?" I waved a hand around to include everything.

"I don't know everything yet, but Henry is giving it his best shot," Jackson chuckled. "I hung around him enough as a child that I at least learned the lingo, and then the army trained me in that area since they were putting me together with a team that would spend time in places where . . ." He paused.

"You could tell me, but then you'd have to kill me," I said. "And then you would forever more remain at number three on my list."

Jackson rolled his eyes. "That just might kill *me*."

"I figured as much. You learned the basics from Henry and some stuff in the army, and now Henry is teaching you whatever he knows that has to do with all those maps on the walls and those big books stacked up on the desk. And that is why you have to take stuff home with you at night. Right?"

He tipped up his bottle and downed a fourth of it. "Absolutely correct. Now, let's talk about you and how I can move up to number one."

Was that a pickup line? Or did he really mean it? I could flirt right back if it was the former, but I wasn't sure what to do with it if it was the latter.

"You'll have to figure that out for yourself. Do you really think you'll be happy doing this for the rest of your life?"

Jackson's expression told me that he was thinking hard about his answer. Finally, he said, "I don't know, Carla. Do you think you would be happy without poker games for the rest of your life?"

"If I had to answer that right now, I'd say no—but in a few months, I might change my mind." I was surprised at my own answer. "What about you?"

He took another drink, which made me think that he was struggling with the answer. "I got a phone call today. The army wants me to come back as an instructor to the new guys who are training for Special Forces. I was tempted to pack my bags, but I couldn't do it. I promised my dad a year. What kind of man doesn't keep his word?"

"But you wanted to, right? Just like I would love to get into a good game of poker."

"I did," he admitted. "However, I've chosen this path, and I have to finish it to the end, or I couldn't live with myself."

"I understand," I said with a nod. "Every day this past week, I've counted my tip money and added my paycheck amount to it. There's not even enough to get me into a small game, much less the high-stakes kind I'm used to playing in. Patience is not my best virtue, but Ada Lou keeps trying to convince me that I'm where I am supposed to be."

"She seems to be quite a character," he said.

"Oh, yeah, but don't ever call her Louise. She got all riled up when Nancy did. Do real friends argue a lot?"

"I will remember to always use Ada Lou," he said, and covered a yawn with the back of his hand. "And yes, honest friends argue when they have a difference of opinion, or when they are just bickering for the sake of joking."

I turned up my beer and finished it. "I'll file that away. Right now, you are tired and still have work to do, so why don't you drive me back to the RV park."

"Will you come back another day and meet Henry?"

"I'd be glad to," I answered. "He might even get added to my list of friends and drop you down to number four."

Jackson chuckled as he stood up and extended his hand to help me. I took it and felt a rush of hot desire that I couldn't blame on the weather.

Chemistry. Either you got it, or you don't. And, honey, you've got it. The voice in my head sounded a lot like Ada Lou this time.

Chapter Nine

The calendar on the kitchen wall beside the coatrack told me that it was Friday—one week and one day since I'd arrived at the Tumbleweed. Not a month or a year like it sometimes felt like, but only eight days. As usual, Rosalie led the way from the trailer to the café with Scarlett right beside her.

Clouds covered the moon and stars like a heavy fog of smoke over a poker table. In my life as a gambler, I saw sunsets but seldom ever caught a glimpse of a sunrise. The games didn't end until the early hours of the morning, and then I had to unwind before going to sleep. So my internal clock was having a horrible time trying to adjust to this new schedule. Had someone told me two weeks ago that I would be getting up before daylight, I would have wondered what they had been smoking.

"Hey, I have a question," I said when we were inside the storage room.

Scarlett pulled a string with a wooden thread spool on the end and lit up the room. She kept on walking into the kitchen, where Rosalie had already switched on the lights. I was beginning to think that she hadn't even heard me.

"Ask whatever you want, but you might not get an answer if it's something personal," she finally said.

Rosalie had already turned on the grill and the oven and, like she had done in previous mornings, had slung a bibbed apron over her

T-shirt and loose-fitting jeans. That day she wore a yellow bonnet with butterflies printed on it.

"What's your question?" she asked.

"What's the difference between a diner and a café? And which one is the Tumbleweed? The sign says TUMBLEWEED BUS STOP AND DINER, but Ada Lou calls it a café."

"I remember asking Matilda that same question," Rosalie answered. "She said that in the beginning, this place was considered a diner since it only served breakfast until about eleven o'clock. And after that, only sandwiches and food that folks on the buses could grab and go. When she began to get business from travelers other than those catching a bus or stopping for a break, she began to fix one hot meal a day and called it the lunch special. It grew from that to the menu we have today."

"Short answer," Scarlett said, "is that the words are now interchangeable."

"Another question." I pressed my luck. "Why doesn't your boyfriend—Gary—ever come into the café?"

Scarlett stopped just short of the swinging doors and turned around. "It's Grady, not Gary—and except for Sunday, he is working when we are open."

I followed her and started putting chairs on the floor while she got the condiment trays ready. "Has Rosalie met him?"

"Of course," she answered. "We've been dating for more than a year."

"Y'all don't dilly-daddle around," Rosalie called out. "Biscuits will be ready in twenty minutes. What do y'all want to go with them?"

"My regular," Scarlett said.

"Sausage gravy and hash browns," I yelled and then focused on Scarlett. "A whole year with one guy?" Not in my wildest imagination could I fathom staying in a relationship that long. Sometimes a weekend was twelve hours too long, and I couldn't wait to tell the guy goodbye at the hotel door.

"You look surprised. You are thirty years old. Surely you've had relationships in the past."

"Not really. To be honest, I've never had a real boyfriend. A few one-night stands, and one guy that I got together with for a whole weekend when our paths crossed. We both knew that it was casual. He got married a couple of years ago, so even that ended. My number one rule is that I don't go to bed with men who are taken."

"Well, you are here now. It's time to change that," Scarlett said.

"I'm still not having sex with a married man," I declared.

"I didn't mean that," Scarlett said with a smile. "I meant it's time to have a boyfriend—a single one that you could fall in love with."

"What does it feel like to have someone in your life for an extended period of time?" I'd read lots of those happy ever after–romance books, but that was just entertaining fiction. Could there be something like that in reality?

"If that person treats you like Grady does me, then it's wonderful," she answered, and then her expression went from warm and fuzzy at his name to cold and tough. "If you get someone who doesn't make you feel like a queen, break it off."

"Do you feel sparks . . ." I hesitated. "I got that word from the romance books I read, so don't judge me, but do you feel all gushy inside when he holds your hand?"

"I do," Scarlett answered. "It seems strange to be answering these questions when you are older than I am."

"Hey, now, I'm not that old," I protested. "But thank you all the same."

"Food is ready," Rosalie called from the kitchen.

Scarlett unlocked the front door and flipped the switch to turn on the flashing Open sign. We went to the kitchen and sat down in our regular places.

"Thank you for always making breakfast for us, Rosalie," I said.

"No problem," she said.

"It seems like I've fallen into a bed of roses. I have everything I need without having to shell out money."

Rosalie chuckled and set a plate of food in front of each of us.

"What's so funny?" I asked.

"That you are finally understanding that you don't need poker to be happy," she answered. "So, are you telling me that you don't need a game of cards anymore?"

I picked up my fork and shook my head. "No, ma'am, I am not saying that at all. If it wasn't for all your good food, I might be driving over to El Paso or up to Carlsbad for a game."

"How do you know you could find something in either of those places?" Scarlett asked.

"I would just need to make a phone call to a guy I know, and he would find a game for me anywhere within a hundred miles. But then you would leave, and I can't cook," I teased.

"Don't you forget it." Rosalie emphasized each word by poking her fork at me.

"Since you hate gambling so much, why didn't you walk away when you realized what Larry was doing with all the money y'all made?" I asked.

"I prayed that he would finally come to his senses or that someone decent would buy this place," she answered. "God answers his children in mysterious ways sometimes."

I didn't think of myself as spiritual, but I agreed with her that morning.

Something totally out of my wheelhouse and comfort zone was surely happening, and I had no control over any of it.

Usually, one or two customers from the buses entertained me with a story throughout the day, but not that Friday. The only potential bright spot had been when Ada Lou rode in on her motorcycle, and even she declared that she was in a bad mood and poor company. I blamed the dreary weather for the ho-hum day when the last customer paid their bill and left to board the bus.

Life does not mean you get to be the statue every time. Today you are the pigeon, the voice in my head said.

"Don't I know it," I muttered. "But a little bit of excitement would be great."

Scarlett had already begun taking the condiment trays to the kitchen to clean them. "What was that?" she asked.

I got busy wiping down the tables. "Nothing. I was just talking to myself."

I finished that job and made a trip to the employee bathroom just off the storage room. When I had washed my hands, I stepped out to the sound of Rosalie yelling at someone to put those guns away and get their sorry butts on down the road. Then Scarlett said something about not opening the cash register in a tone I didn't recognize.

"We are being robbed," I muttered, and my chest tightened. There were people out there with guns. Or was this a drill that Rosalie had thought up to see how I would react? I tiptoed back into the kitchen and was about to peek out through the service window when I heard a feminine voice say, "Old woman, I told you to get over there to that cash register beside the waitress."

I counted to ten and raised up again to take another look. This was no drill. There were two people in masks, and each of them held a gun sideways, like gangsters in the movies.

"Move, old woman!" the one with a masculine voice demanded.

Nobody talked to my friend that way if I could do anything about it. Rosalie was not old by any stretch of the word, which told me that the two robbers were punk-ass kids. I took another quick look from the side of the window and saw Scarlett at the cash register. I couldn't see her face, but her back was ramrod straight. From that angle, it was difficult to see if she was scared or angry, or both. Rosalie had a clean condiment tray still in her hands and was facing the service window. When she noticed me, she glanced down at the counter where she kept the sawed-off shotgun. Was she telling me to try to get to the gun?

Fat chance. I had to make it over to the counter without being seen. The two masked people had guns with what looked like high-capacity magazines attached to them. Were those even legal in the state of Texas?

Robbery isn't legal, either, so I'm sure they don't obey rules. Ada Lou was back in my head.

I checked them both out from my hiding place. One was tall and skinny. The shorter one wore a T-shirt so short that it showed a belly button ring. If they thought they were taking money from us, they had cotton candy for brains—not when I needed every dime to move on with my life.

It's time to prove if Rosalie and Scarlett are your friends. Will you do anything to protect them? the irritating voice in my head asked.

I stopped myself before I blurted out, "Yes, and hush before they realize I'm here."

There was no way I could get to that weapon, not even if I laid on my belly and crawled under the door like a snake. Bonnie and Clyde out there would see me for sure.

"Keep your hands up, or I swear I will shoot you," the girl growled loudly.

All I had in the way of a weapon was a wooden spoon, a butcher knife, and what was left of a pot of hot baked-potato soup. I doubted that the spoon would do much damage. I hated the sight of blood, and besides, I would be dead the minute I rushed at them with the knife. The hot soup might slow one of them down, but the other one could shoot Rosalie or Scarlett without a single thought if I burned his or her partner.

That was when I remembered the pistol in my purse. It hadn't been fired in years, but it was loaded, and I was a good shot back when I could find a range to practice at.

"If either of them lowers their hands, I'll take out the waitress," the guy said. "Now, open that cash register and then take us to the safe and open the damned thing."

"There is no safe," Rosalie lied.

"There better be, or the next customer will find y'all's dead bodies in the back room," he threatened.

Oh, my. She will be spending every day for a week in confession for lying, I thought as I eased away from the window, then tiptoed across the kitchen and back into the storage room, where my purse was located. I carefully unzipped the concealed compartment, removed my five-shot .38, and then took my phone from the side pocket. I wasn't sure if Dell City even had a police department, but I tiptoed into the bathroom and dialed 911. A man answered and I whispered, "I own the Tumbleweed café, and there are two people with guns trying to rob the place."

"Where are you right now?" he asked.

"In the bathroom, but they are threatening to shoot Rosalie and Scarlett," I answered.

"I know the place and both of those ladies. I'm sending someone down there right now. Stay on the phone with me until they get there."

"I can't." I ended the call, took a deep breath, and slowly made my way back to the window.

I took a quick peek and saw that everyone was still in the same place they had been when I left. Rosalie caught my eye again and shifted her gaze back to the counter for the second time.

"You really don't want to do this," Scarlett said as she opened the cash register. "Two policemen come in about this time every day for a slice of pie and some coffee. They'll be here any minute."

Rosalie didn't make the sign of the cross or roll her eyes toward the ceiling as she addressed the robbers.

"Jesus sees everything you are doing," she said. "Ev-ry-thing."

I bit back a nervous giggle because what she said played right into my plan.

"They are bluffing. We should have been out of here five minutes ago. Go on over there and get the money," the man said.

The woman kept her gun up and used the other hand to put the money from the cash register into her big purse. "Where is your tip jar?"

"We don't have one," Scarlett answered.

"Then give me what you have stashed in your purse or pockets," the girl said.

Scarlett set the tip box on the counter and opened it.

Anger shot through me like a lightning strike. Those punk kids would walk out of here with our tip money over my dead body.

"I got it," the girl said. "Now, let's go to the back room where they keep more than just today's cash, and they will open the safe or else they'll bleed out on the floor."

Such big talk for such a little person, I thought as I plastered myself against the wall beside the swinging doors and listened to the guy tell Rosalie and Scarlett to go ahead of them into the kitchen. Rosalie walked past me. Scarlett cut her eyes around and saw me, but she didn't say a word or miss a step. When those two sorry-ass kids came through the doors, I touched the screen on my phone. The next second, the sound of a dog the size of Cujo started barking and growling like it was coming right out of the storage room. A man's voice yelled, "Go get 'em, Jesus. Tear 'em up. Don't quit until they are on the ground."

Both would-be robbers froze. Before the dog stopped barking, the cold barrel of my pistol was pressed against the guy's neck.

"You move, and I shoot. Have you ever heard of the apricot?" I didn't give him time to answer. That episode of *Justified* had better be based on truth. That was the one where Raylan Givens explains that the apricot is a place at the base of the skull, and when someone pulls the trigger, the person is instantly dead.

"If I shoot you right here in the apricot, you will have breathed your last breath," I said, in a voice so calm that it surprised me. "Both of you will drop your guns now and start backing up real slow like. I've got an itchy trigger finger."

"You won't shoot me—and if you do, my partner will kill the old woman," he said, but he backed up into the dining room.

The girl took a couple of steps back, but she turned her gun away from Rosalie and toward me. That was when Scarlett slipped past them and brought the sawed-off shotgun out from under the counter. The clacking sound when she cocked that thing sent shivers down my spine. The steely look in her eyes told me that she was angry, not scared.

"Both of you will very gently lay your guns on the floor and take a seat in a chair. If you don't, I will shoot the girl first, and my friend's bullet will find that apricot. This ends right here and now," Scarlett said.

Apparently they did not want to die, because they obeyed. When they were seated, Rosalie hurried to the kitchen and brought out a roll of duct tape. When she had wrapped it around their hands and ankles, she ripped their masks off. They both looked like they were about sixteen. The girl had blue hair, and the guy had a scraggly beard that reminded me of Shaggy from *Scooby-Doo*. They both had lip rings, nose rings, and hoops in their eyebrows. That they hadn't been pulled out when Rosalie yanked the masks away was a miracle.

"I ought to take a switch to you both," Rosalie snapped.

"I should have shot you," Shaggy growled. "You wouldn't have been the first one, neither."

"I can't believe that we've been caught because I'm afraid of dogs," the girlfriend groaned. "But we'll only do a couple of years in juvie."

"Not for murder, if you are telling the truth," Rosalie said just as a police car pulled up and two officers got out, one with a bullhorn.

"This is Deputy James Carson. I need you to come out with your hands in the air," he said.

Rosalie opened the door and motioned them inside. "Hello, Jimmy and Luis. Come on in and get them. We've got them tied up and ready for you."

Jimmy tossed the bullhorn back into the car and followed her back into the café. When he saw the two kids tied up, he smiled and said, "You've done our job for us."

"She wasn't lying about them coming for pie and coffee," the young girl said. "Next time we need to be more careful."

Jimmy pulled his phone from his hip pocket, looked at a couple of pictures, and then showed them to Luis. "Little lady, I don't reckon there will be a next time. Even out here in the boonies, we get photos and write-ups for who the FBI has on their Most Wanted list." He whipped the phone around to show her the screen. "I believe this is you and your boyfriend. The FBI is involved now since you've crossed several state lines on this spree. Did you think you were reenacting Bonnie and Clyde?"

"We're better than they were." She scowled at him.

"I doubt that, Lisa McAdams," he said.

Evil poured from her eyes. "So, you know my name and that I'm a juvenile."

"Me too, and we are still alive to start again when we get out of juvie," the boy said.

"Not so, Stanley Mason," Luis said. "You don't get to go to juvie when you have murdered two people."

"Allegedly—and prove it," Stanley growled.

"I don't have to. Those guns on the floor will do that for the FBI," Luis told him.

Rosalie had sunk down into a chair and had turned so pale that I was afraid she would faint. I rushed over to the counter, poured a glass of water, and took it to her. She took a couple of sips and then took several deep breaths. At that point, I wished that Rosalie *had* cut a switch, or even a piece of cow's tongue cactus, and beat on them for a while before the authorities arrived. The pompous little snots needed some discipline.

Luis bent down and cut the tape from the girl's ankles. When she was free, she kicked him hard in the shins with her free feet. He fell backward, and she popped up on her feet and tried to kick him again. Jimmy grabbed her from behind and held her while Scarlett wrapped more tape around her legs.

"I'm going to get a lawyer and sue the bunch of you for brutality," Shaggy screamed.

I crossed the room and leaned down until my nose was only an inch from his. "You do that. When you do, I'll gladly be in court to testify that you held my friends at gunpoint and threatened to kill them."

He leaned as far back as possible in the chair. I figured he was either going to headbutt me or spit in my face, so I moved to the side. He was nothing more than a blur when he shot forward, but since I had moved, he couldn't stop the momentum and fell out onto the floor in a heap—screaming and wiggling like a two-year-old having a tantrum.

"Looks to me like we're going to have to carry them out rather than let them walk," Jimmy said.

Lisa started screeching, too, so Scarlett taped her mouth shut and then bent down and did the same with Shaggy Stanley. "They might try to chew through each other's tape or bite one of you. Then you'd have to go all the way to El Paso for a rabies test. It might not be a bad idea, when you get them over there, for the Feds to go ahead and have both checked."

"She's right." Rosalie stood up from her chair. "Something has made them *murciélago mierda loco*."

"What does that mean, Luis?" Jimmy asked.

Luis picked up the guy's feet. "It means they are bat-shit crazy, and I'm surprised that Rosie said something like that."

Rosalie shrugged. "The words ain't nice, but that's the only ones that work on these two feral children. Get them out of here and in your car."

"We'll be locking them up in our jail, but they won't be there long. There are two agents coming to take custody of them in a few hours. I can't believe that y'all caught them," Luis said.

"You can give Carla the credit. She was the one who really caught them," Rosalie said.

I draped an arm around Scarlett's shoulders. "It was a team effort."

Jimmy got the skinny Shaggy kid by the shoulders, and he and Luis carried him out. The way he tried to wiggle free reminded me of a worm in hot ashes. The same thing happened with the girl. The two policemen waved from the car when they finally had them secured in the back seat and drove away.

The adrenaline rush inside my body bottomed out so fast that I either had to sit down or fall on the floor in a heap. I laid my gun on the table. Scarlett shoved the shotgun under the bar and slid into the chair closest to me. Rosalie sat down beside me and draped an arm over my shoulders.

"I was scared out of my mind," Scarlett whispered. "Matilda always told us to never go to the back room with anyone, because nine times out of ten that meant they would kill you."

"I thought you were both very brave," I said.

"So were you, Carla," Rosalie said. "I didn't know if you would get my message or not, but you did."

"Did you know I had a gun in my purse?" I asked.

"I moved it to one side this morning when I grabbed a bag of flour," she answered between deep breaths. "It seemed heavy, and then I saw the zipper on the side. I figured you carried a weapon for protection. I'm glad it was there. I worried that you wouldn't get my message and they would kill us once I opened the safe."

I patted her on the arm. "Me and Jesus took care of things."

She gave my shoulder a gentle squeeze. "I want that recording put on my phone."

"Me too," Scarlett said. "And if I ever get a dog, I'm naming him Jesus."

"Don't you dare!" Rosalie had clearly found her second wind. "That is sacrilegious."

Scarlett slapped her hand over her mouth.

"What?" I asked.

"If they need someone from here to testify in a trial, you will have to go, Carla. Neither Rosalie nor I can do that."

"I will be more than glad to tell the jury what happened," I said. "But why can't you go?"

Why can't they go to court? Does it have something to do with why they are so content to stay in this remote area of the state? I wondered, but I didn't ask.

Scarlett glanced over at Rosalie.

Rosalie shook her head.

"Today is not the time to tell those stories. We're all still too nervous to open those cans of worms," Scarlett finally said.

"Right," Rosalie said. "Let's leave this cleanup until morning. We can come out half an hour early and get it done then. I just want to go home for now. That dog of yours scared me so badly, I peed my pants."

"It helped when you told them that Jesus could see them."

She stood up and headed for the kitchen. By the time Scarlett and I caught up to her, she was already in the trailer. She started down the hallway but then turned around. "I was so flustered that I forgot to pick up the sack with the leftovers in it. Y'all can go get it when you get hungry. And, Carla . . . you can call me Rosie."

Chapter Ten

The tumbleweeds were out in full force that day. We had to push them off the porch, kick them away from us, and then throw them away from the back door of the café to even open for the day. I checked each one for scorpions or a bug of any kind hitching a ride to points south.

"If someone could figure out a use for these things other than starting a bonfire or spray-painting them gold for decorations, we could make a million dollars harvesting them," Rosie said.

Scarlett opened the door and stood to the side to let us enter first. Before I could take two steps, a tumbleweed as big as a bushel basket flew into the storage room.

Rosie picked it up and tossed it back outside. "That one's got a roach the size of a lizard hanging on to it. I don't know why Noah ever let the nasty things on the ark."

I nodded in agreement and forgot all about what she said until I headed to Sierra Blanca to take care of the banking. I had fought with the tumbleweeds on the way to my SUV, and they scooted down the highway in front of me like they were leading the way.

Every time I looked in the rearview mirror, I could see them still chasing me. I swore at a few when they flew up and hit the windshield, but I'd had a good night's sleep and didn't mistake one for a dead body when I crushed them beneath my tires.

I raised my fist and shook it. "Why didn't you kill the damn things off with Noah's flood?"

Hey, now, you have been nothing more than a tumbleweed for many years, my mother's voice scolded me. *Just flitting around from one city to another. And you are cussing because you are disappointed, not because you don't like bugs and tumbleweeds.*

I couldn't argue with that. I *was* frustrated. I had looked forward to spending the afternoon with Jackson. But then, an hour before he was to pick me up, he'd sent a text saying that he was tied up at the rig and couldn't make it that day. I just wanted to go to the bank and back home, where I could pout in silence in my bedroom, not blink every time something came flying up to crash into my windshield.

So, you are calling that area home now? Mama's voice was still there.

The café and trailer were the only permanent homes I'd known in more than a decade. I made less money there than I ever had in my poker games—and that included what I won my sophomore year playing during lunch at school. I could visualize my mother tapping her foot as she waited for an answer.

"Okay, okay, it's home, but that could still be temporary," I answered out loud.

The father of all tumbleweeds slammed against my windshield and then bounced off the side, startling me so badly that I swerved over into the next lane. Thank goodness nothing was coming at me on the two-lane road.

"If I have to live with these blasted things every year, I'm not so sure I want this to be my home for all eternity," I fumed.

The odometer on my SUV could testify that I had spent miles and miles all alone on the road with nothing but my playlist to keep me company. Scarlett was the only other person who had ever been behind the wheel, and that was just a short drive around to the back of the café. No one—not one single soul—had ever sat in the passenger seat.

"So, why am I lonely today? Is this what friends do for a person? Does having them make a person crave company all the time?" I muttered as I started my playlist. Music had always put me in a better mood.

The first song that came through the speakers was "Starting Over" by Chris Stapleton, one of my favorite artists. The lyrics talked about him being a lucky penny and his girl his four-leaf clover.

"Dammit!" I swore when the song ended. "I was *forced* to start over. It wasn't my decision. And besides, that song makes me think about Jackson, and I don't want him on my mind. I sure don't want to get into a relationship that I would regret after a year or two."

I had bewailed my losses in Tucson, but more than a week had now passed since that fateful night. If I'd known then what I knew now, would I have kept driving to Vegas?

I parked in the bank parking lot and sighed because I didn't know the answer. If I had listened to my heart and Lady Luck, I would have my old lifestyle back and wouldn't even be disappointed that Jackson wasn't meeting me for a late lunch. By not knowing and letting the universe have a hand in things, I had five new friends. I held out my palms and imagined the left one filled with hundred-dollar bills and the right one with Scarlett, Rosie, Jackson, Ada Lou, and Nancy in it.

I slowly closed my left hand. Money was just dirty paper with dead presidents' pictures on it. Friends were more precious than that. I grabbed my purse and opened the door. I wouldn't have missed this experience for all the money in the world. Not even that robbery! Now I got to call Rosalie *Rosie*. That was one step closer to getting them to trust me enough to tell me why they didn't want to appear in court. I suspected the answer wasn't great.

I finished my business in record time and decided to walk down to the Mexican café for a late lunch. I had eaten alone for years and had proven that I didn't need to look across the table at anyone else. But suddenly, I experienced a new feeling—loneliness. I had sworn that I would never yearn for company again after six months of living with Frank's wife, Paula, who wanted to control every single thing about me.

A different waitress from the one that took care of Jackson and me looked up from behind the cash register and waved. "Sit anywhere you like. As you can see, you are the only customer we have right now."

I told myself that I was a big girl who made my own way, paid for my own meals, and was totally independent. I repeated it a couple of times as I crossed the room and sat down at the same table where Jackson and I had sat just a week before.

That little pep talk was fine and good until I glanced over, and he wasn't there. The saying about the heart not missing what the eyes don't see popped into my mind. But now I *had* seen the joys of having friends, and my heart missed them.

The waitress who had waved at me appeared at my elbow with one lone menu and a single packet of silverware. "I'm Katy, and I'll be taking care of you today. What can I get you to drink?"

"I'll have a beer," I answered. "Whatever you have on tap is good, and I want the taco platter."

"I'll be right back with that and a glass of water, plus some corn bread muffins for you to nibble on while we fix your food," she said.

"Thank you, Katy."

"Sure thing." She left and returned with a mug of beer and a basket of muffins. "I've lived here all my life, but I don't think I've ever seen you around. Are you just passing through?"

"I'm living south of Dell City. I own the Tumbleweed," I answered.

"Mind if I sit with you?" Katy asked when she brought my food. "I really don't like this time of day. The lunch rush is over, and everything is quiet for a couple of hours. When I get the place cleaned up, it's just a matter of waiting. I'm not known for patience."

I nodded toward the chair across the table. "Have a seat. I'm learning that I don't like to eat alone." Since arriving at the Tumbleweed, I hadn't had to eat alone even once.

She pulled out a chair and sat down. "So, when did you buy the café?"

"I didn't buy it," I answered between bites. "I won it in a poker game."

Her blue eyes got wider and wider until they looked like they might pop right out of her head. She clamped a hand over her mouth and whispered. "Please tell me you won it from Larry, and then he was so broke that he has to live in his truck—or better yet, in a box under a bridge."

"It was from Larry, but he wasn't totally broke when he left that night. Why does that shock you?"

"Larry is a pompous ass who was a friend to one of my ex-boyfriends," she answered. "I'm glad that he lost the café in a poker game. He was about to run it into bankruptcy, and Miz Matilda would be sad. Even in heaven, where everything is supposed to be all joyous, she would be sad. She loved that little place."

"Wow!" I whispered. "It seems like no one around these parts has any good words to say about him."

"You can't find blood in a turnip, and you can't say good things about a man like Larry," she said.

I spooned some salsa onto my tacos. "Not even one little thing?"

"There is one thing . . ." She grinned. "He's gone." She stood up when the bell above the door jingled and a whole group of folks came inside. "Welcome. Are y'all all together?"

"Yes, we are, and we'd like a table for ten," the older woman in the group said.

"Give me a moment to get you set up," Katy said, and got moving.

The woman saw me and came right over to my table. "Hi. I'm hoping you can help. I'm taking a group of teenagers back home from a Christian retreat in Carlsbad. Do you have any recommendations for what to order—these teens are so picky!"

"I've only had the taco platter, but it's awesome. Last week my friend had the enchiladas, and he said they were great," I answered.

"Thank you so much, and have a blessed day," she said.

"You are welcome." I took a sip of my beer and went back to eating.

That's another thing you missed out on. My mama had returned.

I knew what she was talking about. I had not had the normal teenage experience of going to church with a bunch of my peers, or attending retreats—whatever those were. Strange thing was, until I saw them sitting across the room from me and laughing together, I didn't even know that it was something I would miss.

Both vehicles were gone, and the trailer was empty when I got home. I put the bank bag with the receipts on the bar and walked right back outside. Rosalie and Scarlett would realize when they got home that I hadn't run away with their money.

I drove up to Ada Lou's place. Her truck was there, but no one answered when I knocked on the door. It was too early for Jackson to be in his trailer, so I went back into my SUV and headed north to Dell City. Rosie's truck was in front of her church, but I didn't see Scarlett's car anywhere.

I sure wasn't ready to go home to an empty trailer, so I kept driving past the oil rig and on into New Mexico. I passed a sign that told me I was heading for Cloudcroft, population 750 and elevation over eight thousand feet. That sounded like a fairy tale after spending so many days in a flat country with only tumbleweeds and yucca plants. Maybe there would be a place where I could grab a hot cup of coffee, and if I was lucky, Rosalie and Scarlett would be home when I got back.

I left the desert country behind and drove up into a brand-new world. No more yucca plants and cactus, but now tall pine trees and mountains were all around me. When I realized that it was almost four o'clock, I told myself to turn around at the next opportunity, but I didn't want to leave the beauty. The roads were clear, but there was a layer of snow on the trees as well as the ground, turning the whole area into what could be on a picturesque Christmas card. A long, winding curve brought me into a small town that looked like the setting for an old Western movie.

"Why couldn't the café be in this place?" I groaned. "I haven't even seen one of those wicked tumbleweeds up here in the mountains."

I parked in front of the Old Apple Barn, beneath a sign that said their fudge factory was open daily. I got out of the SUV and started up the steps to a porch with all kinds of pottery hanging between the posts.

If you made a home in these parts, you could buy things like these to decorate your house with. Mama was back again, and there was no doubt that she was ready for me to put down roots.

"Why are you talking to me now?" I muttered.

Because I don't want you to play poker. I never did, and I hate Frank for taking you out of school, and I hate his new wife for being so hard on you that you couldn't live a normal life with them. I want grandchildren. I want to see you break this chain of only children by having a yardful of kids. I won't rest in peace until you do, and if you go back to your old lifestyle, I won't pop into your head again.

"Well, imagine finding you here!" Nancy stepped outside as I started in.

"Right back at you." I was glad to see a familiar face so I wouldn't have to argue with my mother.

It had never occurred to me that my mother would have been disappointed in my choice to go out on my own. Had she really expected me to live with Frank and Paula and all their asinine rules?

"Look who I found," Nancy yelled over her shoulder.

"I might not be thirty anymore, but I hear just fine, so don't holler at me. I'm right behind you. What are you doing up here, Carla?" Ada Lou asked.

"I started driving and wound up in this place," I answered.

Ada Lou stopped in her tracks. "Are you going to keep driving, or maybe find a poker game?"

"Hadn't planned on it," I said. "What are y'all doing here?"

"We make the drive once a month to get out of the desert." Ada Lou looped her arm through mine. "We've got two more stops to make, and then we're starting home. You can follow us. That way, if Nancy runs off the road, we'll have someone to drag our cold dead bodies out of her car."

"Hush!" Nancy snapped. "I don't like to drive after dark, but when it's light I am better than you are behind the wheel."

"In your dreams," Ada Lou shot back at her, and then said, "We need to be back on flat land before it gets dark. The roads are so windy and steep that I don't know why I ever let her take a turn when we come up here."

She started walking, and I let her take the lead. "Where are we going?"

We passed a couple of places and then she pointed at a sign: Happy Ever After. "This is where we get our honey while we are here. It's the best in the whole area and goes right fine on biscuits," Nancy said. "If Ada Lou isn't in a pissy mood, I take a pan full of 'em to her house for supper on Tuesday nights."

"What if she is?"

"Then she doesn't get biscuits, or she can bake them herself. She is still using the crutch about losing her daughter to avoid turning on the oven and making anything," Nancy said.

Ada Lou's eyes had become mere slits when she whipped around to glare at Nancy. "We don't tease about that, and you know it. If you say another word about Robin, I will ride home with Carla."

Nancy hip-bumped her. "You know you love me more than your motorcycle."

"Bullshit!" Ada Lou said and steered me inside.

I was mesmerized by all the merchandise. I was used to convenience stores, where I could buy gas, use the restroom, and maybe purchase some food to nibble on while I drove to the next hotel.

"I'll have a big jar of honey," Ada Lou told the lady behind the counter.

"So will I," Nancy added.

"Me too." The idea of drizzling honey on some of Rosie's biscuits for breakfast sounded so good that I told the lady to make it two jars.

"Now, do we go home?" I was already planning to come back when I could spend more time shopping in all the stores.

"Just a quick run into the Burro Street Exchange," Ada Lou answered. "I want a cup of good strong coffee and a lemon pie. I have to be awake when Nancy is driving."

"I won't mention Robin the rest of the day if you'll give my driving a rest," Nancy snapped.

Ada Lou's wrinkles deepened around her mouth as she clamped it shut. "Deal. But because you brought it up in the first place, I'm not going to share my lemon pie with you."

"I can always take a pan of biscuits to Jackson instead of bringing them to you." Nancy shook a finger at her.

"I can always put my honey on a bagel that I make in the toaster," Ada Lou countered.

The aroma of coffee and something that smelled like pumpkin pie swept over me the moment we were inside. I could have easily whiled away a whole day in the store and spent every dollar on my debit card.

"I'll have two cups of the strongest coffee you have and a lemon pie," Ada Lou told the young barista.

"Are you treating me to a coffee, or are they both for you?" Nancy asked.

Ada Lou eyes twinkled even though she frowned. "I have to keep you awake. I'm not ready to meet my maker just yet."

"We agreed not to argue," Nancy reminded her.

"I'll take a salted caramel latte and a pumpkin pie," I said.

"Have that ready in a jiffy," the barista said with a smile.

I hated to leave the store, but like Ada Lou said, it would be dark in a little while, and the crooked roads could be dangerous to those of us who weren't used to driving on them. When we were back at the Old Apple Barn, they got into Nancy's small compact car and waved goodbye to me. I set my pie on the floorboard behind the driver's seat and put my cup of coffee in the cupholder on the console.

"Well, that was an adventure," I said as I backed out of the space and told the GPS to take me back to the Tumbleweed.

"I do not find a city named Tumbleweed," she said in her usual tinny voice.

"Take me to Dell City," I said.

Once I was back on the road going south, I didn't pay any attention to her directions and let my mind wander. I thought about helping Mama make pumpkin pies to take to Frank's Thanksgiving family gatherings. She'd let me use a tiny metal cookie cutter to make little maple leaves out of the leftover dough to scatter around the edge. When there was more than we needed, she would let me sprinkle them with sugar and cinnamon and bake them like cookies.

"I miss you, Mama," I whispered and realized that I was back on flat land with a gorgeous sunset all around me. Shades of orange, purple, pink, and yellow filled the sky. The only way I could describe it was that, had it been music, it would have been like a surround sound on a stereo coming at me from every direction. I imagined that I was sitting on a small island in the middle of the ocean, and someone had poured several buckets of paint from out there in the universe into the sky.

The GPS lady angered me when she spoke and broke the magic: "You have a message from Jackson Armstrong. Shall I read it?"

"Yes!" I snapped, and half expected her to tell me not to be hateful, but she didn't—thank goodness.

"*I apologize again about today. Can I take you to dinner tomorrow evening to make up for such short notice about going to Sierra Blanca today? Pick you up at six?* End of message. Do you want to send a return message?"

"Yes," I answered. "Tell him he is forgiven, and I will be ready."

"Sent. He says, *thank you*. Do you want to send a return message?"

"No," I answered, and got a whiff of the pie behind me.

"Why are all these memories coming back to me since I arrived in this desolate place?" I asked. The GPS lady didn't even try to answer that, but I could almost feel Mama's presence beside me.

No matter how far you go or where you are, memories will be with you or follow you. I heard her voice as plain as if she really was sitting in the passenger seat. *They are what keep a person alive in your heart.*

Chapter Eleven

The three hours from the time we left the café until six, when Jackson was supposed to arrive, were worse than the times I'd spent in a hotel room before I went to a poker game. I shuffled my lucky deck of cards a dozen times, not to bring me good fortune in a poker game, but hopefully for a bit of luck on my first-ever real date.

I hadn't seen a restaurant in Dell City fancy enough for one of the dresses I wore to my card games, but I still changed my clothes five times. A pile of discarded things lay on the bed, along with three pairs of shoes and a dozen pieces of jewelry. I finally decided to go casual with a pair of jeans and a mossy-green sweater, but I added a pair of heels to dress the outfit up and give me a little more height.

At the last minute, I twisted my hair up into a messy bun and let two tendrils fall to frame my face. With fresh lipstick application and one final check in the mirror, I reached the end of the hallway at the same time Jackson knocked on the door, but Scarlett opened it before I could get there.

"Come on in, Jackson. Most of us are ready to go, but Rosie is still redoing her hair," she said. "It takes a while to get her dark curls tamed after wearing it in a bonnet all day. I can fix you a glass of tea or a cup of coffee while we wait."

The poor man looked thunderstruck, and it wasn't from my beauty or lack of it. "I . . . well . . . ," he stammered.

"Carla didn't tell you that we were going with y'all, did she? It's not that we don't trust you. Don't get that idea in your mind, because we do. This is just what we always do."

Rosalie came down the hall wearing her faded chenille robe that she changed into every evening when we got to the trailer. Her hair looked like it had been combed with a garden rake, and she was barefoot.

"I'm running a little late," she said, and went into the bathroom.

"Did you think we were going to let Carla go out without chaperones?" Scarlett asked. "That doesn't happen until the third date. Rosie went with me on my first two with Grady to be sure that he was a decent man."

"Whoa! Y'all wait a minute." My voice sounded like a hoot owl in my own ears. "I am *thirty years old*, and you are not going on a date with me. No way! No how! So back off."

"Neither of us knew the rules, but it's okay," Jackson said calmly. "I will call the café and tell them that we need a table for four."

Scarlett hip-bumped me. "They don't take reservations—and we're just messin' with you. But rest assured that Rosie and I will come looking for you if she's not home by midnight."

I popped my hands on my hips. "Oh, no, you will not!"

"Okay, okay, she can stay out until one o'clock, but not a minute longer," she teased. "And yes, I'm joking."

"Thank God!" Jackson grinned.

"I will get even," I whispered as I passed Scarlett and got my coat from the rack.

"I'm sure you will try," she said.

Jackson helped me with my coat, opened the door for me, and then heaved a sigh when we were in his truck. "I thought she was serious."

"So did I, but it was not happening."

He started the engine and then turned to look at me. "You look beautiful."

"You clean up pretty good yourself." I wanted to put the words right back into my mouth and swallow them. "And that sounded like a line from a bad movie."

He made a U-turn and drove out to the road. "So did what I said, but I meant it. And, honey, I'll take a compliment however I can get it."

"Forget what I said before," I told him. "You are one handsome, sexy guy, and that green shirt makes your eyes sparkle."

His smile got wider. "So, you think I'm sexy, do you?"

"I have twenty-twenty vision."

"What does that have to do with me being sexy?" he asked.

"It means that you are probably used to seeing women's heads turn when you walk into a room. That means you know you are sexy."

"Maybe so, but I like that *you* think I am," he said and pointed ahead. "Look at that."

"It's dark, Jackson. I don't see anything. Did a deer run across the road in front of us? I saw a whole herd of them on my way back from Cloudcroft last evening."

"No, it's starting to snow. I wonder if the blizzard is arriving a little early. Have you heard the weather report today?"

No, I was too busy worrying about this date and what to wear.

That's what I thought, but my reply was, "No, I haven't. Ada Lou talked about it but said it was supposed to hit tomorrow morning."

He eased into a parking spot in front of a small café in Dell City. "That's the last report I got, too. We've shut down all the work at the rig until the storm blows through."

I had always loved snow. There's something about it that brings peace to my soul when it covers the world with a beautiful white blanket. And there was plenty of ugly in this area that badly needed it. I stopped in the middle of the parking lot and caught a few flakes on my tongue.

"I'm so glad you did that," Jackson said.

I started walking toward the small building. "Why?"

He opened the door, and warm air rushed out to greet us. "Because you don't put on airs and pretend to be something you are not."

"I don't know how to be anyone else but me," I told him.

The place was packed, but the waitress led the way to a booth in the back corner. Jackson ushered me with his hand on my back, and again, his touch sent shock waves of desire down my spine. I might not have been on a real date before, but that didn't mean I was stupid when it came to attraction for a sexy man. He helped me with my coat and then looked around for a coatrack or a place to hang it.

I held out a hand. "Just give it to me, and I'll put it right here beside me."

"Looks like everyone in town has gone out to eat before they get stuck at home for a few days," he said as he slid into the booth across from me. "Do all the women in here have twenty-twenty vision, too?"

"Probably not, but I bet most of them have a lot of common sense," I shot back.

He chuckled and then laughed out loud. "I guess they do at that."

"Hello, Jackson." A waitress appeared at our table with two menus, a basket of chips, and a bowl of salsa. She was somewhere between fifty and sixty years old, but the way she lowered her voice to make it sexier and batted her fake eyelashes didn't leave a single doubt that she was flirting with him.

He concentrated on the menu. "How are you tonight, Yolanda?"

"I'd be fine if you'd ask me to marry you," she answered.

He looked up and slid a sly wink toward me. "I hired your husband at the drilling site last week. He could break me in half like a twig."

Her dark eyes twinkled. "I should have never married that man. He won't let me have any fun."

"That's not the truth. You love him," Jackson said.

"Yeah, and only God knows why," she said.

Jackson laid the menu to the side. "Come on, now. He's got lots of good qualities."

"Yes, he does, and he's almost as pretty as you are—but since you won't run away with me, then tell me what y'all want to drink."

"Sweet tea for me, and bring us a bowl of queso," Jackson answered and glanced over at me.

"I'll have sweet tea, too."

"Okay, then, I'll get that ready while y'all look over the menu." She shifted her gaze to me. "You are the new owner of the Tumbleweed, aren't you?"

When she eyed me from my hair all the way down to my waist, I knew how a bug would feel under a microscope. "Yes, I am, as of New Year's Day."

I must have passed a test of some kind, because she smiled. "I clean the church with Rosie, and she has good things to say about you. Treat Jackson right, and I might have good things to say about you, too." She turned around and headed for the drink fountain.

"Point proven?" I said when she was across the room.

He met my eyes and smiled. "What?"

"That all women flirt with you," I answered.

"Yolanda and I always joke around," he said. "Not all women."

Two girls who couldn't have been more than sixteen passed by our table and smiled at him. I could hear their giggles the moment they were in the small hallway leading to the ladies' room. It didn't take much imagination to know what they were whispering about.

"Want to retract that now or argue about it?" I tried to be serious but lost the battle with a grin.

"I don't quarrel on second dates. I save that for the eighth or ninth."

"Why? And this is our first date, not second."

"Our first date was a week ago yesterday, when we broke corn bread together."

"I told you that was not a date," I disagreed.

"Even if the man does not get a kiss and he pays for the meal, it is a date. Check the rule book," he teased.

"There's a rule book?" There was no doubt in my mind that he was joking, but still I wished one existed—official, as in a paperback book, or unofficial, as in handed down by word of mouth through the ages.

"Of course, and on the eighth or ninth date, we will have a big fight. I don't know what it will be about yet, but it will happen."

"If we have all of those dates and we get along all of the others, why would we fight?" I asked.

"Rule book," he answered.

"Then we break up?"

"No, then we have some great makeup sex," he said.

Yolanda brought our drinks, took our orders, and rushed to the cash register to take care of the half dozen people waiting to pay their checks. I took a long gulp of my tea and hoped the chill from it would keep my cheeks from catching on fire.

"You really think we'll have all those dates?" I finally asked.

"Yes, ma'am, and I'm looking forward to every one of them," he answered. "We need each other."

"Why do you say that?"

"We have to help one another decide which path to take for our future."

"Well, there is that," I agreed.

"Now, tell me about your visit to Cloudcroft. I hear it's a great place to ski, and with a blizzard coming at us, the slopes should be good in a few days."

"It's kind of quaint, and I bought two jars of honey. Scarlett and I gorged ourselves this morning by drizzling it on Rosie's hot biscuits." And I went on to describe the stores that Ada Lou took me to.

"I missed big stores when I was on deployment," he said.

"I was so intrigued by the places that Ada Lou, Nancy, and I went that I even thought about learning to cook."

"I bet Rosie could teach you," Jackson said, "and I would be willing to trade lessons."

"For what?"

"Kisses, of course." He winked.

"My kisses are expensive. Will you throw in ski lessons, too?"

"No, ma'am," he answered quickly. "I've only tried that one time. Broke my arm and didn't ever give it another try for fear of breaking a leg. I was planning to play football in college, and I was afraid I wouldn't pass the physical if I shattered a knee or a hip. If you are a ski pro, we might find something to disagree about if we hit the slopes at Cloudcroft."

"I'm not a pro at anything other than playing poker. If you want to have a game of that, I will be glad to take your money," I told him.

"I'm not good at cards, but I would be willing to give you cooking lessons for a few hands of strip poker," he said.

"Absolutely not!" I was not ready for Jackson to see the ace of hearts card tattooed on my hip. I'd gotten the tat right after I went out on my own as a kind of symbol that made me feel like a lucky wild card. Besides, we hadn't known each other long enough for me to play that game with him—or anyone else, for that matter.

"Why? Is that too forward a suggestion for a second date?"

"I wouldn't know about that, but I do *not* play strip poker." I was totally flustered.

"Got a reason why?"

"Yes, I do. I like you too much to embarrass you, and I don't know you well enough to want to see you naked," I barked.

He studied me seriously for several seconds. "You are pretty confident about that."

"Yes, I am."

Yolanda brought out our food but didn't have time to flirt with Jackson or ask me any more questions. The combination platter looked and smelled delicious. I took a bite and nodded. "It's wonderful. Why are you so interested in us having an argument and then having makeup sex or playing strip poker, anyway?"

"Gives me something to look forward to. And I could see if you had any tattoos."

"You might be surprised, and unless you have a heart on your butt with your first love's initials in the center of it, then I've seen your only tat."

"I might have a surprise in store for you on our eighth date," he teased.

Why wait until the eighth date? the niggling voice in my head whispered.

Because I want to do this according to the rules, I fired back, and kept eating.

The little voice in my head told me again to wait until the eighth date when Jackson asked me to go to his trailer and watch a movie after we left the café. But the night was still young, and I didn't want to answer dozens of questions from Rosie and Scarlett. I was selfish and wanted to keep all these memories to myself for a little while longer.

The snowflakes had gotten a little heavier when we left the café. The truck's headlights lit them up in hundreds of patterns, reminding me of a cheap kaleidoscope that I'd won at a carnival the summer before my mother died. I'd laid out in the backyard and played with that thing until the cardboard came apart in my hands.

When we reached the trailer park, the ground was almost covered with a layer of snow. I still wasn't worried, because it was three hours until midnight, and that was when the weatherman had originally said the blizzard would hit in our area. Even thinking the words *our area* sounded strange in my head. Living in a place for two weeks did not make it my home, and yet I could practically feel roots beginning to sink into the desert land.

"Welcome to my home away from home," he said when we were inside his trailer.

He helped me remove my coat and hung it on a rack right inside the door. I took in the place in one sweeping glance—a tiny living space with a recliner sofa facing a television on the wall, a table for two on my left, a galley kitchen a couple of feet from it, and a door leading into a bedroom on the other end.

"This is bigger than Ada Lou's place," I said.

"Since I'm going to have to live in it for a while, I opted for one with a little more space." He opened the fridge and turned toward me. "Something to drink? Sweet tea, beer, water, or I can make hot chocolate or coffee."

"Water is fine," I said.

"Have a seat on the sofa, and we'll pick out a movie together. I have a whole collection that my mother sent me the last time I was on six months' deployment. Most of them are older, but they sure beat trying to watch anything from the local stations over there. I loaned them out to the guys and ladies I was stationed with, so they've been played a lot."

Some of the hotels I'd stayed in offered pay-per-view movies, but I seldom turned on the television. I really didn't care if what he had on hand was old or had just come out a month ago. Watching anything with him by my side would be a treat. Perhaps our big eighth-date fight might come along on the second date if we disagreed over what movie we wanted to see that night.

No! I shouted in my head. *I'm not ready for that yet.*

Even with my mind emphatically telling me no, a visual appeared in my head of us tangled in the sheets on his bed after hot makeup sex. I couldn't remember the last time I'd had an argument with any guy I'd slept with, because two nights had always been the limit. That said, I had no idea if the "after" stuff was as fabulous as he claimed. But I was surely willing to find out—just not that night. I blinked several times to make the image disappear, but I hated to let it go.

"With this comfortable sofa, we can pretend we are in an up-to-date theater," I said to cool down my imagination.

"I haven't been in a real theater in years," he admitted and handed me a bottle of cold water. "I haven't had time for dates or movies or anything else but getting things up and running on this project since I retired from the army."

"Does that make me a military-rebound woman?"

"No, ma'am," he answered. "That makes you a very interesting lady I want to get to know much better. Now, what would you like to watch?

This is our own private theater tonight, and we have a remote"—he held one up for me to see—"which means we can pause for bathroom or food breaks. I have popcorn for later, and even a few candy bars, if you get hungry." He pulled a drawer out from under the middle of the sofa to reveal a whole assortment of DVDs arranged in alphabetical order.

"How long has it been since you've seen *The Bourne Identity*?" I asked.

"About four or five years," he answered as he slipped it out and put it in the player. "I expected you to choose a girlie movie like one of the Hallmark shows. You really are an interesting woman."

"Thank you . . . I think." I kicked off my shoes and pulled my feet up onto the sofa. "I've never admitted this before, but when I watch a movie, I study the characters and pretend I'm playing poker with them. I pay attention to their expressions and the way they deliver their lines."

"Yes, ma'am, you *do* fascinate me," he said.

Somewhere in the middle of the movie, Jackson fell asleep. I finished my bottle of water and needed to make a trip to the bathroom. Although I'd seen the movie several times, I hated to miss the next couple of scenes. But I didn't want to wake Jackson by pausing it, so I left it running and made a hasty trip to the other end of the trailer. When I got back, he had stretched out and pulled a throw over himself. He didn't even move when I picked up his feet, sat down, and held them in my lap.

Sometime before the end of the movie, I went to sleep. Several hours later, I woke up spooned next to him, with my back against his chest and heat rushing through my body like I had fire in my veins. The television screen showed the main DVD menu again, and a tiny night-light in the hallway didn't do much to get rid of the darkness.

I shook Jackson awake and whispered, "Time to wake up and take Cinderella home before your truck turns into a pumpkin."

He sat up and rubbed sleep from his eyes. "Some date I am, falling asleep and leaving you to watch the movie alone. And look at the time." He pointed to the clock on the microwave. "It's already past midnight. So my truck is definitely now a pumpkin."

I slipped my feet into my shoes and picked up my coat. "Not to worry. I'm not Cinderella, so I'm sure your truck . . ." I glanced out the window and saw nothing but white snow. At first I thought it was the reflection of the television screen, but then I realized that the blizzard had snuck up on us while we were sleeping.

Jackson must have realized the same thing, because he was on his feet in an instant and heading for the door. He slung it open, and a hard wind blew snow all over him. He slammed it shut and groaned. "We aren't going anywhere until the storm passes. The snow is coming down so hard that I can't even see my truck or Ada Lou's trailer, and it's only a few yards away."

"I shouldn't have fallen asleep," I groaned. "Rosie and Scarlett will have to run the café alone."

"I'm sure the roads are closed, so there will be no buses or people out," Jackson said. "If the snowplows could get out in this kind of weather—which they can't—it would be a useless job. The roads would be covered again before they could go a hundred feet. You are stuck with me until the storm passes on through."

"Well, then I guess you better make some popcorn, because I'm hungry. Do you have hot chocolate to go with it?" I said with a sigh.

"Does that long sigh mean that you would rather be anywhere else?"

"No, it does not," I answered. "I'm already dreading all the questions that Rosie and Scarlett will ask. Friends are great until they get all up in my business."

"You can add family to that," Jackson chuckled. "With four nosy sisters and a meddling mother, I can relate to what you are saying. Is Rosie going to be mad at me when you don't come home for a couple of days, at the least?" He opened the cabinet above the stove and brought out a package of microwave popcorn and a box of hot chocolate mix.

"She would be more upset if you tried to drive in this mess," I assured him. "We can have a snack, and then you can take me home in the morning. I'll send Rosie and Scarlett a text telling them that I'll stay here until tomorrow." I dug around in my purse and found my phone.

There were two texts, both sent at midnight. One from Rosalie: If you are inside a place, stay there. No one should be on the roads in this weather.

The other was from Scarlett: I will expect details when you come home.

I sent one back to each of them saying that I was at Jackson's trailer and would be home as soon as the weather cleared up. Rosie couldn't fuss too loudly, since she'd told me to stay wherever I was. Scarlett could possibly get some details, but depending on what happened, the story might not be unabridged.

"I'll make the chocolate," I said to take my mind off what could happen in the next couple of days.

He nodded toward the teakettle on the back burner. "Water will be hot when it whistles. I'll get the mugs. You're too short to reach them." Stretching his hand to the top shelf was nothing for a tall man like Jackson.

I opened the box of chocolate and glanced at the size of the mugs. "Those are too big for one package."

"And you said you couldn't cook," he teased.

"I can make a mean cup of coffee, hot chocolate—but not from scratch—and a bologna sandwich to die for," I told him.

Jackson removed the bag of popcorn from the microwave. "That's a start. Your first lesson beyond that might be scrambling eggs."

"Sounds complicated." I tore the tops off two packets of mix and dumped the contents into a mug, then repeated the process.

He chuckled. "You are right. Maybe we should start with a ham and cheese sandwich."

"You are a funny man, Jackson Armstrong."

His green eyes twinkled. "The tip jar is on the bar."

"There is no bar."

He wiggled his eyebrows. "Whoops! I guess I left it in the bedroom."

"No tips for you tonight, then," I said. "But I would like to steal one of your pillows, since I won't have your arm to prop my head on."

The humor left his eyes. "You can have the bed, and I'll take the sofa."

"Nonsense! I'm short. The sofa is fine. Just toss a pillow out here, and all will be good." I wondered if that could be considered an argument. If so, could we have makeup sex, then fall asleep together in his bed? I frowned and mentally scolded myself for entertaining such an idea. This could be a real relationship, and jumping into bed too fast could ruin it forever.

"Are you sure?" he asked.

"Very much so," I answered. "That settled, tell me: Do you cook? Are we going to starve if the storm doesn't pass for a couple of days?"

"I promise that we won't go hungry." He made a dramatic gesture of crossing his heart. "I'm a very good cook, and my pantry is well stocked. Like I've already told you, I have four older sisters, and my folks believed we had to learn to do everything. My sisters can change flat tires, check the oil, mow the lawn, and all those things. I can cook and clean. I really can teach you how to get around in the kitchen."

"Okay, but that might be a big undertaking," I said, remembering an inspirational quote that I'd read on a plaque when I was in Cloudcroft with Ada Lou and Nancy: *Be inspired. There's always a way to do the impossible.*

"Are you saying that you can't learn to cook or that you don't want to?" he asked.

When the teakettle whistled, I picked it up and poured hot water into each mug. "Neither. That was for you, not me. I'll give it my best shot if you want to teach me, but don't expect miracles. I'm already a pro at making hot chocolate."

Chapter Twelve

Time stood still. I called 911 and waited in total silence for what seemed like hours. Then everything was chaotic. Only, I was a grown woman, and it was me lying on the floor, not my mother. Jackson ran into the kitchen and gathered me in his arms. Tears rolled down his cheeks and landed on my face. They burned my skin where they landed, but I couldn't tell him to stop weeping. When I woke up, I was sitting straight up. My chest was so tight that it felt like it might explode. I sucked in big gulps of air. That helped relieve the pain, but I still couldn't stop trembling. I was dead. I couldn't console Jackson in his grief.

You are not dead! Ada Lou's voice screamed at me.

I blinked a few times and scanned the room. Ada Lou was right. I was alive, but was the dream an omen that I would follow in my mother's footsteps and die at a young age? I pictured the expression I had seen on Jackson's face in the dream. Tears welled up in my own eyes. I couldn't bear to cause that kind of pain to anyone I cared about.

Stop being silly. I fell and hit my head. It was my expiration date and could have happened anywhere, my mother said, so clearly that she could have been sitting beside me.

My phone rang, and I almost sent up a prayer of thankfulness for anything to take my mind off the very vivid dream.

"Hello?" I said.

"Well, hello to you," a man's voice said cheerfully. "Where are you? I haven't seen you in weeks. Did you fall off the face of the earth?"

I finally recognized the voice as Isaac's, one of my poker buddies. "Not quite, but almost. I'm in northern Texas in the middle of a blizzard. I own a café now," I blurted out.

He laughed so hard that I had to hold the phone away from my ear. "I don't believe you. First, you've hated Texas after that game when you almost lost everything. And second, you are not made to settle down to normal work. So where are you really?"

"In Canada, and . . ." I checked the time on my phone. "I'm getting ready to go to a high-stakes game that has a fifty-thousand-dollar buy-in. Wish me luck. Where are you?"

"San Diego, about to go for a walk on the beach," he answered. "Good luck, darlin', and maybe I'll see you soon."

"Not if I see you first."

"You always say that," Isaac said with a snort. "Have a wonderful evening, and think of me sitting across the table from you. I'll do the same here in sunny California."

"Sounds good. Goodbye." I ended the call and realized that, for the first time since I was a little girl, I had not shuffled my lucky deck of cards the night before. No wonder a blizzard had hit the area.

I was so deep in my own thoughts that I didn't know Jackson was awake until he flipped on the light above the stove. I shoved the throw off me and stood up. "Good afternoon."

"It looks like it's about to quit snowing, but I'm guessing we have about eighteen inches on the ground," he said. "We might not be able to get you out of here today after all. Did you sleep well?"

"I had a nightmare," I answered.

"Want to talk about it?" he asked as he made a pot of coffee.

"Not really. How did you sleep?"

"I dreamed that we had a big argument about what we were going to name our first child. It was on our eighth date." He didn't crack even the faintest hint of a smile.

I was totally speechless for the first time in my life. I prided myself on nothing being able to shock me and never showing anything in my perfect poker face.

"Gotcha!" He chuckled. "I slept like a hibernating bear. If Henry hadn't woken me up with a phone call, I would still be snoozing."

I grabbed a handful of popcorn from the table and put a kernel in my mouth. It wasn't nearly as good as it had been when it was hot, but it kept me from swearing at him for a couple of minutes.

"No comeback?" he finally asked and set a cup of steaming-hot coffee in front of me.

"I had my heart set on naming my first son Leroy Jethro after Gibbs on the *NCIS* television show. Or maybe Barney Huckleberry, after the purple dinosaur and Huckleberry Finn."

"Well, darlin'," he drawled, "I think that's enough to warrant our big eighth-date fight right there."

I took a sip of my coffee and held it in my mouth for a second before swallowing. I'd teach him to shock me like that. "Great! Now we have the foundation laid for our famous argument, and we don't have to worry about it until summer."

He sat down beside me and frowned. "Summer?"

"I don't have a rule book, but that seems about right for an eighth date, don't you think? We are both busy trying to settle into our new lives. A date every two weeks would be twelve weeks from now."

"That's spring, not summer," he protested.

Ada Lou singing an old song about snow—off-key and out of tune—caused us both to stop and go to the door.

Jackson threw it open, and we found Ada Lou clearing a narrow path from her back door. She finished with the steps to his trailer and then slung the shovel over her shoulder. "Y'all put on your shoes and come over to my place. I just took a pan of hot cinnamon rolls from the oven and made a pot of coffee. We can have a midafternoon snack and play a game of Scrabble."

"You baked?" I gasped. "Does that mean you lost the bet? Did Nancy get a red velvet cake?"

"I did not lose. We called it a tie, so this is the first time I've turned on the oven in years. I'll expect you in five minutes." She turned around and followed the trail back to her trailer.

Jackson came out of his room wearing rubber boots. I looked down at my high heels and hoped I wouldn't fall out into the deep snow on either side of the narrow pathway. The worry didn't last long, because Jackson scooped me up in his arms like a new bride and carried me outside.

"Is this an omen?" I asked.

"I don't want you to ruin your shoes. My sister says that the ones with red soles are not cheap," he said.

"Instead of carrying me over the threshold, you are taking me away. Does that mean there won't be another date?"

"Definitely not," he declared.

He almost slipped when we reached the first step on Ada Lou's porch, but he regained his balance and knocked on the door with the toe of his boot.

"Come on in!" Ada Lou opened the door for us. "What a gentleman you are to not let Carla ruin her high-dollar shoes."

Jackson set me down. "This place smells so good."

"Yes, it does—and I want to hear what made you start baking again, Ada Lou," I said.

She pointed across the room at the line of hooks on the wall. "Take off your coats and hang them over there. I've already set up the card table and chairs. When I heard y'all coming, I poured up some coffee. So we can sit down right now, and y'all can tell me if I've lost my touch after decades of not baking."

I didn't have to be asked twice, not when any kind of pastry was my greatest weakness. I was sure it was because we were in a cramped space, but when Jackson sat down, he seemed to be taller and even more muscular.

Ada Lou cut out one of the enormous rolls and set it on Jackson's plate, then she served me and, lastly, herself. "I'm afraid to take a bite for fear I'll be disappointed. So . . ." She pointed at Jackson. "You go first."

"Oh, my God!" he said when he had swallowed. "This is amazing. You should put a bakery in Dell City. People would go crazy for these."

She nodded at me, and I forked a bite into my mouth. "I will pay you to make these for the Tumbleweed."

"I'm not going back into the business at my age, but I will teach you to make them," she offered.

I cut off another bite. "Rosie won't let me near her kitchen."

"That doesn't mean you can't make them at home," Ada Lou said. "I had a dream last night."

"So did Carla, but she said it was a nightmare," Jackson said.

"What does your dream have to do with cinnamon rolls?" I asked, trying to deflect the conversation away from the shivers dancing through my body at the vision of seeing myself dead on the floor. I had to swallow hard to get the lump in my throat to disappear when I thought of how broken Jackson had been.

"Everything," Ada Lou answered, and retold the story of her daughter in a shorter form for Jackson's benefit. "That said, Robin came to me last night. She looked like she did when she went off to college."

"Is this the first time you dreamed about her?" Jackson asked and helped himself to a second cinnamon roll.

"No, but I haven't done so in a long, long time. She and I were taking a hike out to the mountains, and she fussed at me for not baking since I came to this area. She told me to listen to Nancy, and . . ." She paused. "That it was okay if Carla reminded me of her. Then she disappeared, leaving me alone out there in snow up to my hip bones."

"How did you feel when you woke up?" Jackson asked.

"Freer than I ever have."

I followed Jackson's example by cutting out another cinnamon roll for myself. "Do I remind you of her?"

"In a lot of ways—but now let's talk about your nightmare," Ada Lou said.

Jackson saved me by saying, "I have a recurring dream. My team and I are on a mission, and I'm the team leader. So I throw a piece of carpet over the top of a razor-wire fence so we can get into the prison and rescue an American scientist. When my feet hit the ground on the other side, I step on a land mine."

I could see the whole scene as if it were showing on a huge movie screen. My chest tightened for the second time that morning, and I had trouble swallowing the bite in my mouth. Tears welled up, but I blinked them back. What did all these dreams really mean? Was the universe trying to tell us something?

"You look like you are about to faint," Ada Lou said. "Do you need to put your head between your knees?"

"I'm good," I lied. "I just swallowed some coffee with an air bubble."

"You sip coffee. You gulp water," she said with a smile. "Now, before we start our game, *you*"—she pointed at me—"are going to go get a quick shower and change clothes. I've laid out a sweatsuit that is too big for me. Wash your hair while you are there. We never know how long it will be until we can get out of here, or when the power might fail us. You don't want to have to live and sleep in them jeans for several days."

"Yes, Grammie," I said.

"*Grammie* sounds old, and I'm not ready for that yet. You can just call me by my name, but when you have kids, they can call me G.G."

"Why would you ever want to be called that? And what makes you think I'm having kids?" I asked.

"Because I want great-grandkids, and G.G. stands for Great-Grandmother, and it's easy to say," she answered.

Someone rapped on the back door. I peeked around the end of the short bar and saw Nancy coming inside without an invitation.

"Well, a fine howdy-do this is. You're having a party, and you didn't even invite me." She sniffed the air. "Did you bake?" She stopped right inside the kitchen area and removed a pair of snowshoes.

"I did—and you leave those big old things on the porch," Ada Lou said. "They'll leak on my floor. Pour yourself a cup of coffee and bring it to the table. There's half a pan of cinnamon rolls left. But be warned, I don't want any back sass about my starting to bake from you."

"Wouldn't dream of it." Nancy grinned.

I finished off the last bite of my second roll, pushed back my chair, and headed to the other end of Ada Lou's trailer. I could hear them still bickering when I closed the pocket door between the tiny bedroom and the bathroom. I could barely turn around in the shower, but I managed to get my hair washed. She had even laid out a pair of bright red lacy panties for me. I wasn't about to guess where those had come from, or when she wore them—maybe to Woodstock, and she hadn't had the heart to throw them away.

Chapter Thirteen

On Thursday morning, Jackson woke me up just before noon by kissing me on the forehead. "It's time for you to wake up, Cinderella. The party is over, and we have to go back to reality now. Henry is bringing the biggest tractor we have at the site to get us. We'll take you home, and then he and I will go back to the office. Even if we can't work at the rig, we have lots of paperwork to do."

I sat up and rubbed my eyes. "What about having lunch with Ada Lou?"

"We have time to do that, but we can't have another game of Scrabble," he said.

I groaned and fell back on my pillow.

"If you like that game so much, I'll buy one and we can play whenever you want," he offered.

"I enjoy the company more than Scrabble, and mostly I just play to make Ada Lou happy. I just now remembered that Rosie said we have to clean if we can't open the café." I didn't go into detail about Paula's rules for cleaning.

"If you don't like cleaning, we will simply have to hire a housekeeper," he chuckled. "Maybe one that wears a tight, short outfit?"

"If we ever hire a housekeeper—and I'm not saying that we will—she will be as round as a basketball and have gray hair." I pointed at him. "And she will boss you around."

Jackson's smile turned into another chuckle. "I wish we could spend more time snowed in."

"With that much time together, we would have more than one argument." I got to my feet and headed for the bathroom to brush my teeth.

He wiggled his dark brows. I didn't have to ask what he was thinking, but keeping the silly grin from my face was not easy.

I got the pink toothbrush that I had claimed from a drawer, squirted toothpaste on it, and stuck it in my mouth. My reflection in the mirror had changed a little from the day before. I could see a couple of frown lines, especially across my forehead. After only knowing him for a short while, Jackson had mentioned hiring a housekeeper and children. He might not realize it yet, but he was ready to put down roots. Even after that horrid nightmare, seeing him standing over me and weeping, I wasn't totally sure what kind of future I wanted.

Chapter Fourteen

"I'm home," I called out when I walked into the trailer.

Scarlett ran down the hall and wrapped me up in a fierce hug. "Thank God. Rosie and I are bored out of our minds. We need someone else to talk to."

Rosie came out of her room with a big smile on her face. "Welcome back, and it's good to hear you say that you are home. Did you see Ada Lou? Is she going stir-crazy? How did you get home, anyway? The roads are still closed, aren't they?"

Scarlett didn't give Carla time to answer Rosie's questions, but went on with her own. "Have you had dinner? We just made sandwiches, but Rosie has a ham in the oven. We figured we could eat it tonight, then slice up what's left to make sandwiches in case we lose power. Are you glad to be back? What's it like living in a trailer with Jackson? And where did you get that sweat suit?"

I could not possibly remember all those questions, so I fired back some at them. "Did you already clean the café? Scarlett, how are you handling not seeing Grady? Rosie, how in the world is the church getting along without you? Did y'all miss me?"

Rosie chuckled. "Looks like we've got a lot to talk about."

"The past forty-eight hours seem like a month," Scarlett said with a sigh. "I didn't realize how much I miss my routine."

Rosie sat down on one of the recliners and patted the sofa arm beside her. "We'll each ask one question and take turns. First, have you seen Ada Lou? I've been praying for her and Nancy, even though Nancy doesn't come to the Tumbleweed very often. Poor soul must be lost without her husband, may he rest in peace."

"I had lunch with Ada Lou before I came home." The word *home* still sounded strange when I said it. "She is sassy as ever. Yesterday she shoveled a path from her back door to Jackson's trailer and invited us over for cinnamon rolls. And . . ." I paused for a breath. "She made them from scratch and baked them herself. Then today she made a pot roast for us to share. Oh, and yesterday, Nancy made her way to the trailer using snowshoes, and all four of us played Scrabble. Now it's my turn. Scarlett, how are you holding up without seeing Grady?"

"Holy smokin' hell!" Scarlett gasped.

"I know," I agreed with a nod. "Now, tell me about Grady."

"I've seen him with FaceTime, but that's not holding him or kissing him good night, or . . ." She blushed. "Did you at least get a few kisses when you were holed up with Jackson?"

"Not a single one," I answered. "But all three of us—Ada Lou, Jackson, and I—had crazy dreams that first night."

Scarlett finally sat down in the recliner at the other end of the sofa. "Rosie is good at interpreting visions. Tell us about them."

I started with Ada Lou's dream and what she thought it meant.

"She is right about the meaning. I've been telling her that same thing for years," Rosie said. "I guess she just needed to hear it from Robin. Maybe now she can really move on."

"She says that I'm like the granddaughter she might have had. Did she say that same thing to you, Scarlett?" I asked.

"Nope, but she has helped me get through some really tough times," she answered. "So, you and Jackson are really just friends?"

The idea of a real house, a yard, and especially children and a kitchen still scared me. After the few role models I'd had, how could I ever be a good—or even decent—mother? "To be honest, I don't really know what we are."

"Now, what did Jackson dream about?" Rosie asked.

I couldn't lie, but repeating what he had shared about his dream still made me sad enough to cry. Did that mean this attraction between us was more than a passing thing? I couldn't remember a single guy I had known in the past who could make me that emotional.

"Okay, here it is . . ." I sighed and told them the details of his dream.

Rosie made the sign of the cross and then said a prayer before she said anything. "That's his inner spirit telling him that it would be dangerous, even fatal, for him to go back into the army."

"I thought that might be the meaning," I whispered.

"You've saved the best for last, haven't you?" Scarlett asked.

"What do you mean?"

"Your dream must be the one that you really don't want to talk about, or you would have started with that one," Rosie replied. "So spit it out."

When I finished the story, tears rolled down my cheeks. Cold chills raced up and down my spine. My grandmother used to shiver and then say, "A goose walked over my grave." As a child, I thought that was so funny, because Granny was not dead. Retelling the dream made me realize that I had seen my own death. I didn't understand what a goose had to do with anything, but reliving that nightmare certainly made me understand Granny's saying.

Rosie crossed herself again, only this time she kept her head down a little longer before she focused on me. "Okay, here's what I see. The dreams are not two, but one. They are tied up together, and everything is going to hinge on your decisions in the next few months."

I braced myself when I felt the next quiver coming on, but I still shuddered.

"Do you want me to go on?" she asked.

"Yes," I whispered.

"If you go back to your old lifestyle, you might not physically pass away like your mother did, but your spirit will die. You will always wonder if you might have had a fuller, happier life if you gave up gambling," Rosie said.

"But when I died in the dream, Jackson and I were together, and he was so sad. I like him too much to get into a relationship and break his heart like that."

"That man could possibly be your soulmate. If you leave him for another poker game, he will go back into the army and die—again, maybe not physically, but mentally. That's why I said your dreams are not two, but one that's intertwined together."

Listen to Rosie, my mother's voice whispered softly in my ear.

"Are you all right?" Scarlett asked. "You have gone really pale. In my opinion, you should go get whatever test the doctors can do to be sure you don't have anything wrong. If you do, they can fix it before it becomes a problem."

"I'm a little bit superstitious, and sometimes I hear voices in my head—not the kind telling me to do evil things, but the ones that advise me," I admitted. "My mother is the one I've been hearing the most often here lately, and Ada Lou's voice screamed at me this morning."

Did I really believe in all this hocus-pocus stuff?

Do you shuffle cards every night? Mama's voice was back.

"I hear God speaking to me," Rosie said. "And sometimes my mother. She tried to steer me right. I didn't listen to her, and that's what got me into trouble. So, in my opinion, we should listen to the voices in our heads. They could be angels, you know."

Scarlett raised a hand toward the ceiling. "Amen and hallelujah. I'm not as good as Rosie, so I'm not sure I hear God talkin' to me, but I do hear my grandmother repeating things that she told me when I was a little girl."

"Okay, then, the consensus is that I need to . . ."

"Follow your heart, not your mind, and don't ever look back," Rosie finished my sentence.

"Amen again!" Scarlett agreed.

"Yes!" Rosie's tone was so excited that I half expected her to start singing gospel music.

"Why does that give you the Holy Ghost?" I asked.

"Because it's what I did," Rosie said with conviction, "and I give thanks every day for the help I've received. I've never had a single regret about my decisions."

Scarlett nodded in agreement. "I have never looked back and yearned for something different. Now, moving on, do you have boots to wade in the snow?"

"I've got a pair of fancy boots that come almost to my hip, but they have four-inch heels," I answered. "Why do you ask?"

"We're going to the café tomorrow even if we have to carry a bag of extra clothing with us to change into if we get wet from here to there. I can't stand to be cooped up in this trailer another day past that," Rosie said with a long sigh. "I can teach you a little about the books, and Scarlett can clean."

"I love cleaning," she said. "I wish my name was Monica."

"Why would you want to have that name?" I asked. "I like Scarlett much better."

"Did you ever watch *Friends* on television?"

I got it then. Monica was the character who was obsessed with cleaning. Well, if Scarlett loved that job, I surely would not fight her for it.

Rosie tilted her head and drew down her dark brows. "How did you get home? I don't see wings on your back, and I know you didn't walk in those shoes."

"Didn't you hear the tractor?" I asked.

"I had my earbuds in, listening to Caylee Hammack sing 'Small Town Hypocrite,'" Scarlett answered. "I wouldn't have heard a freight train."

Rosie stood up and headed for the kitchen. "I heard something and hoped that it was a snowplow so we can hang out the Open sign in the morning. I guess I didn't get my wish. Did a tractor bring you home, then?"

I covered a yawn with my hand. "I'm sorry. I've slept on a couch for two nights. But back to your question: Henry needed Jackson at the workplace, so he drove a tractor from the rig and picked us up. Jackson carried me to the trailer so I wouldn't have to wade in snow up to my hip. Before that, Henry cleared a path from here to the café, which means if we can get the snow off the porch steps and what's about two feet in front of the back door of the Tumbleweed, I won't need wading boots."

Scarlett looked like she was about to swoon. "That is so romantic."

"Romantic, nothing," Rosie huffed. "Those shoes she's wearing didn't cost two bucks at a thrift store."

Scarlett went over to the door and looked out the window. "You are right. We just need to clear off the porch and a little bit at the café. That was sweet of Henry to do what he did. Next time he comes into the café, his meal is free. If it wasn't so late, I would go start cleaning this afternoon."

I checked the microwave clock. "It's only a few minutes after two."

"We'll start fresh tomorrow morning," Rosie said. "The ham comes out of the oven in a couple of hours, so Scarlett wouldn't get much done in that length of time."

Scarlett glanced over at the clock on the microwave. "You are right, Rosie—and Grady is calling in fifteen minutes to FaceTime with me."

Rosie pointed at me. "Your eyes tell me that you need a nap between now and supper. You go get a nice warm shower and get into a real bed for a couple of hours."

No one had bossed me since Paula came into the picture. I'd hated it when she got that look in her eyes and laid down the law. But with Rosie, it was different.

One did it because she wanted to make you miserable enough to leave. She didn't want to deal with a teenager when she had children of her own. I didn't recognize the voice, but it sure explained a lot.

Rosie poked me on the shoulder. "How far do you think the nearest hospital or doctor is?"

"What has that got to do with me being sleepy?"

"Over fifty miles," Scarlett answered for me.

"That's right," Rosie said. "That means if you fall asleep on your way to your room and fall and crack your head wide open, I'll have to stitch it up with a sewing needle and thread. Before that, I'll have to shave a patch of your hair away."

A vision of my mother lying in a pool of blood flashed through my mind and sent a shiver down my spine.

"She's not joking," Scarlett said.

"No, I am not," Rosie declared. "I'll wake you up when supper is ready."

"Thank you," I muttered. "But why do you think I need a shower?"

"I washed all our bedding yesterday. You are not crawling in between clean sheets in a sweat suit that you've probably already slept in," Rosie answered.

"Thank you, again," I said on my way down the hall.

I stripped out of my borrowed clothing and made a mental note to wash them the next day. The warm water flowing down over my body was so relaxing that I closed my eyes. I jerked awake when my shoulder hit the shower wall to my right. I quickly turned off the water, stepped out, and wrapped a towel around my body, then rubbed the moisture off the mirror with my palm. I leaned in and stared at my reflection in the semi-fog.

"Why am I so sleepy?"

Because the adrenaline rushing through your body has bottomed out, my mother answered.

Not once in all my traveling years had a bed felt as wonderful as mine did that afternoon. Sleep came as soon as my head hit the pillow, but it wasn't the good kind. Jackson's dream popped into my head in color. Only this time, I was with him. Well, not really right there beside him, but standing back behind a tree so green that it seemed surreal. Unbearable heat caused me to sweat so badly that my shirt and cargo pants stuck to my skin. Jackson was alone when he tossed what looked like carpet over the razor wire, but it could have been something made specifically for that purpose.

My heart pounded so loudly, I was sure the guard patrolling around the ramshackle building would hear it. It was then that I realized something was wrong, and I stepped out from my hiding spot to yell at Jackson: "Don't do it. Come back to me, and let's give us a second chance."

He didn't hear me and barreled over the fence. The next minute, a red haze filled the area, and a gun fired bullets so rapidly that there was no time between the shots. Had that stupid guard lost his mind? There was nothing left of Jackson to shoot. In one instant, he was dead, and I would never feel his lips on mine again.

I awoke with a jerk and sat up so quickly that it made me dizzy. Tears made wet circles when they dripped off my jaw onto my nightshirt. Until I came to my senses and figured out that I had been dreaming, grief like I had never known before filled my whole body. My heart still thumped so hard that my chest ached. I buried my face in a pillow and sobbed until I got the hiccups.

"This is too much responsibility. I need to go back to a lifestyle where I was not responsible for anyone but myself," I whispered.

"Hey," Rosie yelled at my door. "Wake up. Supper is ready and going on the table in ten minutes."

"Surely not. I only fell asleep five minutes ago," I whispered and glanced over at my phone to see 4:45 in big numbers and a couple of text messages.

"Be right there," I shouted and threw back the covers.

I dressed in a pair of pajama bottoms and an oversized T-shirt and went straight to the bathroom. Not even splashing cold water on my face five times helped my red, swollen eyes. I finally gave up and patted my cheeks with a hand towel. I rationalized the dream by telling myself that it was simply showing me the mental pain that could possibly be involved if I chose to leave the Tumbleweed.

"She's alive!" Scarlett said when I walked into the living area.

I forced a smile. "Barely, but I wouldn't want to miss a meal like this, so thanks for waking me."

"If you'd have slept any longer, you would have trouble sleeping tonight. You need a good night's rest, because we have a big day tomorrow," Rosie said. "Take a seat, and we'll say grace."

She bowed her head and said words. I was glad that no one was going to test me on Rosie's short prayer. Whatever came out of her mouth didn't register, because that crazy dream kept replaying on a continuous loop in my head.

"You've been crying," Rosie said when she raised her head.

"I was there with Jackson in his dream this time," I told her. "I saw it all in color."

Scarlett laid a large piece of ham on her plate and then passed the platter to me. "I can't imagine having a dream like that."

"They will quit when you decide to stay at the Tumbleweed," Rosie said.

"I really don't want to talk about it anymore." I put a piece of ham on my plate. "This is nice. We should do this more often."

"We eat together at the café every day," Rosie reminded me.

"But not family-style like this," I argued. "When was the last time any of us sat down to a meal here at the trailer?"

Scarlett shrugged and frowned. "I can't remember."

Rosie sent a bowl of candied sweet potatoes over to Scarlett. "You go to church and dinner at Grady's mama's house every Sunday."

"There's over thirty people there, so his mama serves it buffet-style. And that's not with just the three of us," Scarlett said.

"How about you, Rosie?" I asked and took a bite of sweet potato.

"Christmas Day," she answered. "I invited Ada Lou and Nancy to dinner at the café. We close the Tumbleweed on that one day of the year, and Scarlett was spending the day in Dell City. So us three ladies had a nice meal, and I served it up homestyle in the kitchen. How about you?"

"At Ada Lou's today. The food was good, but we had to rush." I didn't tell them about practically hyperventilating every time Jackson's leg brushed against mine under the table. "Before that, the last time would have been fourteen years ago. I had supper with Frank and his wife, Paula. That was the night I was given an ultimatum."

"Which was?" Scarlett asked.

"To burn my lucky deck of cards, promise to never play poker again, and get my grades up to passing by the semester's end," I answered. "Strange thing was that I had already finished all the classes with my online courses, and I was bored to death having to repeat them."

Rosie's eyes bored into mine. "Or?"

"I asked the same one-word question. That's when the lecture came about appreciating the fact that Frank had taken care of me. How he could have put me in foster care and still could if I didn't quit playing cards. Then she said that she had put a roof over our heads and given me a stable environment. If I didn't like it, I could leave. I chose the latter. And before today, that was the last homestyle meal I had."

"Why would anyone you had spent so much time with let a woman run you off? Was he your uncle or stepdad or what?" Scarlett asked.

The air suddenly seemed almost too heavy to breathe. My chest tightened, and my hands clenched into fists. Admitting what he was, other than my poker mentor, was something I didn't even do to myself. I opened my mouth, but nothing came out. Finally, I inhaled deeply and let it out slowly.

"You don't have to answer that," Scarlett said.

"Yes, I do. Just give me a minute," I whispered.

Rosie covered my hand with hers. "Take all the time you need."

"He *is* my father," I blurted out. "He and my mother were young when they had me. Long story short is that Mama called him Frank, so I did, too. He was fine with that because he never wanted to be a daddy anyway."

Rosie crossed herself and shook her head slowly. "Bless your heart. No wonder you shy away from letting folks get to know you. A father who would turn his daughter out in the cruel world doesn't deserve to be a daddy, anyway. It's a wonder that you survived out there on your own."

I pulled my phone from my pocket and scrolled through my pictures. "Look at this. How old is that person?"

Rosie took the phone from my hand and studied the picture. "It's your mother, isn't it? You look so much like her. She was very beautiful."

"That is the photograph on my first fake ID when I was fourteen," I answered. "Scroll up to the next one, which is the one that I use when I play poker these days. That's how I survived. I studied women who did not need fake papers and mimicked their mannerisms. I attended the card games with Frank at first and had to show my ID, but not always. When I started going by myself, the players that knew him would ask where he was. I always told them that he'd left the game for a woman. We would all laugh, and then forget all about him when we got serious about playing."

"What made that so funny?" Scarlett asked.

"Frank liked his booze and young women, and he had declared many times that he would never marry again," I answered.

Scarlett's eyes got as big and round as saucers. "Did he . . . ?"

I shook my head so that she didn't have to finish. "If we won money, he would blow part of it at a bar until closing time. If he picked up a woman, they took care of their business somewhere other than our hotel or motel room. He would stagger in in the early-morning hours, reeking of whiskey and/or perfume, fall into the extra bed, and sleep. I would be very quiet and work on my studies, wake him up an hour before we had to check out, and make him drink coffee to get semi-awake. He would drive out of the town or city, and then I would take over while he slept off the hangover in the back of the van. That was my life back then."

"Sweet Jesus," Rosie muttered.

"That's why you have trust issues," Scarlett said.

I could feel myself bristling. "Who said I have issues of any kind?"

Rosie reached over and patted me on the shoulder. "Everyone around this table has or has had problems. Matilda rescued us, and the Tumbleweed saved you. There's no way you would trust men the way that Frank floated from one poker game and woman to another."

"I'm still mad at him for not standing up for me when Paula laid down the ultimatum, and didn't even ask me not to leave." I took a sip of tea before I went on. "But he promised my mother that he would take care of me. I guess in his mind, he was doing that. At least he taught me to play cards, and that gave me the ability to support myself."

Scarlett shook her head in disbelief. "You were sixteen, and he let you drive away?"

"Yep. I was sixteen. He was thirty-eight, and Paula was thirteen years younger than that. That meant she was only eight years older than me, and she came from a strict religious background. Looking back, I guess she was trying to be like her folks. But you are right," I said. "Trust is something I don't have much of."

Rosie handed the plate of ham over to me. "You are preaching to the choir."

It seemed like a dam had broken; words poured out of me. "I often envied little girls my age who had a family around them, but I would convince myself that they were probably jealous of me. After all, I didn't have to go to public school. I didn't have to go to bed at any certain time. I could order room service to my hotel room. When Frank finally came home in the wee hours of the morning and collapsed on the other queen-sized bed, I was free to go to the swimming pool. Those girls couldn't do any of that."

"Matilda would tell you that you were growing a shell around your heart to protect you from the pain of losing your mother so suddenly," Rosie said.

"Shall we have a game of Scrabble after supper?" I asked to take my mind off the past.

"Not me," Scarlett answered. "I'm going to FaceTime with Grady again this evening. When the snow finally melts, you"—she pointed at me—"are going to church with me and to Sunday supper with his family."

"O . . . kay," I said.

"Or you can go to evening Mass with me, and then over to their house for Sunday supper," Rosie offered.

"What if I just drove up there in time to meet Grady after y'all go to church?"

"Oh, no!" Scarlett said. "You have to get some Jesus in your soul before supper. Jesus delivered a message to the multitude before he broke up the fishes and loaves to feed them. That means you listen to the preacher before we go to Grady's mama's house."

"I guess I'll pay my dues, then," I agreed.

Chapter Fifteen

The sound of drizzling rain lulled me into a deep, dreamless sleep that night. I awoke the next morning fully aware of where I was. Evidently, two weeks and two days was the magic number for me to be in one place before I got used to it. As usual, the aroma of coffee wafted down the hallway, but that morning it was mixed with bacon and cinnamon. I didn't waste any time getting out of bed.

Rosalie was in the kitchen with one of her bright-colored caps covering her hair. This one had snowmen printed on a crimson background. She smiled and pointed to the coffeepot. "Help yourself. There is bacon on the bar, and I'm making oven cinnamon toast. We'll have a quick bite of something before we go to the café. According to the television weatherman, this freezing rain is supposed to stop by seven o'clock. It's going to make for a slick pathway from here to the café."

Scarlett went straight to the coffeepot and filled up a mug. "Your bonnet is appropriate for today, Rosie."

"Thank you. It seemed like the right one." She removed a pan of toast from the oven and set it on the stove. "This one is getting faded like all the rest, though. If I had the fabric, I would have dragged out the sewing machine and whipped up a few more while we've been stuck in the house. Next time we get to El Paso, I'll stock up again. I hate going over there to all that hustle and bustle."

I loaded a plate with four slices of toast and six of bacon and refilled my coffee. I hated to think about leaving the coziness of the trailer or driving in the snow. But if Rosie had cabin fever and wanted to get out, I would gladly take her. "This looks great. Thank you for making breakfast before we go to the café. Rosie, all you have to do is choose a day, and I'll drive you anywhere you want to go."

"Thank you," Rosie said. "I just might take you up on that when the roads clear up."

I picked up a piece of crispy bacon and bit off the end, glad that she didn't want to go anywhere that day. "Why do you wear those things instead of a hairnet?"

"Hairnets are for old women," she answered. "Eat your toast so we can slip and slide out to the café."

"There will be none of that. If you broke a bone, we would have to close the café permanently," I said.

"Or else just serve hamburgers and fries. I think I could manage that," Scarlett said. "But you and I would get tired of the same old thing every day. We could tie a rope to a cookie sheet, use it for a sled, and pull Rosie out to the café."

"You will not!" she protested. "We'll go slow and watch our steps. There's not a cooking pan in this place big enough for my butt anyway."

"We could wrap you in Bubble Wrap," I suggested.

"Hush!" she snapped. "Besides, all our big pans are out in the café, so one of you would have to go out there."

I shoved another bite of bacon into my mouth, chewed, and swallowed. "You scare me, Miz Rosie."

"I'm glad that I do, but don't call me that," she said. "It makes me feel as old as hairnets. I'm just Rosie Smith, a common name that no one even looks at twice."

I finished off my last piece of toast and looked out the window on my way down the hall. A sliver of light out there on the horizon promised the first sunrise we had seen in three days. What looked like diamond dust sparkled on the snow. Even when I traveled alone, I had followed Frank's rule of thumb, staying in the eastern part of the States during summer and early fall and slowly making my way west for the winter months. I'd gotten a late start this year because I wanted to sit in on a couple of games up near Niagara Falls.

The mountains of snow heaped up on each side of the pathway Henry had cleared caused me to remember a Sunday school story about how God parted the sea for his children to cross over into the promised land. I hadn't thought about that story in years, so why was it coming back to me now?

Was the café my promised land? I wondered. Even if Jackson and I were never anything but friends, was this where I was supposed to be for the rest of my life?

"Is there a shovel in the trailer?" I asked without turning around.

"No, but there is one in the storage room," Scarlett answered.

"Then I'll go get it and clear the rest of the path for y'all."

Scarlett handed me the key to the back door. "You really are scared that Rosie will get hurt, aren't you?"

I removed my coat from the hook, slipped it on, and tucked the key into the pocket. "Don't come out until I finish."

Before I got off the bottom porch step, I wished I had been wearing cleats instead of leather-soled cowboy boots. I stepped out onto the ice-covered layer of snow, and my feet went right out from under me. I crashed into the snow on the right side of the path. Nothing but my pride was hurt, but a visual of Mama and me making snow angels in our backyard flashed through my mind. I'd been about six years old in northern Kentucky, and Mama and I had put socks over our shoes and pretended we were ice-skating.

"Step and slide," I muttered as I got back on my feet. "Or get a good fast start and slide all the way."

I opted for the latter and made it all the way to the snowdrift in front of the café door before I crashed and burned a second time. I got up and fetched the key from my pocket, but by then my hands were freezing.

Mental note to self: Buy a pair of gloves next time you are in a place where they are sold.

Lady Luck must have decided to go to a warmer place, like Florida or maybe Southern California, because she certainly was not there with me when I dropped the key into a snowdrift. Thank goodness for the layer of ice, because it lay there on the top like a piece of gold. I carefully retrieved it, unlocked the door, and used the door to push back enough to wiggle through and get inside the place.

"Holy hell!" I shivered and shook like a dog coming up out of a lake. "Come to think of it, I could use a little of hell's heat right now," I muttered when I was finally inside the warm room. I shot a dirty look toward the ceiling. "Don't you dare tell Rosie that I swore. I'm trying my damnedest to keep her safe, so that should account for a lot." I rubbed my hands together to get the circulation going.

The shovel stood over in the corner, and on a shelf next to it was a pair of brown work gloves. "Hot damn! And that's meant as a wonderful saying, not a dirty phrase."

I shoved my hands down into the gloves, picked up the shovel, and headed back outside. By the time I'd removed the snow out to the edge of the path and chipped away at the ice, I was panting—and appreciating Ada Lou a whole lot more. The freezing-cold air made my chest hurt, and I was thoroughly convinced that icicles were hanging on my eyelashes when I finished the job.

"Okay, y'all can come out now," I yelled. I was right proud of myself for the job I'd done, and I hummed the tune to "Hell on Heels" by Pistol Annies. I might not have been able to even hum on pitch, and I sure wasn't looking for a sugar daddy like the lyrics said, but I felt like I could conquer anything—like I really was hell on heels at that moment.

I had barely returned the shovel to its rightful corner and reluctantly taken off the gloves when Scarlett and Rosie appeared. Rosie frowned at the gloves, and one side of her nose twitched. "Those things should have been tossed a long time ago. We had a big old rat in the kitchen before Matilda passed away. I set a trap and caught it."

My skin had already begun to crawl before Scarlett said, "She used those gloves to pick the critter up and take him to the dumpster. You should wash your hands before you do anything else."

I tossed the gloves in a nearby trash can fast and ran to the bathroom. I didn't even wait for the water to get warm to stick my hands under the faucet. By the time I had soaped them up three times, the mirror above the sink had fogged over.

"Don't judge a book by the cover—or a pair of gloves by what they handled the last time they were used," I told my distorted reflection in the mirror.

Rosie looked up from the grill when I finally reached the kitchen. "I don't even know why I turned on the grill and the oven. Habit, I guess," she said with a sigh.

"We'll be hungry in a couple of hours, and I'm already craving a pan of hot biscuits and some sausage gravy," I told her.

"Breakfast for lunch?" she asked.

"How about brunch? I don't think that toast is going to hold me until noon."

Scarlett pushed through the swinging doors into the kitchen and plopped down into a chair. "I went ahead and set the chairs all up to be for business, but there's no need to put money in the cash register. I'll get started doing some deep cleaning in a few minutes."

"You said you liked to clean. Why do you look so sad?" I asked.

"I got stranded in Dallas on the way here five years ago. Not snow, but black ice, and the buses had to sit still and wait for it to melt. There were so many people milling around in that place that . . ." She hesitated, took a deep breath, and then went on, "Well, I was terrified. Everything I owned in a small suitcase. I was afraid to go to sleep and had only a few dollars left for food, so I bought a bag of chips and a chicken sandwich. I found a corner and sat with my back against the wall all night and part of the next day when they finally announced that the bus was ready to load. I just feel sorry for anyone who is in that position these days."

"I used the last of the change that I'd thrown into the console to buy gas to get here, so I can relate to your story." I went on to tell them about being so sleepy that I thought I had killed a person but found out it was a tumbleweed. "I had one package of crackers in the car, and I filled my water bottle in a bathroom sink at a service station."

"You really weren't kidding when you said you were starving when you got here," Rosie said.

"I was not—but why were you coming here on a bus, anyway, Scarlett?"

"Can I trust you to keep my secret?" she asked.

She couldn't be in witness protection, because they must sign their former life away. That meant Scarlett wouldn't have told anyone, not even Rosie.

"I can keep a secret," I finally answered.

"This goes back to Matilda," Scarlett said. "She helped support more than one women's shelter in several states. She had friends who knew how to go about getting women in really bad situations what they needed—like new papers, jobs, homes, and so on. I'm one of those women. I came here from Louisiana and changed my name to Scarlett because of the heroine in *Gone with the Wind*. I wanted to be tough like her instead of a frightened little rabbit who let a man beat on her."

I felt as if someone had knocked the wind clean out of me. No one had ever laid a hand on me. If they had, they would probably be lying in a shallow grave somewhere. "Did you . . . What . . . How . . . ," I stammered.

"I am not a victim—not anymore, so don't pity me," Scarlett scolded. "I am a strong woman who will never let a man make me feel less than what I am."

"Can I ask what happened?" I asked.

"My mother went to prison for drugs. There was no father in the picture. Not ever. My grandmother took me in, but she had to hold down two jobs to support the two of us. So I moved out to live with my boyfriend Billy before I graduated. I worked at a convenience store after school and on weekends, and I handed over my paycheck to him every

Friday night. By Sunday morning, he had used all of it for liquor and beer for him and his sleazy friends. And I had more than a few bruises to prove that he was a mean drunk, but by that time my grandmother had passed away, and even if I left him, I didn't have a place to go or the money to get away from him."

Rosie laid a hand on her arm. "You are strong . . ."

"Yes, and I am independent. I don't need anyone to complete me," she said, finishing the statement. "That's what you and Matilda taught me to say to myself every morning before I even got out of bed."

"And it worked, right?" I asked.

"It did," she answered. "I was a victim when I put up with Billy's abuse. My grandmother had tried to talk sense into me, but I wouldn't listen. He loved me, and I loved him—or so I thought. I graduated from high school, and he thought I would work full-time and make more money. But the store only needed a part-time clerk. He got so angry that when he got tired of hitting me with his fists, he picked up a ball bat and worked on me with it. If a neighbor hadn't heard the ruckus, he would have killed me. He ran when the cops showed up, and an ambulance took me to the hospital."

"Holy . . ." I stopped myself from completing that thought.

Scarlett forced a weak smile. "A sweet nurse and a lady police officer talked me into filing charges and going to a battered women's home. Billy took a plea deal and went to jail, and Matilda took me in when I was able to travel. End of story."

"No wonder you have trust issues," I whispered.

"Yep, and that's why Grady and I have dated for a year. I wanted to be sure that he was the kind of man who would never hurt me, physically or mentally."

"What happened when you had your first argument?" I asked, still in a bit of a shock that she was telling me something so personal.

"We didn't see each other for several days. Both of us were miserable, and I finally drove up to his house and told him that he wasn't ever to raise his voice to me again over something so trivial as him sitting in the passenger seat of my car. We talked . . ." She really smiled this time. "Plug your ears, Rosie."

"I'm a grown woman," Rosie said. "I know that you had hot and heavy makeup sex."

Rosie might have known all about it, or maybe just guessed, but she still blushed as she spoke.

"You've had makeup sex, right?" Scarlett asked.

"Nope," I answered honestly. "If you never get to that magic date when you have a fight, you don't ever get to experience that kind of thing. I've only had one-night stands and a few forty-eight-hour relationships. Always with guys I knew and trusted from poker games, so don't be thinking I picked up men in bars. I never sleep with married men, and I'm up front about there being no strings attached."

Scarlett and Rosie both nodded in agreement.

"What about Jackson? Did you shake hands at the end of the time you spent at his trailer?" Rosie asked.

"No, he raised my hand to his lips and kissed my knuckles when he dropped me off at the trailer yesterday. From the romance novels I have read, that's not even first base."

"But it is *super* romantic," Scarlett said.

Rosie stood up and brought out the biscuit-making bowl. "Enough about all this. I'm going to make our brunch, and then we'll get down to business."

"One more question, Scarlett."

"Just one?" Rosie frowned.

I crossed my heart with my forefinger. "I promise. What was your name before you became Scarlett?"

"My name was Stacy, and the son of a bitch—sorry, Rosie—that put me in the hospital said that when he got out of jail, he would hunt me down and kill me. So Matilda worked with the woman at the women's shelter where I was living, and the two of them got me new papers. Scarlett rose out of the ashes that used to be Stacy."

Was I ready to burn my poker identity, Clara Williams? Not just yet.

Chapter Sixteen

Scientists say that the brain does not feel anything.

I would argue that point after spending the whole day with Rosie at the kitchen table. I had taken pages of notes on which vendors arrived on what days, how to figure taxes and send them in quarterly, and everything that went into running a small café like the Tumbleweed.

Even though my head ached from looking at numbers all day, I was amazed beyond words at how much profit came in each month. If I let all that sit in the bank, or invested some of it to bring in even more, I could sell the place in six months and take what money was in the bank for more than one high-stakes game.

What about Rosie and Scarlett? the voice in my head asked.

There were all kinds of possibilities to use for an answer, but I didn't like any of them. Not even the idea of making sure the new owners didn't fire them helped. They were my friends, the first adult ones I'd ever had. I wanted to get back in the game, but I did not want to leave Rosie and Scarlett behind.

You can't ride two horses with one ass, the same voice reminded me.

It took a few seconds for me to understand just what that meant. "Okay, okay!" I muttered.

"Okay about what?" Rosie asked.

"I need a card game." Playing always helped me make difficult decisions.

"Oh, no, you do not!" Rosie said.

"I could teach you how to play," I offered.

Scarlett brought a bucket of soapy water from the dining room and dumped it down the drain. "It's not that she doesn't know how, but rather that she won't."

"We don't have to play for money, so it won't be a sin." I remembered the candy rack beside the cash register. "We could play for candy. An M&M is worth a dollar. A whole candy bar is five hundred dollars, and a section of Twix could be a hundred."

Rosie cut her eyes around at me. "For candy only. No money?"

"Absolutely," I agreed.

"And if I play, you will promise to stay here until July 4?"

"Why until then?" I asked.

"That's my birthday," Rosie said.

"Oh . . . okay." That was within the year that Jackson and I had more or less agreed on, so I nodded. I would stick around until Rosie's birthday and then face the tough decision of leaving or putting down roots. I went to the storage room and got my lucky deck of cards from my purse.

"Blackjack or Texas Hold'em?" I took a chair and handed the cards to Rosie to cut.

"Texas," Rosie answered, and shuffled the cards with such expertise that it shocked me speechless. "Go get some candy, Scarlett. A bag of M&M'S, two Twix bars, and one Snickers for each of us. And get a York Peppermint Pattie to use for the dealer's button."

"Close your mouth," Scarlett whispered when she returned with fistfuls of candy. "I told you so."

"Well-worn deck," Rosie said. "They aren't marked, are they?"

"No, ma'am, this is their virgin cruise."

Scarlett passed out the candy and then sat down on Rosie's right. "What does that mean?"

"I'm sorry. I was off in la-la land. That deck is my lucky charm. I shuffle them every night and before I go to a game. They have never been used for anything else." I wondered if using them would nullify their power. But being on Rosie's left meant that I was required to put up the small blind. I ripped open my package of M&M'S and put ten in the middle of the table.

Scarlett, being the big blind, laid out twenty.

Rosie chose twenty pieces of candy—all red ones—and pushed them out into the middle of the table. "That's my lucky color. Rule number one is that I don't cheat, and I do not abide cheaters, so don't even think about it. No card counting," she said, looking right at me.

I locked eyes with her. "I do not cheat or count cards." I pushed up my shirtsleeves. "See? No aces."

She dealt us each two cards—the hole cards. I checked mine and wished that the pot was fifty dollars instead of that many M&M'S, because I was sure to win this hand.

I did not.

When the bets were all in, Rosie had a whole pile of M&M'S plus a fourth of a Twix bar in front of her. Scarlett won the next round, and I took the third one. But at the end of the fourth, Scarlett and I both folded, and Rosie raked every bit of that candy into a Ziploc bag. She tucked it into her purse and handed my cards back to me.

"You are right. That is a lucky deck of cards. Now, let's go home, make ourselves some fried potatoes to go with the leftover ham, and have supper," she said. "There are some apples that need to be used, so I could fry up some fritters for dessert."

"That sounds wonderful," I said as I slipped my coat on and started for the back door. "Who taught you to play poker like that?"

"What's important about the game is that you promised to stay around until my birthday, not that I know how to play," Rosie answered.

"I keep my word," I said with more sharpness than I intended.

She followed behind me and carefully watched her step. "This is going to be a muddy mess when the temperatures rise."

Even though the sun had done little to melt the snow piles, the porch steps were dry. The wind didn't cut through my face like sandpaper, and we only had to be out in it for a few minutes. My thoughts stayed on the fact that I had just promised to stay at the Tumbleweed until summer, and I'd done so without even the slightest hesitation.

Rosie removed her coat and hung it on one of the three hooks, tucked her bonnet into a pocket, and went straight for the kitchen. "I don't know about y'all, but that brunch this morning is all used up, and I'm hungry."

I hung my coat beside hers, still wondering about the next few months. "I'm starving, too, but are you sure there's not another reason other than your birthday for wanting me to stay until summer?"

"God told me that you need to settle down, and I'm doing what I can to help Him out. In six months, it will be harder for you to leave than it is today or even next month. Besides, I like you being around," she said. "Now, you girls peel some potatoes, and I'll get the fritter batter whipped up."

Same old, same old! Rise, work, eat, sleep, and start all over again. But today was different. I'd played poker and the adrenaline rush wasn't there. Nor was the absolute sadness when I didn't win. Something had changed in me, and that was confusing, because without poker, I didn't know who I was. Ada Lou had said that obsession was an addiction and that living in this area was like medicine. But did I want to be cured?

Scarlett handed me a potato and a peeler. "You look like you are a million miles away. What are you thinking about?"

"Life, decisions, and bewilderment," I answered.

"Those are all heavy topics."

"Yep, they are. You said Matilda helped you. How?"

"She listened to me," Scarlett answered. "Between her and Ada Lou, they made me understand that not all men were like my boyfriend. And that maybe he had seen his father treat women like he did me and thought that was normal. I forgave him, but I still never want to see him again."

I watched her peel a potato and followed her example. "If you did, he would find that you are so strong now that he had better be scared of *you*."

I was so proud of myself for peeling one potato, and then I realized that she had done four and already cut them up for frying. She took mine from my hands, sliced it, and added it to the bowl. "I just hope that theory of yours is never tested. I didn't realize until now that all three of us came from dysfunctional backgrounds. Here I am, dating a guy who has a big loving family, and for a while I've been worried that I might be wanting to marry him because everything is normal in the Mendoza household."

"Shhhh . . . ," Rosie shushed us. "Do you hear that?"

"Praise the Lord!" Scarlett shouted.

I didn't hear anything, but I figured Jesus must be coming to earth for a second time, or maybe God was about to let Rosie see Him in person. I had read *Left Behind* years and years ago, and as excited as they were, I wouldn't have been surprised to see them grow wings.

"What is it?" I whispered.

"That sound is the snowplows on the highway, and I even hear one going north, which means that I might get to see Grady tomorrow," Scarlett squealed and danced around the floor. "And you can see Jackson, and Rosie can go to confession and ask for forgiveness because she played poker with us."

Rosie did her cross thing and bowed her head. Scarlett kept jumping around like a kid on a sugar high. New friends, new rhythms, I guessed.

Long after dark, the snowplows had finished, and everything was quiet again. I could hear Scarlett talking to Grady on her phone and Rosie singing hymns as I went from the bathroom to my bedroom. My phone was ringing, so I picked it up and hit the "Accept" button without checking to see who was calling.

"Well, hello, gorgeous." Jackson's face filled the screen.

"Don't lie to me," I said. "I just got out of the shower and my hair is dripping wet."

"No lies, just facts," he chuckled. "What's going on in your world?"

"Then thank you for that. I played poker today," I answered.

"With whom?" His eyes got wide, and his smile faded.

"Rosie and Scarlett. We played with candy instead of money, and Rosie wiped me and Scarlett out. She's going to have a sugar high if she's eating it all tonight back in her room."

"I can't believe she even considered touching cards. Ada Lou said she was so religious that she wouldn't even bet on Scrabble games," Jackson said.

I stretched out on the bed, propped pillows up behind me, and was very careful to only show my face. He didn't need to see that I was only wearing a Minnie Mouse T-shirt that barely covered my faded panties.

"There was a condition," I admitted. "I had to promise that I would stay in this area until her birthday on July 4."

"Well, then, God bless Rosie," he chuckled. "Neither of us will be leaving for a while, since I've promised my dad to stick around for a year."

"How did your day go?"

"Fast and furious. The crew living in the trailers is getting cabin fever and ready to get back to work. We've fielded calls all day from the local staff. They work on wages, not salary, so they lose a lot of money when the rig is shut down. I'm so glad to be back in my trailer tonight. I slept on the sofa in the office last night, and I feel like I owe you an apology."

"For what?" I asked.

"I should have insisted that you take the bed those two nights you stayed with me."

"No apology necessary. The couch was fine, and it beat the last motel I rented. I had to deal with a rat in the parking lot, and a roach and spider in the room."

"Sounds like a few places I've been. Have you seen a picture of those spiders bigger than a dinner plate over in Africa?"

"No, and I don't want to. A granddaddy longlegs is only slightly smaller than a full-grown lion in my eyes."

"Then instead of a knight in shining armor, I'll be your spider slayer in shiny armor," he teased.

"Hey, Carla, you've got to see this," Scarlett called out.

"I heard that," Jackson said. "If it's a spider, call me and I'll saddle up the white horse."

"Be ready, and I'll see you later," I said.

"How about tomorrow afternoon at four? We can drive to El Paso for a steak?"

"I will be ready," I said, and ended the call. I pulled on a pair of sweatpants and hoped like hell that Scarlett didn't have a spider cornered in the kitchen.

"What's up?" I asked when I found her peeking out the front window. I edged up to her side and leaned forward. If there was a spider or a bug of any kind between the blinds and the glass, she was going to be in big trouble. "What is Rosie doing out there in the cold with a shovel?"

"I asked her if she was going to eat the candy she won today or if she would share it with us," Scarlett answered.

"What has that got to do with . . ."

Scarlett stepped back. "She told me it was blood candy and not a single bite would go into any of our bodies. The only good thing that would ever come of that game is that you now had to stay until summer. So she's out there burying it like it was a dead person."

"It's in a plastic bag. We could dig it up while she's at church," I suggested.

"I already thought of that, and she said she's going to unwrap it all and make sure it's unfit for even a coyote if he tries to dig it up."

I watched her finish chipping a shallow hole out of the frozen earth and dump all the candy into it. Then she filled it up again and took the shovel back to the café. When she came into the trailer, she went straight to the kitchen sink and washed her hands twice.

"That evil stuff is now gone from the house. While it was here, I felt like I should call my priest and have him perform a cleansing for the trailer," she said. "I'm going to take a shower now. I will see y'all in the morning. We will open the café at the normal time."

I was speechless as I watched her disappear down the hallway and into the bathroom. "Do you think she'll burn the clothes she wore today?" I asked in a low voice.

"I wouldn't be surprised," Scarlett said. "Her faith in what's right and what's wrong is pretty strong. I'd hate to be the devil if he ever did materialize in front of her."

"But burying candy?" I frowned.

"I don't know which is worse: her playing cards to get you to stay, or wasting all that good chocolate," Scarlett said with a sigh.

Chapter Seventeen

When Mama had said that things happen for a reason, I was too young to know what she was talking about. Before daylight on Saturday morning, I was so eager to get back to work that what she had said so long ago finally made sense. I had needed to be away from the Tumbleweed for a few days to realize how much it meant to me. Had I not practically lost my shirt, then I would have never found my new family.

"Good morning! Are we ready to get back into our routine?" I asked as I poured a cup of coffee.

"Thank you, Jesus!" Rosie said.

"Does that mean yes?"

"Absolutely," she said. "The café hasn't been closed this long since I've been here. The Good Book talks about everything in life having a time."

I took a sip of my coffee. "What has all this been a time for?"

Could it be that the same snowstorm could have a different meaning for all of us?

"For me, it's been a few days of getting to know you better—and realizing that you aren't only a boss, but a friend."

I set my mug on the bar and wrapped Rosie up in a fierce hug. "Thank you for that," I said around the lump in my throat when I took a step back.

"There ain't no reason to get all mushy," she muttered.

Scarlett went straight to the coffeepot. "What are we talking about?"

I picked up my coffee and took another sip, but it didn't completely get rid of the lump. "That basically, everything happens for a reason, and that Rosie just called me her friend."

"I believe that with my whole heart," Scarlett said. "If all that with Billy hadn't happened then, I wouldn't be here. I would have never met Grady and found out that there are good men in the world. And these past few days when I couldn't see him, except for his face on the phone screen, have taught me that I want to be with him forever."

One blizzard.

Three different meanings.

I wondered what Ada Lou and Nancy's interpretations would be, and then a picture of Jackson flashed across my mind. Did he believe that things happened for a reason? Or did he think that everything was happenstance?

"Grady asked me to move in with him," Scarlett blurted out.

"Are you going to?" Rosie asked.

"That would mean that I have to tell him about . . ." She inhaled deeply. "Couples committed enough to live together shouldn't have secrets."

"I figured you had done that a long time ago," Rosie said.

"I tried, but the words wouldn't come out of my mouth," Scarlett said.

I slipped an arm around her and gave her a sideways hug. Women empowering women—that was what we were to each other.

"If it is laid on your heart to tell him about your past, then you won't be happy until you do," Rosie told her.

"Billy gets out of prison this spring. What if he finds me and hurts Grady?"

"None of us can worry about *what-ifs*," Rosie said.

"He got five years for assault?" I asked.

"No, he only got a few months for that, but he got caught drunk driving with cocaine in his truck and an underage girl in the passenger seat," Scarlett answered. "It wasn't his first time to stand before the judge for driving under the influence."

"I don't mind spending my last days in jail," Rosie said with enough conviction in her voice to make me shiver.

"What does that mean?"

"Before I would let him hurt you, I would work him over with a ball bat myself," she answered without blinking an eye. "Ilene sent me the pictures of you in the hospital. God would not lay that sin to my charge."

"That all happened before you were Scarlett," I assured her. "Just promise me that if you do move in with Grady that you won't quit working at the Tumbleweed."

"I promise. Now, let's go to work and get our minds on something else."

I could handle Scarlett moving out of the trailer, but I sure hoped that Rosalie wouldn't decide to become a nun. Was there such a thing as a part-time holy woman? If she did feel the call from God to join the church in that capacity, could she work at the café and be a nun in the evenings?

Excitement—right along with the aroma of good food—filled the Tumbleweed that morning when the first bus pulled into the parking lot. The worst lot of tired, frazzled customers we'd had since I arrived at the Tumbleweed straggled through the door. There were no big smiles about winning money in Vegas. Even the children were too tired to whine.

"Clara, darlin', I'm so sorry . . ." a masculine voice that sounded a lot like Frank said.

When I heard my poker name, I came close to dropping the tray of coffee cups I was holding. I whipped around to find an older couple sitting side by side in a booth. The woman patted him on the shoulder and said, "It's all right, Vincent. A few sore muscles and bones from getting stuck in a bus stop are worth the memories that we made on this trip."

I set two cups on the table. "Do I hear a story?"

"Yes, you do." This particular Clara looked up at me with unshed tears in her eyes. "My arthritic knees and back are aching from trying to sleep in a chair. If there had been room on the floor, I would have stretched out there even if it made for a hard bed."

"But it was wall-to-wall people," Vincent explained. "The place reminded me of the POW camp in Vietnam. But we survived, and we will be home this afternoon in Pecos. We won't even unpack until later because our recliners are calling our names."

"A hot shower and *then* my recliner," Clara said. "And our kids and grandchildren that all live in Las Vegas are going to come see us from now on. We won't be traveling more than a hundred miles in any direction again."

"I'm so sorry," I told them. "Can I start you off with a cup of hot coffee? On the house."

"That would be great," Vincent said.

"Coming right up—and thank you for your service, sir."

He smiled and nodded.

I headed for the bar to pick up a full pot of coffee and whispered to Scarlett, "The couple at booth number eight are not paying for their breakfast. Take it out of my tip money or else just tear up the ticket."

"You act more like Matilda every day you are here," Scarlett said with a smile. "We'll tear up the ticket, but why that one?"

"He's a POW from the Vietnam era, and her name is Clara, and they had to sleep in chairs, and they haven't even had a shower, and . . ." I paused to catch my breath.

"Enough said. They are eating on the house today," Scarlett said. "You can tell me later why you reacted to that name—Clara, was it?"

"Yes, and how did you—"

"You turned a little pale. Was that your mother's name?"

"No, but we'll talk about that later." Change was all I'd ever known. Stability was not ever mine to have. But something made me yearn for the past when I heard that name.

I carried the pot over to Clara and Vincent's table and poured two cups full, took their order, and hung it on the carousel. Then I made my way back through the rest of the dining room, taking drink orders first. Scarlett finished waiting on the bar and then helped with the booths, running back and forth between her own customers and what was supposed to be mine.

When the bus finally reloaded and pulled away, I could commiserate with Clara when it came to aching bones. Scarlett and I went straight to the kitchen and slumped down into chairs.

Rosie set a plate of hot biscuits in the middle of the table. "Has a couple of days away from work made y'all soft?"

I split a biscuit in half, slathered both sides with butter, and reached for the jar of honey. "Yes, it has, but one or two of these will perk me right up."

Before I even took a bite, the phone—a landline that hung on the wall across the room—rang, and Rosalie hurried over to answer it. "Tumbleweed," she said, and listened for a minute, then told whoever was on the other end that Matilda had passed away.

She said yes a couple of times and turned to motion to me. "You are the boss, so you need to talk to Ilene."

"Who is Ilene?" I asked Scarlett.

"Go talk to her. Someone must be needing help," she answered.

"He . . . llo?" I answered cautiously when Rosie handed the receiver to me. I hadn't used a phone like that since my grandparents were alive, and started to walk away before I realized the cord only went so far.

"This is Ilene Wilder," the woman on the other end of the line said, "and I understand you are the new boss at the Tumbleweed."

"Yes, ma'am, that's right," I answered.

"I supervise several women's shelters, and I'm the one that helped Rosalie and Scarlett relocate to your area. I have another young woman in bad need of help, and it is very necessary that she gets far away. Her name is Tressa. She is twenty-two years old, and she has no job skills to speak of, but she is a fast learner. Are you willing to take her?"

"Can you give me an hour to think about it and then call me back?" I asked. "Before I say yes, I'd like to talk to Rosie and get her advice."

"Rosalie must respect you if she lets you call her Rosie," Ilene said. "I will call you tomorrow unless you make up your mind earlier and get in touch with me." She clicked off.

Before I could say a word, Scarlett squealed and got up so quickly that she knocked her chair over backward. She raced across the kitchen toward a tall, thin guy standing with his arms open wide. He picked her up and swung her around a couple of times before bending her over in a true Hollywood kiss.

"What are you doing here?" she panted when he set her down.

"I couldn't wait until this afternoon to tell you the news. That house that you have admired in Dell City is going up for sale tomorrow. I'll write a check for the down payment if you'll move in with me. We can look at it this afternoon when you get off work. I was so happy that I had to drive down here and tell you. I've got to go"—he gave her another kiss—"but . . ."

"Grady, you already know Rosie, but I want you to meet Carla, our new boss and friend," she said.

There was no doubt in my mind that she was stalling for two reasons. One was that she didn't want to answer him about moving in, and the other was that she didn't want him to leave.

"Hello. I'm so glad to finally meet you," I told him.

"Likewise," he said with a nod. "I understand you are coming to church with Scarlett tomorrow evening and then to supper with us. You can meet my whole family then. They all love Scarlett as much as I do."

"Hey, what's going on in here?" Ada Lou called out from the dining room. "It looks like a tornado struck this place."

"Y'all want us to bus these tables?" Nancy yelled.

"You talk to Rosie and then come help me." Scarlett picked up a bin and backed through the swinging doors with Grady right behind her.

"Hello, Miz Ada Lou and Nancy. You ladies have a nice day," he said on his way outside.

Rosie washed and dried her hands at the sink. "I know what you are thinking, and I know that Ilene wants to place a new young woman with us. My vote is to try to help her. Scarlett is about to move out, so her room will be empty, if you are worried about logistics."

"Things happen for a reason," I muttered as I picked up a bin. "I will tell her yes when she calls back, if you think that's the wise thing to do. Have you done this before?"

Rosie held up four fingers. "Matilda and I helped four young women before Scarlett came to us. We don't have room or finances to take in a lot, but Matilda supported the shelters that Ilene takes care of. When the café is stable again, you might think of doing the same for a charity tax write-off."

"That's a good idea."

"Hey, did y'all have a big crowd, or are you slow from having so many days off?" Ada Lou asked when I made it to the kitchen.

"A little of both. Are y'all glad to be out and about today?"

"Definitely," Nancy answered. "We are going to drive over to El Paso to do some shopping."

"There's no *we* to the driving," Ada Lou declared. "That pregnant roller skate you call a car shouldn't be on the roads in weather like this. Besides, if a coyote ran across in front of the car, you would swerve and we'd end up buried in a snowdrift. I'm driving my truck, and you are buying our brunch."

Nancy chuckled. "She's in a bitchy mood until she gets fed."

Scarlett had already cleaned off their table and poured coffee for them. She sat down across the table while they studied the menu. "Grady asked me to move in with him, and he wants to buy the house not far from our church," she blurted out.

Both menus were a blur when the older women dropped them on the table.

"Are you going to do it?" Nancy asked.

Ada Lou looked Scarlett right in the eyes. "What's keeping you from saying yes? It's just a matter of sleeping with him all night or getting up and leaving in time to get back here before you have to go to work in the morning."

"I want to do it. I love him so much, but I don't want to make a mistake," she answered.

"Move into the house he's renting now and see if y'all can live together before you sign the final papers on buying that house," Ada Lou suggested. "It will take a couple of weeks to close on a real estate deal. By then, you'll either be ready to wring his neck or marry him for better or for worse."

"Has he proposed?" Nancy asked.

"Too many times to count in the past six months," Ada Lou answered.

"Good Lord!" Nancy gasped. "Why didn't you tell me about that, Ada Lou? You aren't supposed to keep news like this from me."

"Guess I didn't remember." Ada Lou shrugged.

"That's excellent advice, Ada Lou," Scarlett said before another argument between the two old gals started. "What are you ladies having this morning?"

"The Supreme Breakfast for me," Nancy said.

"The same here," Ada Lou answered, then focused on me. "You look like you are having one of them internal fights with yourself."

"I am," I admitted.

Nancy leaned forward, and her perfectly manicured nails clicked on the table when she put her hands down. "Tell us your troubles, darlin'."

"I got a Matilda call a few minutes ago," I answered.

"A young woman needs help, right?" Ada Lou asked.

"We could sublet the fifth trailer," Nancy suggested. "Ada Lou owns it and leases it to a couple, but she could sweet-talk them into letting her move someone else in if it is short term."

"If Scarlett moves out like I think she will, we have a room for her. My problem is that I'm new at this. I'm not Matilda." I felt like someone had thrown me into cold, deep water and expected me to swim to shore. I needed a life jacket, and I sure hoped Rosie had one.

"You are a woman who got help when you needed it, and now it's time to pay it forward. Us women, no matter age or experience, should always stick together and uplift one another," Rosie called from the other room.

"Yes, we should," I agreed with a nod and carried a full bin back to the kitchen.

Rosie heaped scrambled eggs onto a couple of platters and set them on the service window. "Order up," she called out, and then turned to face me. "Have you changed your mind?"

"I haven't, but all this responsibility coming on so quickly . . ."

"God don't pile no more on a person than He will help them to endure." Rosie patted me on the back. "I'm proud of you, Carla."

"Thank you, but I wouldn't even consider it if . . ." I slapped a hand over my mouth at the same time Scarlett came into the kitchen with another bin of dirty dishes.

"Are you all right, Carla?" Scarlett asked.

"Please tell me again that you aren't going to quit working here," I whispered.

"I will work here as long as the Tumbleweed stands," she said. "Unless you tell me that when I have babies, I can't bring them to work."

"We'll turn the storage room into a nursery and buy one of those portable buildings to keep our supplies in. We could even hire a lady from Dell City to be our nanny."

"If we get a new girl, I would like to take Sundays off after we get her trained," Scarlett said.

"Done," I said without hesitation.

Chapter Eighteen

I had to push Scarlett's boxes away from the door when I heard Jackson drive up that evening. She had mulled over the idea of moving in with Grady all day, but by closing time she had made up her mind, and in a couple of hours she had completely cleaned out her bedroom.

"When you make up your mind, you don't mess around," I said.

"That's right. I forge full speed ahead."

I had lived out of two suitcases for more than half my life, and I could be packed up and gone in fifteen minutes or less, but Scarlett had lived in the trailer for five years.

"Where did all this stuff come from?" I asked. "Your room is smaller than mine."

"You accumulate stuff when you live in one place for more than a few days," she answered.

"But how did you get it all in one small bedroom?"

"*Tetris*," she said with a shrug.

"What does that have to do with anything?"

"It's called organization, and utilizing every single space," she answered.

I opened the door expecting to find Jackson, but instead he and Grady stood side by side on the porch. The idea of the boxes being like a game of *Tetris* flitted away at the sight of the powerful testosterone before me.

"I'd invite you both inside, but I'm not sure there's room," I teased.

"I'll start loading the stuff in my truck," Grady said. "Don't bother with introducing us. Jackson and I met each other in the café last week."

"From what all you have to load, you should have brought a semi," I told him.

"Hey, I've got a truck if you need more room, and I can help carry stuff out," Jackson offered.

"I never turn down help," Grady said. "And I really do appreciate the help. It's supposed to start raining in a couple of hours, and I'd hate for any of Scarlett's things to get wet. Let me repay you by asking you to supper Sunday evening at my folks' house."

"No problem, but you don't owe me anything."

The guys each picked up a box and headed toward Grady's truck. In a few minutes they had everything loaded.

"Carla is coming to the supper, too," Scarlett said with a wink. "And you'll know a lot of the people, because they work for you out at the rig."

"Then thank you. I would love to have supper with your family," Jackson said.

"You could come to church with us, too," Scarlett said. "It starts at six in the winter, and supper is at seven."

"I'll be there," Jackson said. "The Baptist or the Catholic?"

"Baptist," Grady answered.

Scarlett handed her house key to me. "This seems so final, and yet I'll see y'all tomorrow morning. I hope that the new girl loves that bedroom. When I first came, it was a refuge—not only for my body, but also for my mind."

"I'm not sure either one of those needed tinkering with for me, but my room is definitely a place I can call my own, which is more than I've had in years," I said, and changed the subject before I started crying. "I bet Rosie hates goodbyes as much as I do, and that's why she conveniently had to go to the church to talk about some kind of fundraiser."

"This is not goodbye," Scarlett frowned. "This is *see you later*."

"I like that better. See you later, then, as in before daylight in the morning."

"Yes," she said with a chuckle and got into her vehicle.

Jackson slipped an arm around my shoulders. "Are you all right?"

"Yes. I am happy for her."

He opened his truck door for me and whistled as he rounded the front of the vehicle and slid in behind the wheel. "Since the roads are clear now, I thought we'd go over to El Paso to my favorite steak house, if that sounds good to you."

"That sounds great." My SUV looked sad, sitting there all alone as we drove away. Tressa would arrive on Monday afternoon by bus, which meant she wouldn't have a vehicle.

"Change is tough," Jackson said as he made a left turn at the end of the lot and then a right onto the highway.

"For everyone?"

"Absolutely," he answered. "I retired from the military in July. For the first three months, I still had trouble getting into a different lifestyle. I missed the thrill of planning a new mission. I longed for my team and even missed mess hall food. I still have the option of going back as a civilian and teaching. That sounded good in the beginning."

"When did all that stop?" I asked.

"It hasn't, but it's getting easier each day. Staying busy helps, and also knowing that the job offer to go back and train new teams is on the table until July 4," he answered.

July 4.

D-Day for both of us. Rosie must have known.

"Independence Day," I whispered.

"Shall we plan to celebrate that day—one way or another?" he asked. "Over a nice dinner with champagne?"

"How about with pizza and beer or a shot of good whiskey? I really don't like champagne."

He nodded. "You got it. Beer in a place where there's dancing, even if the music is coming from a jukebox."

"I would like that. Only let's do it the day after the holiday. I want to see fireworks somewhere that evening." Consenting to a date was a little scary—but then, so was traveling from Tucson to the Tumbleweed on a prayer and a few crackers. "No, that's not right. I don't want to just see them. I want to set them off like kids do. Mama was too afraid that I would get hurt to let me play with them when I was a little girl."

"You've never gotten to light a firecracker or hold a Roman candle?"

I shook my head. "I usually watched them from the window or balcony of whatever hotel we were in until I was fourteen."

"And then?" he asked.

"Then I was playing poker in a room that seldom had windows," I answered. "So, this year, I want to go to one of those roadside stands, spend money on fireworks, and set them off myself."

"It's a date. I'll bring the beer and pizza," Jackson said, "and find a good place for us to celebrate."

What will happen in the five months ahead of us? Will I have put down more roots in that time?

"Will that be our eighth date?" I asked.

"No, ma'am."

"So, is this our last date?"

"No, ma'am," he repeated with a chuckle. "Independence Day will not be the date when we have a fight the first time. It could be our thirtieth one, but definitely not the eighth. That is, if you are willing to keep going out with me."

"Depends," I replied with my best poker face.

"On what?"

"By your standards, this is our third date, and you still haven't kissed me," I answered.

"Well . . ." He braked and pulled the truck over close to the piled-up snow on the side of the road. "I expect it's time to remedy that problem." He got out, rounded the front of the vehicle, and opened the passenger door. His arm brushed against mine when he reached across my body to unfasten my seat belt.

I put my hand in his when he held it out, and a huge tumbleweed floated over the six-foot-high bank of dirty snow. He helped me out of the truck, cupped my cheeks in his hands, and his eyes fluttered shut. I moistened my lips with the tip of my tongue, and his mouth closed on mine. Heat like I had never known before shot through my body, and I leaned in to him so close that I could hear his heartbeat pounding against my chest.

When the kiss ended, he scooped me up and set me back in the seat. "Does that help you make up your mind about dating me?"

"It does, but I would like to know if we are exclusive." My voice had gone high and squeaky.

"I don't have the time, energy, or want-to for anyone else in my life," he answered. "How about you?"

"Same," I told him.

He started the engine and pulled back out onto the road. "Then tonight we will celebrate our decision to date—that kiss was hotter'n blue blazes."

"Yes, we should—and yes, it was." I didn't tell him that I'd never been in a committed relationship before. Or that he was the one person that might make me get off the fence concerning spreading my wings and going back to my familiar lifestyle or falling over to the other side and putting down roots.

"Feels a little surreal out here, doesn't it?" Jackson said. "I don't think I've ever seen snow piled up this high. Seems like we're driving through a tunnel."

"If we had a full moon, it might be different, but that little sliver up there doesn't give us much light," I answered. "But I kind of like it this way. It seems so intimate and private."

"Me too. Like we're the only two people in the whole world," he said.

"Exactly. You were with your team when you went on missions. Did you ever wish for more alone time?" I asked.

"You had lots of alone time," he said in return. "Did you ever wish for family?"

"Not the kind that Frank had," I chuckled.

"Why not? What was wrong with his kinfolk?"

"I only saw them four times a year. Easter, Independence Day, Thanksgiving, and sometime close to Christmas. They all came down from the hills for the holidays with a truckload of casseroles, their Bibles, and moonshine. They would argue about religion, politics . . . and it got louder every time they emptied a quart jar of 'shine."

"Sounds like a hoot to me," Jackson said.

"As an eight-year-old little girl, believe me it was not." I shook my head, trying to shake away the thoughts that arose about Frank's abandonment. "Now, where is this steak house that we're headed toward?"

"On the other side of El Paso, not far from the Mexican border," he answered. "Are you hungry? We could always stop at some place before that."

"No, I'm good. A steak sounds great."

He was almost too good to be true. He didn't make me feel awkward about sleeping in his house. He helped Grady load up boxes. And he was concerned about me. Something had to be wrong with him, and makeup sex or not, I intended to be cautious.

What about that kiss? my inner voice asked.

"Too hot for words," I whispered before I realized I was talking out loud.

"What was that?" Jackson asked.

"I was muttering to myself," I answered. "Like you said earlier, I've spent a lot of time alone. Sometimes I forget to keep my thoughts in my head."

"I do the same, and I've been around family of one kind or another my whole life."

The two tall glasses of sweet tea I had drunk before he arrived were making me wiggle in my seat. I could surely sympathize with the folks who got off the bus and did a fast trot all the way to the restroom. I saw a sign advertising a gift store and café just up ahead. It pained me and my dignity to ask him to stop so I could use the restroom, but it was either swallow my pride or arrive at a nice steak house with wet spots on my denim skirt.

He braked and turned right into the parking lot of a conglomeration of buildings. "This is the last stop before we get to El Paso, and I need to find a restroom."

"Have you been here before?" I unbuckled my seat belt before he even turned off the engine.

"Nope, I always stop at the Tumbleweed," he answered, got out of the truck, and opened the door for me.

According to the signs, one side of the long, low-slung building in front of us was May's Café. The other was a gift shop. I'd been in enough convenience stores to figure out that in cases like this, the café was probably built first. Therefore the bathrooms were most likely in that part of the place.

Jackson laced his fingers with mine and headed for the first entrance. The sign on the window said that they were open from eight a.m. to five p.m. He pushed the door, and it opened. I almost made the sign of the cross and sent up a prayer of thanks that they weren't closed.

"We are closing in five minutes," the lady behind the register said.

"We just need to make a fast trip through the bathrooms," I told her and headed across the room.

I hadn't ever been in a store or café that was so crowded—not with people, but with stuff everywhere. There wasn't a square inch of empty space on the walls or on the countertop. I would have loved to come back some afternoon and get a better look at everything, but Scarlett would have had a heart attack thinking about dusting all the merchandise.

Jackson was sitting at a booth when I came out of the ladies' room. "Ready?"

I nodded and smiled at the lady. "Thank you. I'll come back another time when you are open."

"Where y'all from?" she asked.

"I live at the Tumbleweed," I answered.

"Over near Dell City," Jackson said.

"You must be the new help over at the Tumbleweed. I heard there was a new woman over there." She followed us to the door. "Come back and see us another time. Like the sign out there says, we make the world's best burger."

"Will do." I waved over my shoulder as we left.

"I doubt very seriously that their burgers are any better than Rosie's," Jackson said on the way across the lot to the truck.

"I agree, but it might be fun to drive back over here and check out the competition. After all, this place and the Tumbleweed are pretty much the only stops for a long time after leaving El Paso."

"Consider it a date for another time," Jackson said.

The scenery along the hour-long drive from Cornudas to El Paso changed very little. With snow piled up on either side of us, it still felt like something out of a paranormal movie.

"Ada Lou says that this is pretty country in the spring when everything begins to bloom," I said after a few minutes.

"I'll believe it when I see it," Jackson chuckled. "I do like the way the bigger yucca plants stick up out of the snow. Look, there's a cardinal."

"Ada Lou told me that when you see one, it means someone who has passed away is thinking of you," I said.

"I've been told that, too, and I'm choosing to think that one is my grandfather. I was away on a mission when he died, and didn't get to come home to the funeral."

"I'm sorry," I whispered.

"Thank you. My grandpa was a blunt old guy, and I could hear his voice telling me not to come home, because he was dead and wouldn't know if I was there anyway. Dad assured me that Grandpa would have wanted me to stay right where I was and save lives," he said.

We seemed to hit every traffic light in town before he finally parked in front of a place called the 170 Degree Steak House.

"We are here," he said.

"How did you ever find this place?" I asked. "And why is it called that?"

"I have no idea. It's only been open for a little while. It's part of the Hotel Paso del Norte, a place where my folks like to stay when they are in this area," he answered.

I was a little worried about whether I was dressed for such a fancy place. My long, straight denim skirt and cowboy boots would have been much better suited to May's Café than in a high-class place like we walked into. When he mentioned steak, I'd figured on something like LongHorn SteakHouse or maybe Saltgrass. I mean, I'd been to some of the fanciest restaurants across the country—from the Odeon in New York City to Top of the World in Las Vegas to Le Pichet in Seattle. I sure wished I'd worn one of my poker-playing dresses that evening. Maybe you can't leave everything behind.

Jackson ushered me inside and told the hostess his name and that he had reservations for two. The paneled walls, crystal chandeliers, and padded leather chairs reminded me of the dining rooms in some of the really fancy hotels I had visited for poker games through the years. I seldom stayed in them, because even when I was flush, I was a little too tight with my money to fork over what a room cost.

"You should have told me that we were going to a place like this," I fussed at Jackson while we followed the lady to our table. "I would have dressed up."

He helped me remove my denim jacket and handed it to the lady, along with his leather jacket. Then he pulled out a chair for me and kissed me on the cheek. "I thought you were dressed up. You are beautiful in that outfit—but, darlin', you would be gorgeous wearing a gunnysack tied up at the waist with a length of baling twine."

"What do you know about either of those things?" I asked.

"Oil isn't the only thing my family is interested in," he answered. "Remember my four older sisters? My folks handed Jenny the reins to the Armstrong Cattle Company a while back. She doesn't only run that business, but she, her husband, and her three sons work right out on the ranch with the hired hands."

"And the other three?" I asked.

"Joy is the prissy one," he said with a smile. "She and her husband are the oil company's lawyers. They live in Dallas, don't have any children, and from what she says, don't intend to ever have them."

I was sure enough out of my league, even if I had eaten in high-class places. "What about the other two?"

"Jaylynn is the oldest child and the bossiest. She wanted to shoot me when I joined the military. She and her family live in Frisco, Texas, a suburb of Dallas, and have three daughters. All of them have business degrees and run the Armstrong Trucking Company."

"Sweet baby Jesus!" I muttered.

"They're all ambitious women," he said, "but when we all get together for holidays, it seems like we revert to when we were kids. They try to boss me, and I retaliate by teasing them."

"And the last one?"

"That would be Jessica, who is a couple of years older than me. She doesn't have a finger in any of the family pies. She and her husband are both doctors and have a son who is studying music in Nashville. He has hopes of being a country music star. He's got the backing from his parents if the industry likes his voice."

"You all have names that start with a *J*?"

"Yep, my Dad is James. Mama is Julia. They thought it was cute," he answered. "If you had five kids, would you do that to them?"

"Would you?"

"Hell no," he said. "None of my sisters did. We didn't mind being the J's, but still . . . Seven J's in one family?"

"Neither would I, but I don't expect that I'd ever have five kids anyway. I'm thirty, so even by spacing them out two years apart, that would mean I would be forty by the time the last one was born. I can't imagine having enough energy to chase five of them around," I said.

The waiter came by and filled two of the stemmed glasses with water. He laid two leather-bound menus on the table and asked if we wanted to see the wine menu.

"No, we'll have two beers," Jackson answered and looked across the table at me. "Imported or . . ."

"Whatever you are having. I'm adventurous."

"DeadBeach it is," he said.

"Never heard of that one," I told him once the waiter left to retrieve our drinks.

"It's a Texas beer. My dad introduced me to it when I was twenty-one. We both pretended that it was the first one I'd ever tasted. Who bought your first legal beer?"

"I did," I answered with a shrug. "On my twenty-first birthday, at the hotel bar. I had my real ID, but the bartender didn't even ask for it. I was very disappointed that I didn't get to flash it."

The waiter brought our beer and two frosted mugs. Then a second server came over to ask if we wanted appetizers.

Jackson looked across the table at me. "I'm ordering a garden salad. Do you want something else?"

"I'll have one, too," I answered and handed the menu back to her. "And I want the eight-ounce filet mignon with grilled asparagus."

"I want the fourteen-ounce New York," Jackson told her. "And truffle mac and cheese."

"Good choices," she said and left with the menus.

"I've told you about the J's," Jackson said. "Now tell me about your family."

"I already did," I answered. "As far as I know, Frank is still alive and living in Kentucky. The closest thing I might have to kinfolk are his people."

"Do you ever go back there for one of the holidays?"

"Absolutely not! I don't think I would enjoy being around them any more than I did when I was forced to attend the events."

"They sound like one of Tucker's family reunions. He's one of my team members who has family living up in West Virginia. I went with him to a reunion years ago. It was quite an experience, but I've got to admit, those folks made some delicious apple pie moonshine."

"Was it good the next morning?" I teased.

"No, ma'am. The hangover was straight from hell."

The waiter brought our salads and set them before us. "Your food will be out shortly. Can I get you anything else?"

"We're good," Jackson told her, and waited for me to take the first bite. Then he cocked his head and looked somewhere between surprised and angry. "I didn't know . . . I didn't plan . . . Please don't be mad," he said and stood up.

"About what?"

"Jackson, this is a wonderful surprise." An older woman with a little bit of gray showing in her black hair hugged him tightly.

"Yes, it is." A man near in age to her clamped a hand on Jackson's shoulder. I could see that Jackson would look like him in another thirty years.

"You didn't tell me you were coming," Jackson said.

"We aren't going to Dell City," the man said. "We spent a couple of days in Denver looking at a new breeder bull and decided to make a stop over here in El Paso before Quinton flies us on home tomorrow."

When they both turned toward me, I felt like crawling under the table, especially when I knew how big that Armstrong pie really was. The only way I could keep my cool was to pretend that they were rich folks at a poker table. When I was in that element, no one had ever taken away my courage.

"This is my date, Carla Wilson. She recently acquired the Tumbleweed. Carla, this is my father, James, and my mother, Julia."

"I'm pleased to meet y'all," I said. "Have you eaten?"

Julia gave Jackson the evil eye and answered, "No, we haven't. We were about to be seated when James noticed y'all."

"Then join us, please," I said. "There's two empty chairs, and I'm sure you would love to visit with Jackson."

"We couldn't impose on your date," James said.

"Why not?" Julia's tone left no doubt that she was annoyed with her husband. "If Clara doesn't mind, it would be lovely to eat with y'all this evening."

"Carla," Jackson corrected her, and mouthed, "Sorry!" in my direction.

I thought it was a hoot that she had called me by my poker name. "I do *not* mind." I patted the arm of the chair beside me. "You sit right here beside me, Mrs. Armstrong. That way, when these men start talking shop, we won't have to raise our voices over them."

"I should have listened closer when Jackson introduced us," she said.

Jackson popped up from his chair and seated his mother, and then he held up a hand for the waitress. When she came over, he said, "Two more have joined us. Would you please hold our food until you bring theirs?"

"No problem. What can I get y'all to drink? Maybe some wine or sweet tea?" she asked James.

"We'd both like the same beer these kids are having," James answered. "No need for a menu."

"Since it opened, this has been our favorite place," Julia said. "I always have the filet, and James gets the rib eye."

"I've never been here before," I said, "but Jackson tells me that this is his favorite steak house."

"Did he tell you that he got engaged in the Hotel Paso del Norte lobby?" Julia asked.

"Mother!" Jackson barked.

"No, ma'am, he didn't—but he's not still engaged, is he?"

"If she's dating you, then she has a right to know about Yvette," Julia snapped. "She was a big part of your life until you went off to the army."

"We were eighteen, and the engagement lasted all of six weeks," Jackson explained.

"They were high school sweethearts and even were crowned king and queen of their high school prom. She's recently divorced, and we had high hopes . . ." Julia let the sentence hang.

"Let's not talk about the past," James said. "What do you do, Clara?"

"Thanks, sir, it's Carla these days, and I own the Tumbleweed Bus Stop and Diner. Most of the time, I'm just a waitress. Rosie calls most of the shots, and she does a fine job of it," I answered.

I would have loved to shuffle a deck of cards and play a few hands of poker with Julia. Her face showed every emotion and every thought that ran through her mind. I bet if I could get her to sit in on a game, I might even own that big sparkly rock on her finger, or maybe even half of one of the Armstrong companies, when the night ended.

"We love the Tumbleweed," James said. "I've offered to pay Rosie triple what she makes at that little café if she would move to Dallas and be our cook. I even offered to give her the guesthouse and hire a staff to work for her. So I guess the Tumbleweed is not for sale anymore?"

"No, sir, it's not," I answered.

"Do you own other small cafés?" Julia asked.

"No, ma'am."

"I thought maybe you bought them and flipped them once you had them financially stable, or something like that," Julia said.

"No, again," I answered. "I wouldn't even have the Tumbleweed, but the previous owner lost it to me in a poker game. I am a professional gambler, and my professional alias is Clara Williams, so you weren't totally wrong when you called me by that name. I'm going to give the business a few months to see if I'm ready to settle down or not."

"I knew you looked familiar," James said. "We were in the same game in Vegas five or six years ago. The buy-in was fifty grand, and I barely broke even."

"That was a long time ago," I said. "But I'm glad you didn't lose all of your money."

Julia looked like she could pass plumb out right there in the restaurant. Her eyes darted from me to Jackson and then to James. "And if you aren't ready to settle down?"

"Then I will either sell the café or give it to Rosie. I promised that I would stay until July 4, and I plan to keep my word."

"I'd love to play another game with you some time," James said.

"Maybe we can do that after July, but until then I'd have to say no. Rosie has threatened to leave if I fall back into my old life," I told him, and hoped that would keep him from asking any more questions.

"I'll keep that in mind," James said with a smile.

I turned toward Jackson. "We were talking about family reunions when y'all arrived. Does the Armstrong family all get together for any holidays?"

"My folks used to have those when I was a kid," James answered. "I loved all the food and seeing my cousins. When my parents passed away, no one picked up the job of organizing one, so they just stopped. These days, we have trouble coordinating schedules even for our own five kids and grandkids to get together on Christmas Eve. Does your family still do that kind of thing?"

"I'm an only child. It's great that all of your kids live close enough that you can see them often." My hands trembled when I picked up my beer. Even if I *had* sat at a poker table with Jackson's dad, I didn't share that much personal information. No, that wasn't right. Other than Rosie and Scarlett, I didn't talk about my old life—period.

I took a sip to keep from saying anything more. These people didn't need to know that they were intimidating the hell out of me and my nerves were beginning to frazzle. I needed to get away, if only for a minute. Anywhere, even a broom closet, where I could replenish my determination to not let anyone, or anything, make me feel inferior.

I laid my napkin on the table and pushed back my chair. "If y'all will excuse me, I need to make a trip to the powder room. If the food comes before I get back, y'all go ahead and eat."

I took several deep breaths on the way to the ladies' room, but even that didn't do much to calm my frayed nerves. The way Julia cut her eyes at me reminded me of Paula's cold stares. I wasn't dumb at sixteen, and certainly not at thirty. I could tell from day one that Paula didn't want me in her house or her life. And I got the same vibe from Julia in the first two seconds after she met me.

The ladies' room was every bit as fancy as the restaurant. I was glad that this one didn't have an attendant to hand me a fancy monogrammed towel after I'd washed my hands. I wanted to be alone, if only for a few minutes. I went into the first stall, put the lid down on the toilet, and sat down.

"Dating is for the birds," I whispered.

"I'm so jealous, I could just cry," a woman with a high voice said.

"Me too. I could use that tip money for a pair of shoes I've had my eye on for weeks." The next one sounded like she was a two-pack-a-day smoker. "Mr. Armstrong always tips in cash, too, and Natalie doesn't even need it. She's got a rich boyfriend and also has the Holt family on her section tonight. They might not be as wealthy as the Armstrongs are, but, honey, they will add at least two hundred dollars to the standard tip."

"If I had the Armstrong table, I would flirt with the son. He's really too old for me, but hey, to get a toe in the door for all his money, I'd rob a pharmacy and take all the little blue pills they had in stock," Miz High Voice said.

"For that kind of cash, I would give up sex," Miz Smoker said.

They giggled and then I heard the door close behind them.

"So, that's what's happening?" I sighed.

I understood a little more about the past and the present—Paula being the past, and Julia, the present. Paula wanted a family with Frank, and it was evident that I would upset the dynamic. She might not have even realized that she wanted me out of her house. Julia saw me as a gold digger like those two women I had just overheard. In her eyes I was nothing more than a glorified waitress—not nearly good enough for her only son.

As I crossed the floor, I gave myself a scolding for letting her affect an evening that Jackson had planned for us. I was almost back to our table when I stopped behind a big plant and assessed the situation. Julia's rings sparkled in the candlelight as she shook her finger at Jackson. James had his arms folded over his chest. Jackson had set his jaw. He shook his head and said something, but I couldn't read lips from that distance.

An eighth date might not ever be in our future, but I wasn't going to let his parents totally ruin our evening. Julia's face went from anger to a fake smile when both men stood up.

"Looks like I timed things perfectly. It does seem strange to be on this side of the game," I said as I sat down.

"What does that mean?" Julia asked with more than a little ice in her tone.

"It means"—I nodded toward two people bringing trays in our direction—"that our food is coming, and I, for one, am starving. If I would have taken a minute longer, my food would have gotten cold, and that's a sorry thing to do to a good steak." I kicked off my high-heeled shoe under the table and ran my foot up Jackson's leg from his ankle to his knee.

That little gesture erased Jackson's frown and put a smile on his face. Even if he never asked me out again, I didn't intend to let these people intimidate me—not again, anyway.

I cut a small bite from the steak in question and popped it into my mouth. When I chewed and swallowed, I nodded toward Jackson. "You are right. I haven't eaten all the steaks in Texas, so I wouldn't know if this is the best in the state. But it beats the ones I got at the Cosmo in Vegas, or even the Renaissance in New York City." I didn't take my eyes off him. “And the company here is so much better than in either of those places.”

“Thank you.” He shot a sexy wink across the table. “I’m glad that our third date is going well.”

“This is the fourth one.” I held up a finger. “Number one was in Sierra Blanca.” A second finger popped up. “The second was in the little Mexican place in Dell City.”

“You are wrong,” he argued. “This has to be at least our seventh date—my lucky number. We can count the two nights we were snowed in at my trailer as three through six, and now we are here.”

My pulse raced, and I was sure that his parents could feel the electricity crackling all around us. “Then we’re getting close to the eighth one. Have you decided what we will argue about?” I ignored his parents and stared into his eyes.

Then Julia popped my pretty bubble.

“Have you really visited New York and Vegas?” she asked.

I slipped my foot back into my shoe and focused on her. “Yes, ma’am, I have, and I’ve played poker in every state except Hawaii. I’m saving it for a trip with someone very special.” I shifted my gaze back over to Jackson.

“Why . . . you aren’t old . . . When . . . ,” she stammered.

“I was fourteen and had a fake ID when I played my first official game.” I figured that I might as well come clean about my past. After all, this was our seventh date. “My father taught me the basics, and the rest is instinct, I guess. I’ve always been good at it. Living in a trailer and working in a café has been quite an experience, on the other hand. I’m finding out that my friends”—I winked at Jackson—“are more important than slapping down thousands of dollars to get into a high-stakes poker game. Y’all know a little about Rosie, but did you know that she’s very religious?” I went on to tell them about talking her into playing poker with me and then burying all the candy she had won from me and Scarlett.

Even Julia laughed, but I had exaggerated the hell out of the story. "Sometimes I feel like Cinderella in reverse," I rambled on. "But I've talked too much. Let's eat before our food gets cold."

"Nothing worse than a lukewarm steak or cold gravy," James said.

"I agree on the steak, but I put away Rosie's biscuits and sausage gravy too fast for it to ever get cold," I said.

Julia laid a hand on Jackson's arm. "You haven't told me how things are going in Dell City."

"No shoptalk, Mother," Jackson said. "I'm officially on a date and have better things to talk about than the company."

I could fall in love with you. I was very glad that neither Jackson nor his mother could read my thoughts. My poker face was still intact.

"You were awesome," Jackson said when we finally left the restaurant and were inside his truck.

"Thank you, but why do you think so?"

"The way you handled my mother was amazing. I love her because she is my mother, but ever since I retired from the army, she has been trying to set me up with women—most of them from her circle in Dallas."

Those two women in the ladies' room came to mind. "Are they interested in you or your inheritance?"

"Most of them want my last name," he chuckled. "You would be surprised how many doors the Armstrong name will open."

"But if they come from your mother's circles, then they also have prominent names and money," I argued.

"Yes, but . . . ," he started and hesitated. "They don't have *my* name. The first thing that I liked in the military was that no one gave a damn where any of us soldiers came from."

"Ever think of changing your name?"

"More than once," he answered. "How about you?"

"Nope, I was glad to be Carla Wilson and not Clara Williams."

"How many guys still know you as Clara?" he asked.

"A lot, but not a one of them know me as Carla. How many women have you introduced to your folks?" I asked.

"Basically, only one, and that's you," he answered.

"Yvette?"

"By all standards, that was an arranged marriage from the time she and I were little kids."

Surely I heard him wrong. "Repeat that, please."

"Not really, but kind of," he said. "Her parents and mine were best friends. They went to parties together. The mamas had lunch together a couple of times a week. Most of the time, they left me and Yvette with my nanny, so we were thrown together a lot. We dated all through junior high and high school. When we were about to go to college, I proposed to her. The plan was for a long engagement, a big wedding after we graduated, and then happy ever after living exactly in the pathway our folks had carved out for us."

"But?"

"I played football with this guy who didn't have the finances for college, so he decided to go into the army. A six-year enlistment would get him enough money from the government to get him started on an education to be a doctor. I went with him to the recruiter, and we both enlisted. I lost him on one of our missions," he answered.

I reached across the console and laid a hand on his shoulder. "I am so sorry. Was Yvette upset about you enlisting?"

Traffic was light at that time of night, so we were on the highway leading east in only a few minutes. For a while, I thought that Jackson wouldn't answer my question, but he finally took a deep breath and let it out slowly.

"She was angry at first, but after she thought about it, she said that everything would work out fine. I could go play my war games, and she could have fun doing the sorority thing. We would have a long-distance relationship and get married in four years. When I came home after basic, she had returned the ring to my mother and had gone off on a trip to Paris with some of her friends before she started at the university. She left a note for me saying that she wanted to enjoy her college experience without being tied down."

The romance books I had read told me that was probably the reason he was thirty-eight and had never married. "And you never got over the heartbreak?"

"I was more relieved than anything. Being away, and in a place where I wasn't any better or worse than any other guy, had already taught me a lot. The major thing was that I was too young to tie myself down, even if the engagement was supposed to last for four years. Now, let's talk about how many old boyfriends you introduced to Frank."

"None," I answered. "You are my first boyfriend."

Jackson braked, pulled the truck over on the side of the road, and stared at me. "You have got to be kidding me."

"I have kissed guys. I slept with a few, but my lifestyle didn't have room for anything that lasted more than forty-eight hours. Until I came here, I didn't realize that it wasn't normal."

He put the truck back into gear and started driving. A couple of long, pregnant moments passed. I thought I'd really like to go out with him again—maybe more than once.

"What are you thinking?" I finally asked.

"That in a lot of respects, we have lived similar lives. I didn't feel like I could get involved with someone for a long-term relationship when I was in the military. It wouldn't be fair for either of us. Sometimes I was gone for six months at a time, and in places where a woman couldn't go. Or would even want to. I had some of those short-lived flings, too. Can I see you again tomorrow?"

"That was abrupt," I answered.

"Well, it was on my mind and just came out," he said.

"We're already committed to go to church with Scarlett and Grady, and have supper with his family after that," I reminded him. "Unless you stand me up."

"Never," he grinned. "Shall I pick you up, or are we meeting at the church?"

"Let's meet there. I'll be the one sitting beside Scarlett."

He turned onto the highway on the west end of the Tumbleweed. "I'll get there early enough to walk inside with you."

"Why?"

"Because a sexier guy might sit down beside you, and then there would be a fight right there in front of the Mendoza family and even God." He held my hand all the way to the door. "Thanks again for being so understanding about my mother crashing our date."

His mouth closed on mine, and the kiss was hot enough to melt all the snow between the trailer and the restaurant in El Paso.

He took a step back. "Was that as good for you as it was for me?"

"If Rosie wasn't home, I would invite you inside and show you how good it was."

"I really like you, Carla Wilson," he whispered.

"I really like you, Jackson Armstrong—and it has nothing to do with your name."

Chapter Nineteen

"How did your date go?" Rosie asked before I even closed the door.

"Were you waiting up for me?" I asked.

"Yep, I was," she answered. "Ada Lou thinks she's your grandmother, and that's all right, but I'm of an age to be your mama, and that outranks her. That means that I can wait up for you to get home, be nosy, and ask questions. Pour yourself a glass of sweet tea and come and tell me all about the evening. You *know* you want to talk to someone."

I hung up my coat, filled a glass with ice and tea, and sat down beside her. "Yes, I do, but it might take a while."

"Let's start with something that's been on my mind and has nothing to do with tonight. You mentioned a while back that men like Buddy made your skin crawl and said you would tell me why sometime."

My nose crinkled at the thought of Buddy and the way his eyes followed me around the Tumbleweed. "Since he hasn't been back in the café in weeks, I had forgotten about that sleazy piece of crap."

"But you've never forgotten about men like him, have you?"

"No, I have not," I answered. "I was almost fourteen, and Frank promised that I could have a fake ID on my birthday so I could play cards. You saw my picture at that age. I matured really early. Anyway, we were at one of those backroom games that drew in the kinds of guys you might expect. Frank was on a losing streak and had thrown his last chips into the pot. He lost again and was ready to leave the table. That's when a man who had been watching me with . . ." I paused and tried to find the right words. "He didn't look like Buddy, but he had those same creepy eyes. Anyway, he said that Frank had something he wanted, and he would give him five thousand dollars in chips for one night with me."

Rosie gasped. "You poor child."

"Of course, Frank said no, and we left the game, but he hesitated and looked over his shoulder at me before he turned the guy down. There were other offers like that, but by that time I had my ID, and I made the decisions, not Frank."

"I'm so sorry that you had to live through that," Rosie said.

I shrugged. "Life is not all rainbows and unicorn farts. I read on a T-shirt once that experience is what you get when you didn't get what you wanted. Do you still want to talk about tonight?"

"Absolutely," she said. "We both need to get that taste out of our mouths."

I took a long drink, and it did help take away the memory. "You are already up past your bedtime."

She patted the place beside her on the sofa. "If you ain't done telling me all about it by midnight, we will stop and finish up tomorrow morning."

"It started out really well," I said, and went on to tell her about the kiss on the side of the road, and the restaurant. "That place was so romantic, Rosie, with crystal chandeliers and fancy leather chairs. And then his parents showed up."

"You are joking, right? Did he know they were coming? I'll strangle him if he sprung this on you out of the clear blue sky."

"I'm serious as a heart attack, and he was as surprised as I was." I told her about Julia and as near as I could remember what had been said.

She scowled and shook her finger at me. "Don't ever let anyone, and I mean no one—not Julia Armstrong, or Jackson, or whichever Armstrong—make you feel inferior. No matter how much you love a person, they are not worth giving up your peace to stay around them.

You handled that situation well, and I couldn't be prouder of you if I was really your mama."

I didn't even try to keep the tears from flowing down my cheeks. "You don't know how much that means to me, Rosie."

She handed me a box of tissues from a tiny end table. "Dry your eyes. I'm speaking the truth."

Black mascara mixed with my tears and left long streaks on the tissue. "How did you get so wise?"

"Like you said, 'Experience is what you get when you didn't get what you wanted,'" she answered.

I pondered over what she said for several seconds. "Amen to that. I wanted to go to Vegas, but I got the Tumbleweed instead."

"I wanted to have a happy ever after marriage, but I got the Tumbleweed instead, so we are enough alike to be kinfolk even if we don't share a drop of that DNA stuff everyone seems to be taken with," she said in a wistful tone.

I gave the tissue box back to her. "I would gladly claim you for my mama."

"Thank you for that, and I meant what I said about not letting anyone control you. I thought if I found a good man in the church, one who had the same values that I had, then I could spend my life with him. Raise a bunch of kids and die with a big family gathered around me, singing hymns when I made that transition from a physical body to a spiritual one."

"I take it that didn't happen, since you wound up at the Tumbleweed, too."

She barely nodded and took a deep breath before she went on. "What I'm about to tell you goes no further than the walls of this trailer. Do you understand?"

I felt a yawn coming on, but I stifled it. No way in the universe would I ever stop her from telling me her story. "Yes, ma'am."

"I will be forty-eight years old in July. Thirty years ago, about the time you were born, I gave birth to a stillborn little girl. She was full term and perfect, but she never took a breath. I was eighteen and had been married for ten months. Her birth broke me. Not spiritually or mentally, but physically. I could never have another child." She stopped talking.

"I'm so sorry." I couldn't help crying more tears.

"I was a smart student and graduated a year early, and I'd grown up with the man I was in love with, so we got married on my eighteenth birthday. We went to church every time the doors were open, volunteered for fundraisers, and even taught the four- to five-year-old Sunday school class."

"Catholics have Sunday school?" I asked.

"No, *they* have catechism, but in those days, I wasn't in the faith that I am now. Fred and I worshipped in a nondenominational place that was very radical in their beliefs. My parents had gone there my whole life, and they abided by the 'rules.'" She air-quoted the last word. "It's what Fred and I both knew, so I was prepared to be a submissive wife."

"You?" I almost choked on the idea.

"Yes, and I did a fairly good job of it, until we got a new preacher who was very charismatic and began to make new rules. The first one was that to keep men's minds pure during services, the women would sit on one side and the men on the other side of the center aisle."

"Good grief! That dates back way more than a hundred years," I gasped.

"Yes, it does, but according to Preacher John, it would keep all our minds on the Holy Father during his sermons and away from lust. Then he took away the Sunday school classes. His theory was that the children should be made to sit still in services and learn obedience to their elders. Things went from bad to worse. But looking back, it all happened because we women were taught from childhood to be submissive wives. Fred and I had been married more than a decade when it all came to a head." She paused again.

She had my absolute attention, and I had to know what happened next, but I waited. From the sadness in her eyes, I could tell that it was not an easy story. She probably would rather keep it buried rather than endure the pain that came along with telling it.

She took a deep breath and went on. "By then Fred was firmly under the preacher's control. He was the head deacon and Preacher John's best friend. They met in private at least twice a week to discuss things. Things between us changed so slowly that I didn't realize it for a couple of years. But then he became verbally abusive, blaming me for being barren like some of the women in the Old Testament. He didn't beat me, but nothing I did was right. Preacher John told him that God was punishing him for past sins for not giving him children and backed it up with scripture. According to Preacher John, Fred was entitled to have a wife who would produce sons for him. Didn't Jacob in the Bible have two wives, and even a mistress or two?"

"Holy crap!" I whispered.

Rosie nodded in agreement. "That's exactly what it was. Mind control and a bunch of crap. Preacher John had four wives by then. Our town was very small, with only the one church, so it became kind of like a commune of sorts. Maybe like that show *Sister Wives* in some respects, only on a bigger scale. When Fred came home from work one evening, he told me that he was taking another wife. Preacher John had picked out a woman for him that would give him sons to carry on his name."

"What did you do?" I asked.

Rosie shrugged. "By what I'd been taught and then brainwashed to believe that was biblical, I should have kept my mouth shut and welcomed a younger woman into our house. But I did not do that. I told Fred that the only way he was moving another woman into the home was if he divorced me. That was the first time I had stood up to him, and he was furious. He screamed that Jesus spoke against divorce."

I thought of what Scarlett had told me about her past. "Did he hit you?"

"Not at first, but when I argued that Preacher John jumped from the Old Testament to the New when it suited his needs and wants . . ." Another long pause. "That's when he jerked off his belt and taught me his form of submission."

The truth is stranger than fiction came to my mind. "Did you leave?"

"Not that time, but I asked for a special meeting with Preacher John, and I told him that I did not want another woman in my house," she answered. "I'm not sure where he got his verses, but it was decided that I should be an example to the other women who didn't want to 'believe.'" More air quotes went around the last word.

"What happened?" I asked.

"I was taken out of town the next night after midnight and stoned by all the men in the congregation. They tied me to a chair and threw big heavy rocks at me until I died."

I had lost my ability to read people for sure if I was to believe that story. She had pulled my leg long enough, and I didn't want to hear any more of this fake tale of woe.

"Only," she went on, "I wasn't as dead as they thought I was. They left me tied to the chair, sitting there on the side of a seldom-used dirt road. I suppose they figured the coyotes and buzzards would take care of my dead body, but there was still a little life left in me. Have you ever read the story of the Good Samaritan?"

I was speechless that something like that could happen outside of a horror film. All I could do was nod.

"Well, I had one. A priest had been down that road to deliver last rites to an old woman who lived way back in the sticks. He stopped and loaded my nearly lifeless body into the back of his vehicle and took me to his church in another town. The nuns nursed me back to health. It took several months. During that time, Preacher John was arrested for fraud. He was using the money donated to the church for sex trafficking. I'm not sure how that worked, but I did remember him sending several young girls off to work in other places. I testified against him in court for trying to kill me. The nuns had the foresight to take pictures before they cleaned me up and called for help to mend all my broken bones and body."

"Didn't you go to the hospital?" I asked.

She shook her head. "I was too terrified to go, so a lady doctor who went to the Catholic church made house calls and took care of me. She called the police, and the rest is history."

"You are in witness protection, then?"

"No," she replied. "I was beaten to death and woke up a new woman. Ilene helped me change my name from Rita Marie Sanchez to Rosalie Smith, and I've been at the Tumbleweed ever since. Matilda, my priest, and Scarlett are the only people who knew or knows all that. Rita died in that chair. Rosalie was born when I looked up through a tiny slit in one bloody eye and realized that I was being treated by a couple of nuns. And now it is midnight, so it's time for us to go get some sleep."

"One more question, please?" I asked.

"Only one, and then that's the last time I want to remember that part of my life."

"Where did you learn to play poker?"

"Matilda had been a dealer at a casino in her past life." Rosie chuckled. "When I first came to the Tumbleweed, I had horrible nightmares, and she taught me the game. The nights when I woke up crying or screaming, she would get out the cards and we would play until I could go back to sleep. I got addicted to the game and wanted to play every night, even after the dreams ended. We decided to give it up one year for Lent. It was only a game to Matilda, but I spent a miserable month going through withdrawal. I learned that the deck of cards was controlling me as much or even more so than Fred, so I never played again until we played for candy."

"Did y'all play for money?"

"That's two questions, but the answer is no, we did not. We bet with dried beans and macaroni. I threw away a gallon jar full when I quit playing, and I've never let anything else control me since then. No more questions, and good night." She got up from her chair and disappeared down the hall.

She might have slept that night, but not me. I kept going back and forth over her story, then flipped to all the events of that evening. Would Julia talk Jackson out of ever seeing me again?

Anything worth having is worth fighting for. Ada Lou was back in my head. *You have won bigger battles in the past. If you really like him, then put up your fists and fight.*

Chapter Twenty

Some folks can't define the very moment that their life changed. To those people, the exact second of clarity, when they knew beyond the faintest shadow of a doubt what they needed to do, didn't come in a flash, but it crept in slowly. For me, it was the total opposite.

I was sitting on a church pew for the first time in over twenty years. Scarlett was to my left, with Grady beside her. Jackson held my hand to my right. The little black dress I wore with a dark green cardigan was too warm, but the heat flooding my body had more to do with his touch than the temperature of the building.

A young couple with kids arrived and sat right in front of us. The mother led the way like a mama duck with four little ducklings behind her, only this was four little blond-haired girls, and then the father took his place at the end next to the aisle. The youngest of the children stood up, put her hands on the back of the pew, and smiled at me.

In that very instant, I knew that the Tumbleweed and Dell City was my forever home. What was more, I wanted a chance to give Jackson a permanent place in my heart, and I wanted kids—lots of them. I might not have had the background to know how to raise children, but I would give them the same kind of love that my mother gave me. That should be enough to start, and the rest could be learned along the way.

The preacher seemed to appear out of nowhere, but then, I hadn't been paying attention to anything except that adorable little girl and my own revelation.

"I'm glad that the roads are finally open enough that we can have services," he said.

"Amen!" someone said from the back.

"Hallelujah!" another person shouted.

I wasn't sure if we were supposed to say something or not. Jackson gave my hand a gentle squeeze and smiled. If he could read my thoughts, then my poker-playing days must have come to an end.

"Yes, amen and hallelujah!" the preacher said. "While you are opening your hymn books to page 189, I'd like to take a moment to welcome our newcomers," he said. "We would be happy to have you make our little church your spiritual home. We are a right friendly and informal bunch who will gladly make you a part of our family. Now, let's sing loud enough that the angels in heaven can hear our praise."

There was that word again—*family*. This time it didn't scare me like before.

Jackson reached for a hymnal from the pocket on the back of the pew in front of us. Scarlett winked when he shared the book with me.

"What?" I whispered.

"I'll tell you later," she answered in a low voice.

I should have paid more attention to the sermon, but my mind drifted back to that moment of clarity. I didn't want to change it, and I did not have any second thoughts. I would have loved to have a real relationship with Jackson, and children with him someday—a year came to mind when I thought of how long Scarlett had been dating Grady.

The preacher jerked me back to the present when he said we would close the services with a moment of prayer. I could hardly believe that thirty minutes had passed so quickly, or that I hadn't heard a word of the sermon. Yet sitting there in that small church had changed my whole perspective on life, and I truly felt at peace.

"Have I paid my dues?" I whispered to Scarlett.

"Did you listen to the message?" she asked.

"I got a message loud and clear, but I'm not sure who it was from," I answered.

"Then you get to break bread with the Mendoza family." She grinned when she stood up. "And just so you know, when you share a hymn book with a guy, that means he's off-limits to the other women. Some floozies might make a play for him, but you faced off with his mama, so you can take care of them."

"Sometimes I feel like a sixteen-year-old who is just learning the ropes," I whispered.

"If I had lived in your world, I would, too," she said. "Oh, and we usually leave our vehicles here and walk to the Mendoza home. It's only a block away, and there's very little parking."

We shook hands with the preacher, and then Jackson slipped an arm around my waist. When we were outside, he removed his arm and laced his gloved hands with mine. Scarlett and Grady walked beside us. A dozen people were ahead of us, including the couple with the four little girls, who ran and slid when they found an icy patch. Several more folks trailed along behind us.

"Do you think we are all headed to the same place?" I asked.

"Yes, and this isn't all of us," Scarlett answered. "Rosie's Mass is over, so I'm sure she's already there, along with the relatives and friends that go to the Catholic church. She brought along that extra peach cobbler that we had left over from the café today."

"Mama always makes enough tamales and enchiladas to feed an army for Sunday supper, and all the relatives bring food of some kind," Grady added.

"Do you do this for Sunday dinner, too?" I asked.

"No, that's just for the immediate family," he answered.

One look at the house told me that all those people would never fit into the place. I was hungry enough that I would have claimed a couple of square feet on the floor and held my plate on my lap. But when we arrived, everyone went through the living room and kitchen and into the garage, where several tables lined the walls, and two over to my right were covered with food.

"We always have Sunday supper out here. After supper, the older folks gather in the living room to talk about old times or fall asleep for a power nap. The young ones get out board games. And those in between take their kids home for a few hours," Scarlett explained and motioned for us to follow her. "Supper is a time of visiting with friends and family, and after cleanup, everyone goes home. Y'all come on and I'll introduce you to some folks."

"I feel like I did when the first busload came into the Tumbleweed," I whispered to Jackson when I looked over the room full of people.

"A little bewildered?" he asked.

"Yep, and I didn't even have to remember all their names."

"Hey, Jackson!" a short guy with graying hair yelled from the back of the room. "I'm sure glad that we got back to work yesterday. I was getting a bad case of cabin fever."

"I think we all were," Jackson said.

"How many of these folks work for you?" I asked.

"A lot—but they work for the company, not me," he answered.

Scarlett made us acquainted with Grady's folks, his sisters, and a few other people, then she grabbed my hand and led me over to the food tables. "Jackson, you can go talk shop with the guys. Carla is going to help me and a couple of other women serve tonight."

For a brief moment, I thought about the church where Rosie grew up, but then I saw a man throw a diaper bag over his shoulder and escort his small son to the restroom at the back of the garage.

Rosie wouldn't let Scarlett worship in a place like that, I assured myself.

Jackson let go of my hand and kissed me on the forehead. "Save me a little bit of Rosie's cobbler."

"I'll do my best," I promised, and turned to Scarlett. "You said this was a buffet. Don't folks serve themselves?"

"Yes, but sometimes the older folks and the children need help taking their plates to the table, and if someone spills something, we are on duty. It's a good time to meet folks," she explained, and introduced Cynthia and Lola, our other two helpers.

"Pleased to meet you," they said in unison.

"My pleasure," I said. "I'm new to this, so y'all might have to guide me."

"You were sitting behind me in church," Cynthia said. "I'm married to one of the Mendoza cousins."

"And I'm married to another one," Lola said. "We are so glad that the Armstrong Company came to our area. My husband had been driving all the way to El Paso for his job. It's nice to have him home an hour earlier in the evenings, and the pay is double."

"That's great." I could almost feel roots growing right down through my feet, into the garage floor, and on into the ground.

"Hey!" Nancy said as she and Ada Lou came into the room. "We're not too late, are we?"

Scarlett shook her head and took a bowl from each of them. She set the one with banana pudding on the dessert table and the one with salad with the side dishes. She tapped on one of the casserole dishes with a spoon, and the whole place went silent.

Mama Mendoza stood up from her place beside Rosie and said, "Tonight, Rosie will say the blessing, and then all y'all can line up and fix your plates."

Rosie pushed back her chair and bowed her head as she got to her feet. "Father, thank you for this food, for the hands that prepared it, and for the fellowship we will enjoy. Amen."

I heard one of the little blond-haired girls say, "I like it when Miz Rosie prays. She don't talk a long time."

"Amen," I whispered under my breath.

"Are most of these people related to the Mendozas?" I asked Scarlett.

"Yes, we are, in some form or another. That tall redhead over there is my cousin's wife, and the lady beside her is her mother. They aren't blood kin, but they are what we call *shirttail kin*," Lola answered.

As people came through the line, they told me their names, but there was no way I would remember all of them. Still, the whole scene reinforced my decision to give up poker and stay in the area. I wanted a family that was not only related by DNA, but some of those shirttail folks, too.

Frank marked you after all. The voice that I didn't like was in my head.

Mama, where are you? I'd think that you would be happy that I'm going to settle down. So why don't you tell me how happy you are rather than letting a different voice tell me that I'm like Frank and his ragtag family.

No answers floated down from the rafters in the garage, so I simply kept smiling and talking to folks as they loaded up their plates. Jackson and Grady had been roped into helping serve drinks, so they were the last two in line. When they finished getting their food, Scarlett and I were done with our job, and we joined them at a nearby table.

"This is a really nice way to end the weekend," Jackson said.

"Good food. Good friends. Good family," Grady said. "We're a pretty tight-knit group here in Dell City."

"Actually, from here all the way to the Tumbleweed, since y'all took us in," Scarlett said.

"Anyone that has a Dell City address is counted in with us," Grady replied.

I had never been included in a town before, and I liked the warm feeling of acceptance that washed over me. Yes, I had made the right decision, and it hadn't taken me all the way to July 4 to do so. I wasn't ready to stand on the top of my trailer and announce it to the world. Not yet, anyway. I wanted to keep it close to my heart for a while and enjoy the peace all to myself.

Grady stood up and extended a hand to Scarlett. She took it and together they walked to the center of the room. Mama Mendoza shushed the folks around her and pointed. Soon the whole room was quieter than the church when the preacher gave his sermon that evening.

Scarlett shot a smile and a wink at me from across the room. My thoughts went in several different directions. Was Grady about to propose? Were they announcing that she was pregnant?

"Since everyone is here, we have an announcement to make," Grady said. "Scarlett has moved in with me, and just this morning she finally said yes when I proposed for the twenty-fifth time. We would like to invite all y'all to attend our wedding in two weeks. The ceremony and the reception will be held at our church."

The applause was probably heard all the way to El Paso, and everyone rushed to congratulate them.

"What do you think about that?" Ada Lou whispered in my ear.

I whipped around to find her right there in person instead of just as a voice in my head. "I am happy for her."

"Aren't you going to miss her at the café?" she asked.

"When she moved in with Grady just yesterday, she promised that she would continue to work at the Tumbleweed."

"What about when she has a baby or babies?" she asked.

"Then we're turning half of the storage room into a nursery and hiring a nanny. You want to apply for the job?"

"I just might."

Her answer shocked me so badly that I didn't even have a comeback for several seconds. Finally, I found my voice and said, "Are you serious?"

"Sure, I am. Rosie told me y'all have a new girl coming tomorrow morning. When she gets trained, you could give Scarlett the weekends free. Then I'd only have to work five days a week. If I can't handle it, I'll talk Nancy into helping me," Ada Lou answered.

"You've already given this some thought, haven't you."

"Yes, I have," she said, then went up to hug the couple.

Jackson leaned over and kissed me on the cheek. "So, you're putting in a nursery? I'd thought we would hire a live-in nanny."

"For Scarlett's kids?" I asked, even though I knew what he was talking about.

He stood and held out a hand. "The nanny I had it mind would be for Leroy Jethro and Barney Huckleberry. Those are strange names for a cute little girl like the one that kept turning around in front of us during church services, but I bet there won't be another girl in her kindergarten class named that."

"It would take a lifetime to get ahead of you," I said on the way to stand in line to congratulate Grady and Scarlett.

"But just think about how much fun it would be," he chuckled.

Chapter Twenty-One

A big, full moon would have made it a perfect night. Stars twinkled in a nearly black velvet sky, but there wasn't even a faint sliver of a moon up there. Jackson and I weren't the only ones who were walking back to the church parking lot. Kids ran along in front of their parents and grandparents. Young couples huddled up so close to each other that cold air couldn't have gotten between them. Jackson held my hand, and I was not a bit surprised at the little rush of heat traveling through our gloves, spreading warmth through my body.

"What are you thinking about right now?" Jackson asked.

"Helping Scarlett plan a wedding in two weeks. She says it's going to be very simple, and that Mama Mendoza and Grady's family are taking care of the reception. But as her family, Rosie and I need to do something. And to be honest, I am worrying a little about the new girl who will be living in the trailer with me and Rosie. I hope she fits in with the dynamic as well as I did."

"That's sweet, but I was hoping you would say you were thinking about me," he said.

"Is that a pickup line?" I asked.

"It could be," he answered. "I've never used it before, but I like it if it's working—and you are certainly thinking about me now. Ask me what's on my mind."

I stopped and looked up at him. "What's on your mind, Jackson?"

"You," he answered and kissed me right there amid all those people. "If you asked me yesterday, or last week, or tomorrow, the answer would be the same. Ever since that first day in the Tumbleweed, you have been on my mind."

"Wow!" I whispered. "That's the most romantic thing I have ever heard."

"It's the truth." His warm breath on my neck sent extra shivers down my spine.

"We've only known each other a couple of weeks," I said.

"When you know, you know." He started walking again. "Now, back to wedding talk. What kind of wedding do you want when you get married?"

"A quick trip to the courthouse would be fine with me—and that is *if*, not *when*."

"Are you against marriage?"

"Nope, but I want to be absolutely sure." I took a couple of steps before I realized that Jackson had stopped in his tracks.

"I'm a patient man, and I understand why you wouldn't want to rush into anything," he finally said and took my hand in his. "I'm going to Dallas on Saturday, which is Valentine's Day, for an oil company meeting. Dad is sending the plane to take me, and I'm staying over until Sunday. One of my army team members is retiring, and we're having a get-together for him." He slowly took a couple of steps closer. "Why don't you come along?"

"I have to work, and we have a new woman arriving, so I need to be there to help train her," I answered. "Can I have a rain check?"

"Of course you can." Jackson stopped at my SUV and opened the door for me. He pulled me close to his chest, tipped my chin up with his knuckles, and kissed me—soft at first and then deeper, with more passion.

A fiery-hot desire rushed through my entire body, and I forgot all about everything else. I leaned in to him. My hands snaked up around his neck, and I tangled my fingers in his hair. He cupped my face in his cold, gloved hands, and we made out like a couple of teenagers in the church parking lot until we were both panting.

"Text me when you get home—or better yet, FaceTime," he whispered when he finally took a step back.

"I will." My body whined for more than kisses all the way back to the trailer. Rosie must have heard me drive up, because she had two cups of hot chocolate sitting on the bar. She motioned me inside and said, "Close the door fast so you don't let all the bought warm air out."

I hung my coat on the rack, picked up one of the cups, and sat down on the sofa. "You know I've been thinking. The Mendoza family is taking care of the reception. We are Scarlett's family, and we should do something. I'm at a loss to know how or what to do. I've only ever been to one wedding. That was Frank and Paula's, and I was just told to sit on the back pew and be good."

Rosie brought her hot chocolate to the living area and sat down on the other end of the sofa. "You are the boss and have the final say-so, but what do you think about the Tumbleweed buying her dress and flowers? It's a tradition for the groom to pay for her bouquet, but we could decorate the church or just call a florist and tell them to do it."

"Are you talented at arranging flowers?" I asked.

"Absolutely not," she answered.

"Me neither, so let's book a florist and go shopping for a dress in El Paso," I suggested.

Rosie tapped her chin with her finger and pursed her lips. "How about we plan on going to find a dress on Friday? Tressa is coming tomorrow, and we need to get her settled for a couple of days. On Wednesday, you need to go to Sierra Blanca to the bank. We don't need to keep so much money in the safe."

"Friday it is," I said. "If Scarlett is agreeable to that. I've never bought flowers or had any delivered to me, but Ada Lou might have some suggestions. We can ask her tomorrow."

"I feel better now that we have a plan," Rosie said. "My priest says that I like to be in control because I wasn't when I was married. But now that we agree, I believe I can sleep. This is going to be a busy week. The Tumbleweed will save one young woman and is sending another one off to a happy ever after. You and Jackson seem to be getting along right fine, but please don't spring an engagement on me like Scarlett did."

"I promise I won't," I said. "We should fuss at her for sure for not telling us first. After all, we are her family."

"Yes, we are." Rosie stood up, put her cup in the dishwasher, and headed down the hallway. "And we will make Tressa part of the family, too."

"Of course we will." I wondered if Rosie was trying to convince herself or me.

Scarlett was already in the café when Rosie and I arrived the next morning. She had put on a pot of coffee and hugged us both as soon as we were in the storage room. "I'm so sorry I didn't call y'all or at least send a text before dinner last night. I had no idea Grady was even thinking about announcing the engagement, but he was so excited. That really was the twenty-fifth time he asked me to marry him. He has every single one marked on last year's calendar. When he asked me if we could do it right then, I couldn't tell him no. Not again!"

"You are forgiven," Rosie said. "Why are you getting married so quickly?"

"We want to start a family, and it means a lot to both of us to be official before we get pregnant," she said.

"That's a good thing," Rosie agreed and went on into the kitchen. She slipped a clean apron over her head and fired up the grill and oven. Then she gave me a look and nodded. "Tell her."

"Tell me what?" Scarlett asked.

"We are your family," I started. "So we want to do something for the wedding. We'd like to make an appointment at a bridal shop on Friday and buy your dress."

"And," Rosie said, "hire a florist to put up some simple decorations in the church for the wedding."

"That is . . . ," she stammered, tears welling up in her eyes.

Rosie handed her a paper towel. "You know I never let anyone cry alone. So stop it! We've got a café to run, and we can't have tears dripping in the food."

"Y'all really are my family," Scarlett said. "Thank you so, so much for offering to do this. I had thought I'd just order a cheap dress online. I told Grady that I wanted a bouquet of roses and figured that was enough. If we started getting corsages for everyone in his family, we'd have to rob a bank."

Rosie got down the big bowl and started making biscuits. "What color roses?"

Scarlett didn't even hesitate. "Red, since it's so close to Valentine's Day. He's going to wear a red tie with his Sunday suit."

I gave her a sideways hug. "Then red it is. Now, let's go get the dining room set up for the breakfast rush."

"If y'all talk about the wedding plans, then raise your voices so I can hear," Rosie told us as we pushed through the swinging doors.

"Yes, ma'am," we said at the same time.

Scarlett switched on the lights, and together we set down the chairs, filled the condiment trays, and took them to the tables, and then I wrote the Monday lunch special on the board—spaghetti and meatballs, hot rolls, salad, a free drink, and a piece of cherry or blackberry pie.

The aroma of biscuits baking in the oven wafted out through the dining room. Even if I moved in with Jackson, I couldn't imagine a life when I didn't work at the café or eat biscuits and gravy for breakfast.

"Are you eating your regular, Scarlett?" Rosie called out.

"No, I made breakfast at home for me and Grady before I drove down here," she said. "But I might have one biscuit with honey."

"I want my regular," I said, raising my voice.

"Biscuits and gravy and a stack of pancakes?"

"Yes, ma'am," I answered.

I made one last scan of the dining room to be sure everything was ready for the first busload of customers before Scarlett and I went to the kitchen. As usual, Rosie had already poured the coffee and had a plate of steaming-hot biscuits in the middle of the table.

"Do y'all think we will have Tressa trained enough that I can take a few days off after the wedding?" Scarlett asked. "Grady would like for us to have a long-weekend honeymoon—maybe up to Cloudcroft to stay in one of those hotels. I could be back to work on Wednesday."

I nodded and chuckled. "Of course you can take those days off for your honeymoon. I'm sure our new girl will catch on quickly. I have been here less than a month, and look at the miracles you and Rosie have worked on me. Besides, y'all ran it with only the two of you before I came along. So yes, we can give you a long weekend for a honeymoon, and after that, you should take Sunday off each week. That way you'll have a family day, and when Tressa is comfortable, you can take off full weekends."

Rosie buttered a biscuit and drizzled honey on it. "I agree. Someday we might get another young woman who needs help, and both of you can have weekends off."

My fork stopped halfway to my mouth. "Why would I want to do that?"

"You and Jackson might want to lay in bed and make a baby after you get married," Rosie answered.

"Bite your tongue," I snapped. "I like him a lot, but marriage is so far down the road that it's nothing but a dot on the horizon."

"Hmph!" Scarlett snorted. "Everyone at the supper last night saw the way he looked at you. You might as well get ready to catch the bouquet when I throw it. That reminds me—as much as I would like for either or both of you to be my bridesmaids, Grady and I are doing something different: We are walking down the aisle together. He's got too many relatives to pick a best man and groomsmen, so we will do it our way."

"I like that idea," Rosie said. "Together from the beginning. I heard the brakes on the bus a minute ago, so it's time to get to work."

Scarlett and I were behind the bar when the parade of people came into the dining room. Like always, about half of them headed toward the bathrooms, while the rest found places to sit. I tied an apron around my waist, slipped an order pad and pen in the pocket, and was on my way to the first table when a tall blonde straggled in behind everyone else.

"Just have a seat anywhere," Scarlett called out.

"I'm here to see Carla Wilson," she said.

"I'm Carla. Are you Tressa?" I asked as I crossed the room.

She nodded.

"We've been expecting you, but we didn't know which bus you'd be arriving on. Grab an apron from behind the counter. Scarlett can show you where they are. And then follow me today. You'll catch on quickly."

"Yes, ma'am," she said in a deep Southern voice.

My first thought was that we would have to beat the men away from the door when they saw her long blond hair and big brown eyes and heard that sexy accent. My second thought was that we would make a lot of money when word got out that a single woman who looked like her worked at the Tumbleweed.

After half an hour, I handed her an order pad and pen and told her to wait on the two tables of travelers who had parked outside beside the bus. I kept a close eye on her. She kept her distance from the men in the last booth by the window and never looked them in the eye. She took their order, pinned it on the carousel, and refilled their coffee cups. Then she went to the next group of four with two sulky teenage girls.

When everyone had left, she got a broom and dustpan from the storage room and swept while Scarlett bused dirty dishes to the kitchen and I wiped down the tables. Yes, sir! She truly was a fast learner.

"You did good, Tressa," I told her.

"Thank you." She smiled for the first time, but it did not reach her eyes. "I've never worked in a café, but I tagged along with my older sister a few times when she did waitress work. How late does this place stay open?"

I was reminded of my first day at the café and how everything seemed surreal. Different time. Different woman. Different circumstances that brought me and Tressa to the same place. Same feelings of bewilderment.

"We just serve breakfast and lunch," Scarlett answered. "So we usually have everything cleaned up and leave between two and three o'clock. Let's go meet Rosalie. Rule number one is that you don't mess around in her kitchen. If you want something, just ask and she will cook it for you. We take home leftovers for supper—today, that is spaghetti—and if we have time, we grab lunch between customers. We get two buses at lunch, so most of the time we either get a bite now and then between waiting on customers, or we eat a late lunch after everyone clears out."

"Okay." Tressa's eyes darted around like mine had done that first day I arrived. "Ilene said I would have room and board. I left my duffel bag over there." She nodded in the direction of the Special of the Day sign. "Where should I put it?"

"In the storage room," I answered. "Do you have a purse?"

"It's in the bag." She blushed. "Ilene gave me twenty dollars to use for emergencies until I got here. I was too nervous to eat, so I just bought a soda out of a vending machine."

I slipped my arm around her waist and gave her a sideways hug. "Honey, that's twenty more than I had when I got here. Come on to the kitchen, and Rosie will fix you up with some breakfast or a burger."

Scarlett picked up her small duffel bag and led the way through the swinging doors to the kitchen. Tressa followed her into the storage room and asked, "Is that futon my bed?"

I opened the back door and pointed to the trailer. "No, you have a bedroom out in that place. You'll be living with me and Rosie. Scarlett just moved in with her fiancé. They'll be getting married the first week in February."

Rosie left the stove and came into the room with us. "I'm Rosalie Smith, the cook, and my number one rule is that if you are on social media, then you do not put pictures of—"

Tressa held up a hand and shook her head. "No social media of any kind. Ilene warned me about that. I only have a prepaid phone, and don't even need it since I don't have anyone to call or text anyway."

"We understand," Rosie said. "But now you have us three to call and text. Just be sure not to let pictures get out on social media. Are you hungry? There's leftover biscuits from breakfast, and I can whip you up an omelet or some gravy. Or if you aren't a breakfast person, I can make you a burger."

"Breakfast sounds wonderful," she said. "I was too nervous to eat anything in the shelter night before last, and I didn't want to use my money yesterday for food in case of an emergency. All I've had is a soda since I boarded the bus."

"Of course," Rosie said. "How about a Carla breakfast? That's biscuits and gravy, and a stack of pancakes and a cup of coffee to go with it?"

"Yes, please," Tressa said. "No coffee, though, but I would like a glass of milk."

"You got it." Rosie hustled back to the kitchen.

"Does she have cancer?" Tressa whispered.

"No, she wears a bonnet to keep any stray hairs out of the food, and you will need to put yours up for the same reason. A messy bun does a good job," I told her.

She opened her bag and pulled out a brush and a big clip. In seconds, she had pulled her hair up and secured it. That was when I saw the faded bruises around her neck. I didn't ask questions. She would tell us her story when she was ready. Until then, we would just let the Tumbleweed heal her.

Chapter Twenty-Two

Not many vehicles were on the road from the Tumbleweed to Sierra Blanca on Wednesday afternoon. Since I could set the cruise control and let my mind wander all over the place, my thoughts jumped around like a sugared-up six-year-old kid.

What Rosie had said about giving me and Scarlett both the weekends off in the future was the first thing that surfaced. "Making babies?" I muttered. "Jackson has teased about a committed relationship, but I need to wrap my mind around that before I think about making babies."

A vision of a little dark-haired boy holding my hand as we crossed the road flashed through my mind. I wondered how Julia would handle a commoner like me being the mother of her grandchild.

That picture faded and my mind went to how well Tressa had settled in just three days. She was meticulous in her cleaning, quick to follow directions, and as proud of her split of the tips as I had been in those first days. She had spent most of her afternoons in her bedroom—but then, she might have been so worried that she couldn't sleep before she came to the Tumbleweed. A few times I heard her crying, but I figured she would tell us her story when she was ready, or maybe never. Whichever would be her decision. She seemed very excited to be included in the trip we'd planned to shop for a wedding dress.

Thinking of Tressa made my thoughts go to Rosie's and Scarlett's pasts. They had done very well in putting that behind them, but Tressa's was still raw enough to make her cry. I had to put up with Paula, but never any physical abuse. However, if the Tumbleweed could cure my poker addiction, it could save Tressa's heart and soul.

I had been driving along without paying much attention to the songs on my playlist, but when Ashley McBryde started singing "Light On in the Kitchen," I listened closely. She sang words that came from a mother to a daughter about trusting herself and loving herself first and foremost. And she would leave the light on in the kitchen in case her child needed her. I'd never thought of that before, but vowed that if I ever had children, I would do the same.

"I promise to treat Tressa like you would," I said out loud.

The song had just ended when my phone rang. Hoping that it was Jackson, I touched the screen to accept the call without even looking to see who was calling and answered, "Hello? The roads are clear. It didn't snow as much down here as it did up where we are."

"Carla?" a vaguely familiar voice asked.

"Yes, this is Carla," I answered.

"This is Paula. I'm calling to tell you that Frank died," she blurted out.

"Do you mean my dad or Frankie?" I was so shocked my voice came out in a high-pitched squeak.

"Frankie and Christian are alive and well, and mourning the loss of their father, as much as I am. That was very rude of you to ask which one—but then, I wouldn't expect much from someone who chose poker over a stable home."

"When is the funeral?" I asked, not knowing whether I should go or not.

"He passed away on the first day of January after a two-year battle with cancer. He wanted to be cremated, and his ashes scattered at the family reunion site. We had a lovely memorial with all his family, and we sang hymns while the boys and I took care of the ashes. I could feel him smiling from heaven. His sweet relatives told stories afterwards and provided a big meal for everyone."

I braked and made a left turn into Sierra Blanca. "Why didn't you call me before now?"

"I didn't want you to be here for his sickness or his memorial, but Frankie thought we should at least let you know that he was gone. After all, you were his daughter," she said.

I slapped the steering wheel out of a mixture of hot anger and sheer confusion. "Yes, I was, and—"

"I've told you," she butted in. "Now you know. Goodbye, Carla."

I was heading east out of town when I realized that I had passed the bank. I made a U-turn and went back, still in a state of numbness. Granted, I hadn't visited him or called except on his birthday.

"If he was sick for two years, why didn't he tell me? And for that matter, why would Paula wait three whole weeks to even let me know that he was dead?" I yelled so loudly that my voice echoed all through the SUV.

After making my deposits, I didn't go to the little café or stop at the convenience store for a cup of hot chocolate. I did not listen to music on the drive back to the Tumbleweed. I tried to sort out my feelings, but it was impossible. Frank had loved my mother enough to give up gambling, and he didn't put me in the system. The mere fact that I was his daughter should have at least warranted a phone call.

He didn't treat you like a daughter, and he didn't try to stop you from leaving when you were only sixteen, I reminded myself.

I still wasn't sure how I was supposed to feel when I parked my SUV in the space between the café and trailer. Scarlett had driven back to Dell City right after work, and Rosie had something that she took care of at the church on Wednesday afternoons, so my vehicle was the only one there. I stormed into the house to find Tressa sitting on the sofa with a bowl of popcorn in her lap.

"You look like you could either cry or kill someone," she said and held out the bowl to share with me.

I took out one kernel and popped it into my mouth. "I'm dealing with both emotions, and I don't know which one is worse."

"I found a stash of movies in the drawer in my bedroom, so I'm watching *Shooter*. It's only five minutes into the story. I can start it all over if you want to see it with me. It could take your mind off whatever is stressing you out."

"Sure," I agreed, then removed my coat and sat down beside her. I dipped into the popcorn and put several kernels in my mouth. "I haven't ever seen this one. Have you?"

"Nope, but I researched it and it's a kick-ass movie. That's what I need today," she said with more conviction in her voice than I'd heard since she arrived.

The popcorn needed something to wash it down, so I stood up and headed for the kitchen. "Don't push play yet. I'm going to get us each a glass of tea to go with this popcorn. I need that kind of movie, too, but why do you?"

"You first," she answered.

I filled two tall glasses with iced tea and carried them to the living area. "I found out on my way to the bank that my father died three weeks ago. They've already had his memorial. I don't know whether to be relieved or mad."

"Why wouldn't your mother tell you? Were y'all estranged?" she asked.

"Long story short is that Mama died when I was eight years old. My father and I had a complicated relationship from the time I was born. I never called him Dad or Daddy, just Frank. Good ol' Frank."

"Why?"

"He and my mama were young when they got pregnant, and he didn't want to be a father or be labeled *Daddy*. So he was Frank. About the only thing we had in common was poker . . ." I told her the bare bones and ended with "I won the Tumbleweed in a poker game, and I've only been here since New Year's Day."

"I guess we've all come from a less-than-normal background," she said. "My boyfriend, Isaac, didn't want to be a dad, either. Today marks one month since I lost my baby. I was only six weeks pregnant. My boyfriend was mad because my birth control pills failed. I wound up in the hospital. There were complications because he had hit me in the stomach so many times and they had to remove my uterus. I can't have children, so I'm damaged goods . . ." Her voice trailed off, and her eyes filled with tears.

I shook my finger at her. "No, you are not! You are a survivor, and the Tumbleweed will heal you, just like it did Rosie, Scarlett, and me. From now on, you are a kick-ass woman who doesn't take crap off anyone, especially a man who doesn't treat you right."

"Will you keep telling me that?"

"Every single day, if necessary," I promised. "Now, turn on this movie, and let's see if we can get some ideas to make us even stronger."

She pushed the button on the remote, and we settled down to watch the movie. Sometime during the first half, I realized I was relieved that I didn't have to deal with Frank's family at his memorial, or his illness. Some people remembered the good things about a person when they were dead, but what came to my mind was the reality of those eight years of traveling. The moment's hesitation in his face when the sleazy man wanted him to sell me for poker chips. The times when I was too young to drive but did anyway, while he slept off a hangover in the back of the van. His expression of relief when I packed up my old used car and drove away from Kentucky.

The old saying *Know the truth, and it will set you free* came to mind.

Those were the cold, hard facts, and I had been set free by admitting that everything wasn't a bed of roses—or maybe it was, with extra thorns.

Tressa cussed the characters who tried to frame Bob Lee Swagger, Mark Wahlberg's character, and paused the movie to refill our tea glasses.

"Be careful," I warned her. "Rosie does not abide swearing or gambling."

"She's not here," Tressa said.

"Honey, Rosie could probably walk in the door and *smell* a cuss word," I said in all seriousness. "She might give you a second chance since you haven't heard the speech, but I'm just giving you fair warning."

She brought back full glasses and started the movie again. "Thanks. I do swear too much, but I'll try to watch my language."

"That would be a good idea." But during the very next scene, I said words that could have blown the windows out of the trailer.

"I won't tell if you don't," she said and crossed her heart like a little girl with a secret.

"I owe you one." I fought back a blush.

It's not the movie, Ada Lou whispered in my head. *You might think the Frank issue is resolved, but you are still angry at Paula. Rightly so. She should have at least given you the option of whether to go to the memorial or not. Remember what I told you about the first family we have and finding your second one?*

"Did you leave behind a family?" I asked.

She paused the movie again. "Just a sister who disowned me several years ago."

I told her what Ada Lou had told me. "I've found mine here in less than a month. No matter how long it takes, I hope you do the same."

"Me too," she said, and turned the movie back on.

Chapter Twenty-Three

Jackson was behind schedule at the rig all week, so all we got was a few minutes of FaceTime each night before we went to sleep. That I missed him was a whole new experience for me. I had cried myself to sleep for weeks after my mother died, but this was a whole new emotional level. I went to sleep thinking about him. I woke up wishing he was next to me. Through the day at work, I relived his kisses and fought the hot desire that just that brought about. When he called on Friday morning to ask me to watch a movie at his trailer that night, it seemed like a month had passed since I'd seen him.

"I'll make shrimp scampi," he said.

"I love all things shrimp, and I would love to, but this is the afternoon for bride dress shopping and supper—or at least wine and dessert afterwards to make it a special day for Scarlett," I answered.

"Then tomorrow night? I could pick you up at six."

"I'll be ready," I said. "But right now, the rush is about to hit us, so I have to go."

"I'll be counting the minutes," he whispered.

His deep drawl fired up my hormones and made me think about makeup sex. I might just start an argument so I could finally fall into bed with him.

At the end of the workday, all four of us piled into my SUV after we had closed the café.

"This makes it real," Scarlett said as she fastened her seat belt. "I am getting married in a few days. I will be Mrs. Grady Mendoza, and we're going to have a bunch of kids and live happily ever after."

"I think I'm as excited as you are," Tressa said from the back, where she sat beside Rosie. "I've never been wedding dress shopping. I hope you are blessed with a lot of children and that you and Grady are married forever."

"We were talking about that last night, and we want to keep up the family traditions of meals on Sunday like his mama and daddy. They will have their fiftieth wedding anniversary in a couple of years, and we want to follow in their footsteps."

I was proud of Tressa for giving Scarlett that blessing about kids. No one in the vehicle knew what that had to have cost her after she had lost her own baby in such a violent way.

"I don't imagine any of us have been dress shopping, have we?" Rosie asked.

"Not me," I answered. "Until I came to the Tumbleweed, I was married to poker, and a woman doesn't have to buy a dress for *that* wedding."

"I was married once," Rosie said. "But my mother made my dress. Since we didn't believe in overdoing things, it was a simple white eyelet outfit with baby-blue trim. That was supposed to be my something blue. My underwear was something old. And Mama loaned me her pretty pearls for something borrowed. Even with all those good-luck things, it didn't work."

I plugged the bridal shop address into the GPS and made a left turn out of the parking lot, then a right onto the highway. "Stay on Highway 62 for the next seventy-five miles," the tinny GPS lady's voice said.

"What's between here and there?" Tressa asked. "I lived in a small town in Mississippi my whole life and never been out of the county until now. This is all new territory for me, and even with the snow, it looks bare. I'm used to trees and lots of green."

"There is one little gift shop and café between the Tumbleweed and the outskirts of El Paso," Scarlett answered.

"Right now, all you will see is some dirty snow and a few really strong tumbleweeds," Rosie chuckled. "When the snow melts and the tumbleweeds all have blown away, you will see dead desert grass and a few straggling yucca plants."

"Are y'all sh . . . teasing me?" Tressa asked. "That many miles with nothing?"

"Welcome to West Texas," I replied and told her about my first drive from El Paso to the Tumbleweed. "But I understand that after this month, there aren't as many of those pesky weeds. Maybe we won't have to kick them out of the way on Scarlett's wedding day."

"I haven't seen any," Tressa said. "What do they look like?"

As if on cue, a couple blew across the road and got stuck in the snowdrift on the south side. "Your wish is my command." I slowed down enough that she could see the thing out the side window.

"It's just a big old round weed," she said.

"Yep, and when the north wind blows, they migrate south in droves," Scarlett told her. "The winter months—especially January—is when they are worse. You'll see for yourself next year."

"I hope so," Tressa said. "I like it so much here that I never want to leave."

I glanced up in the rearview mirror and saw Rosie reach over and pat her on the shoulder. "That's music to my ears. Some of us took a while longer to trust each other."

Tressa asked Scarlett what kind of dress she had in mind, and the conversation between them went from there. The word *trust* stuck in my mind. I believed in Rosie and Scarlett more than anyone I had known in my life. I wanted to feel the same for Jackson, but a small part of my heart was still guarded. I'd only known him for a short time, and there was real chemistry there. Even knowing that, I could not put him through the agony I'd seen in my dream.

"You look sad, Carla," Tressa said. "Did I say something wrong?"

"Not at all. I was thinking about how glad I am that you showed up when you did so that Scarlett can have a few days off."

"Me too," Scarlett said. "Matilda told me that some folks come into your life for a season, and some for a reason. I'm glad that y'all are in my life for more than a season, and I believe the reason is because we are a family, as Ada Lou says."

"Thank you. I haven't even been with y'all a week, and I already feel that . . ." Tressa paused.

I looked into the rearview mirror to see if she was crying, but she had a beautiful smile on her face.

"That," she went on, "I'm a part of a family. How does the Tumbleweed do that?"

"It's not the café," Rosie answered. "It's Matilda's spirit."

"Who?" Tressa asked.

Scarlett and Rosie took turns telling stories about Matilda and the adages she had passed along to them. A little over an hour later, they were still talking when the GPS lady said, "You have arrived."

A woman greeted us with a smile when we walked inside the shop. Racks and racks of white dresses were to our right. How on earth was Scarlett ever going to go through all those gowns? She would be exhausted by the time the shop closed. "Y'all must be with the Scarlett Jones group. I'm Mary Beth, and I will be helping you. Which one of you is the bride?"

Scarlett raised her hand. "That would be me, and I'm already bewildered by all this."

"Don't you worry about anything. I will take good care of you." She looped her arm through Scarlett's and led her toward the back. "Two of your group have already arrived and are waiting for you."

We rounded a corner to find Ada Lou and Nancy sitting in a semicircle of pink velvet wingback chairs and drinking champagne from crystal flutes. Ada Lou raised her glass. "Since we are part of the family, we decided to crash the party."

I looked over at Rosie, who shrugged and said, "I always make an exception for a wedding."

A stage with a bank of mirrors on three sides and two open doors leading into dressing rooms was right ahead of the chairs. A crystal chandelier with what looked like thousands of prisms hanging from it threw out light over the whole area. I heard a short gasp from Tressa and turned to find her blushing.

"I feel like I should run back to Mississippi. Folks like me don't belong in places like this," she whispered.

"You will do fine," I assured her with a pat on her back. "This is not the norm for the Tumbleweed folks. It's just a dress-up day."

"We crashed for two reasons," Nancy said as all of us took a seat. "We wanted to get in on the excitement, and we both need to buy a new dress for the wedding."

That was when it dawned on me that I would need something suitable to wear, too. The little black dresses that I wore to poker games wouldn't be appropriate. Neither would my denim skirt or jeans. The only things left in my closet were work clothes.

I could feel Tressa squirming next to me and remembered the duffel bag full of secondhand things. "Then I guess we'll all need something decent to wear," I said. "After we get Scarlett all set, the rest of us can try on outfits. Maybe we should all wear shades of red since that is Scarlett's color."

"Since y'all are paying for the wedding dress, I'm picking up the bill for the rest," Ada Lou said. "Don't argue with me. This is something I didn't get to do for my daughter."

I bent down, gave Ada Lou a hug, and whispered, "Thank you. Tressa is super nervous."

Mary Beth whipped out a white notebook and a pen. "You all have a seat, and then the bride can tell me what she has in mind. I'll gather up a couple of dozen dresses and bring them back for her to try on. But first, what is your budget?"

"She doesn't have one," Rosie said. "If she likes it, then she has it."

"Nothing too elaborate. I like things that are more vintage than modern," Scarlett said.

Mary Beth poured four more flutes of champagne and handed one to each of us. She set the half-full bottle on a low coffee table along with an assortment of cute little petit four cakes and a carafe of water with six small glasses arranged around it.

"This is the fanciest place I've ever been in," Tressa whispered.

"Me too," Scarlett agreed and set her flute on the table. "I don't really like champagne. Does anyone want mine?"

"I'll take it," Nancy said. "Ada Lou is driving, so she can only have one drink, but I'll take whatever any of y'all don't want. This is the good stuff."

Tressa also passed her glass down to Nancy. "Ada Lou, I will pay you back for my dress as soon as I get a paycheck."

"Nonsense." Ada Lou waved her off with a flick of her wrist. "Family takes care of family. You can pay me back by coming to my trailer sometime and playing Scrabble with me and Nancy."

Mary Beth rolled a rack up to the side of a platform and showed us all the first dress. It had pearls scattered on the skirt and looked like it came out of a 1960s fashion catalog.

Scarlett shook her head on that one, as well as the second one, but the third was the charm. Her sudden intake of breath told me that she had picked out the perfect dress before she'd even tried it on. But the expression on her face said everything when she walked out of the dressing room in a dress that fit her like it had been tailor made for her figure.

"That is gorgeous," Ada Lou gasped. "Please keep it as a maybe, if not a yes."

"I'm afraid to look at the price tag, but this is my dream dress." Scarlett's voice was filled with awe. "I never thought I would find something so perfect."

"Then you will have it," Rosie said. "Now, pick out a veil?"

"I don't think I want one. The dress is enough by itself." She held out her arms, and the bell sleeves fell halfway to her knees. "If it gets warm, I can remove this"—she took off the jacket, leaving behind a sleeveless V-neck dress—"and dance all night with Grady."

"How about red and white rosebuds tucked into your hair?" Tressa suggested.

Scarlett turned around to check out her reflection in all the mirrors. "I like that idea, Tressa. I haven't been to many weddings, but the dresses look stiff and uncomfortable with all the satin, beads, and lace. The lace on this one is soft and moves with me."

I could clearly see her walking down the aisle with a bouquet of red roses in her hands.

"What kind of dress do you want when you marry Jackson?" Ada Lou whispered.

"Shhh . . . ," I shushed her. "This is Scarlett's day, not mine."

Ada Lou nodded and winked. "If that's *the* dress, then we should find something in red for the rest of us. Mary Beth, can you roll that rack away and bring us something to look at that would be fitting for the mother, sisters, and grandmothers of this beautiful bride?"

"Absolutely. Long or short?" she asked.

"Short," Ada Lou said. "Two of us—and I'm talking about me and you, Nancy—would get tangled up in the hems of something that's dragging on the floor and fall on our faces."

"Of course," Mary Beth nodded. "Scarlett, if you are sure about the dress, we will put it in a garment bag for you."

"I want to keep it on until you come back with something for the rest of the family," she said. "But you can take the others away. This is the one."

We'd gone into the store intending to buy one dress. We left with six. Mine was a white rose print on a red background. I'd never worn anything quite like it, but when I tried it on, it fit and Scarlett loved it. As we were walking out with our garment bags draped over our arms, I suggested that we put them all in the back of my SUV.

"That sounds like a wonderful idea," Ada Lou agreed. "That will leave room for Rosie to ride with me. I might need her to help me haul Nancy's drunk butt out of the truck."

"I am not drunk," Nancy declared. "It would take more than six of those skinny glasses of champagne to make me dizzy."

"Then why did I have to help you get into that crimson dress?" Rosie asked with a bit of edge in her voice.

"I'm old. I can't zip up a dress from the back. That does not make me drunk," Nancy snapped.

Ada Lou made sure that Nancy was in the back seat and then turned to face us. "I wanted to take y'all to a really nice place, but this is Scarlett's day, and she wants pizza."

"All of you have spent way too much money today for us to go to a swanky restaurant—and besides, I like pizza," Scarlett said as she slid into the passenger seat. "I already feel like a princess."

"So do I," Tressa said. "If I'm dreaming, don't wake me up."

"Me either," I whispered under my breath.

Chapter Twenty-Four

The adrenaline rush of the whole day hadn't ebbed by the time I went to bed. After a brief conversation with Jackson, I tried to sleep that night, but nothing worked. Finally, I pushed back the covers and tiptoed to the kitchen. Rather than switching on a light, I used the one in the refrigerator to pour a glass of milk, and carried it to the living room in the dark.

"Couldn't sleep, either?" Tressa asked.

Her voice startled me so badly that I jumped and had to do some fancy footwork to keep from spilling milk all over her.

"Didn't mean to scare you," she said.

I sat down on the other end of the sofa and turned on the lamp beside me. "No problem. I thought I was the only one who had a dose of insomnia tonight. All the excitement of the day hasn't settled, I guess."

"I had another nightmare," she whispered.

"Want to talk about it? I had one a few days back, and it helped me to talk about it."

"You go first," she said.

I told her about the dream I had when Jackson was so upset. "Sometimes I worry that I'll end up like my mother, dead at an early age . . ." I then went on to tell her about the accident that took Mama's life. I remembered part of a quote that said something about paying it forward, and hoped that I could help Tressa as much as my newly found family had helped me.

"That's so sad, but . . ." She paused and swiped a tear from her eye. "At least you had a few years of good."

Poker had taught me to be patient. I waited and sipped on my milk.

"I had four stepfathers, and too many boyfriends to count came and went in my mama's life. They were all cut from the same cloth. Sweet as sugar cookies until she married them or let them move into the house with us. Meaner than a snake when they got drunk or high. They slapped Mama around and eventually did the same to me. There are a few good memories, but those are centered around when Mama was between men."

"I guess I should be thankful for those good years," I said.

Tressa nodded. "Yes, you should. Cherish them. What happened after your mother died?"

"Frank—that was my father—and I went on the road for eight years and played poker," I answered. "Is your mother still living?"

"Last I heard. She disowned me for going to the cops when one of her boyfriends almost raped me," Tressa said. "It wasn't hard to leave her behind and promise Miz Ilene that I wouldn't look back, but it's tougher than I imagined. Memories keep popping up, and nightmares about my baby blaming me for not living."

I scooted over and draped an arm around her shoulders. "I understand, but you can't blame yourself for what is not your fault."

"I made the choice to live with a man who had already abused me, so how is it not my fault?" she asked.

"We had crazy role models. You lived with abuse and rejection. That's what you knew. I lived with a father who loved poker more than his kid. Putting the next card game ahead of everything in the world—including happiness, roots, and a family—is what I knew. We can help each other take baby steps forward until the past is so far back there that it's not even a blip on the radar."

"I don't know that I'd be much help to you," Tressa said.

I gave her shoulders a gentle squeeze. "Honey, when four women stick together, we're stronger than a three-ply rope. Nothing can keep us back. We empower each other, and with every conversation, we get tougher."

"Like that therapy stuff people talk about?" she asked.

"Absolutely," I agreed.

"So, I can talk to you anytime?"

"Yes, ma'am, even in the middle of the night—and even if I'm out with Jackson."

"I wouldn't do that unless it's an emergency," she promised. "You can do the same."

"Thank you," I said as I stood up. "We are here for each other. Always remember that."

"I will, but it'll take a while for the idea to really soak in. I've never had that kind of friends or family before." She yawned. "I think I can sleep now."

"Me too. Thanks for the therapy session."

"Right back at you," she said.

The aroma of hot cheese and pepperoni wafted out from the back seat to meet me when Jackson opened the door. Plain old pepperoni used to be a staple in my poker days. I could order it online and have it delivered directly to my room. Supper could be before or after a game, if it didn't last past midnight, and I could eat in my pajamas. Pizza, biscuits and gravy, and anything Italian was food that I would never grow tired of. Even if I had eaten the same thing with all the ladies the night before, I was more than ready to have it again.

"I've missed you this week," Jackson said when he slid in behind the steering wheel. "I've got cold beers at the trailer, and the pizza is—"

"I know," I butted in. "It smells so good, and I'm hungry. The special at the café on Saturday is beef tips and noodles, and there wasn't a single bite left in the pot after the second bus came and went."

"Well?" he asked.

"What?"

"Did you miss me at all?"

I unfastened my seat belt and leaned over the console to kiss him on the cheek. "You are the last person in my thoughts when I go to sleep and the first one when I wake up in the morning. When I'm at work, every little thing reminds me of something you said or that we shared. So yes, I missed you, and yes, I'm glad to have this time to spend with you tonight, and yes, I do want a proper kiss when we get to the trailer. Until I met you, I thought that these kinds of feelings were only found in romance books."

I caught myself before I added, "Especially after hearing stories of Rosie's, Tressa's, and Scarlett's pasts."

He chuckled. "I don't read romance books."

"Life can sure have some twists and turns, and turn into a mystery, can't it?" I asked.

"Do you want to solve it?" he asked.

"Solve what?"

"The mystery."

"It was a figure of speech," I told him. "I'll admit that there was chemistry between us from the beginning, but most couples aren't where we are now until a year down the road. Do you want to explain that?"

"Are you a little testy tonight?" he asked.

"If testy and hungry are the same thing, then yes, and . . ." I stopped long enough to flash a grin toward him. "I'm hungry for more than pizza and beer. I want a couple of those toe-curling kisses to keep me from being so grouchy. I have missed them very much."

He chuckled and made a turn into the trailer park. "You say what's on your mind, and I like that."

"I'm glad, because I don't know how to do anything else," I said. "But honestly, it seems like we're moving too fast, doesn't it? I can tell you everything about any kind of poker you want to talk about, but this is a whole new game for me. Do people really get this serious after less than a month?"

He parked in the narrow space between his and Ada Lou's trailers. "Sometimes they do. I knew the first time I laid eyes on you that there were vibes between us. The stars aligned for us, and we can either ignore them like you did Lady Luck, or we can give thanks for them."

He got out of the truck, but I didn't wait for him to open the door for me that night.

He handed the pizza to me on the porch, unlocked the door, and swung it open. I went inside and set the two boxes on the stove. But when I turned around, he was right behind me with open arms. I took a step forward and his mouth landed on mine. For several minutes, we made out right there in the tiny kitchen area, and then he took a step back.

"I was starving for your kisses, even more than the pizza, so we had dessert first." He kissed me on the forehead and took two beers from the refrigerator. He twisted the tops off both and handed one to me.

My body was still tingling when I took a long gulp, but not even the icy cold soothed the heat in my body. With the few sexual encounters I'd had through the years, nothing had ever affected me like kissing Jackson Armstrong. I wanted to take it further, but suddenly I had second thoughts, so I blinked away the idea of this being the night to go to the next level with a sigh.

"Let's take the pizza and beer to the living room and get a movie going. What do you want to watch tonight?"

Nothing with a lot of kissing or falling into bed.

I removed my coat, crossed over to the living area, and eased down on the sofa. He brought the pizza and set it between us.

"How did you know that I liked pepperoni?" I took the first slice out of the box and bit into the pointed end. Strings of hot cheese strung out and stuck to my chin. Jackson moved closer to me and wiped it away with one of the paper napkins the pizza place had given him. "I'm as graceful as a drunk elephant on ice."

"That's a joke. I watched you at the steak house, and you moved across that dining room like a ballerina when you came back from the ladies' room."

"Thank you, but I was being very careful that evening. I didn't want your mother to see me fall, jerk one of those white cloths off a table, and wind up on the floor with tomato bisque or whatever other fancy soup they served all over me."

He laughed out loud. "Is Clara Williams as funny as Carla Wilson?"

"No, sir. Clara is dead serious. She doesn't smile except when she's trying to throw another player off his game."

The laughter stopped. "Does that mean that when you give me one of your smiles, you are trying to manipulate me?"

"I'm Carla when I'm with you, not Clara," I answered. "You never did answer my question about knowing that pepperoni is my favorite."

"I don't know about Clara, but Carla doesn't look like a pineapple and ham person to me, or a black olive and sausage," he answered and opened the movie drawer.

"You are right about that. And Clara doesn't watch much television, but Carla loves it, so what have you got in mind for us tonight?"

The twinkle in his eyes told me that his thoughts weren't on picking out a movie. "We could argue about what movie to watch and then . . ."

"Do you really believe that nonsense about the eighth date? We could break up after the seventh date in an amicable way and never argue," I told him.

"That would be a crying shame," he said. "I'm looking forward to the makeup sex."

"What if we've made such a big deal out of it that we are both disappointed?" I asked.

"Has anything disappointed you so far?" he fired back.

"No, not with you, or any of my new friends since settling down here."

"Whoa!" He jerked his head around to stare at me. "Did you say what I think you said? When did you make that decision?"

"I got a revelation in church last Sunday. I figured out that poker doesn't mean as much to me as what I've found here. I'm ready to put down roots," I answered and took another bite of the slice in my hands. "Are you going to take all the way to summer to decide what you want to do?"

"No, ma'am," he answered. "I made up my mind at the Mendoza family supper. This is where I want to settle down and raise a family."

Alert! Alert! He's talking about a family. Are you ready for that?

"I want my kids to have friends that aren't separated by social standards," Jackson said. "I want to do more than have an oil company in Dell City. It will take a few years, but eventually I want to bring in a doctor or two and build a health clinic. Maybe even a small hospital. I want to support the school system and bring life into the place."

"Jackson, you are the boss here," I told him. "Your children will be considered the rich ones no matter what you do. Maybe not like they would in Dallas, but in this place, you are a big fish. Your dreams are great, but even here, you are an Armstrong."

"Carla, I don't care how long it takes you to make up your mind about us. I'm a patient man," Jackson said. "Which reminds me, my former team has been called out on a mission, so we won't have that get-together that I invited you to. I'm already planning something for early summer, though, so keep your calendar open."

"We'll see where we are in this relationship at that time," I told him.

"I can appreciate your independence, but I want to introduce you to my friends and my sisters."

"And I said we'd see where things were," I said with a bit of an edge in my tone. No one was ever going to make plans for me—with me, maybe, but not *for* me. I would not be a submissive wife, not after what Rosie had told me about her life.

I put the rest of my uneaten slice of pizza in the box, stood up, and put my coat on. "I think it would be best if you take me home before we say things that we will regret later."

"I'm not taking you home until we talk this through."

I opened the door and took a step out onto the porch. "Then I'll get Ada Lou to drive me back to my trailer."

"Okay, okay!" he growled. "I will take you, but I don't like leaving things unfinished."

In the romance books that I had read, when a couple had an argument, tears were involved. When they broke up for good, the heroine laid around in her pajamas for days and grieved for the love she had lost. Whoever wrote those books did not know Carla Wilson or Clara Williams.

I eyed the pizza when the urge to throw something at the walls came over me. "Just take me home. I'm through talking, and I need some space. We might revisit this someday, but not tonight or tomorrow. And, Jackson, I will not be manipulated or told how to live my life—not ever." I stormed out to the truck, got inside on my own, and almost apologized for being so stubborn. But my pride wouldn't let me say a word all the way back home.

"Can I call you or FaceTime with you?" he asked and opened his door.

"Give me a couple of days—and I'm quite capable of getting out of this vehicle on my own." I got out of the truck before he could even unfasten his seat belt, and walked to the trailer without looking back.

An old song came to my mind from my playlist as I entered the house. The lyrics to Terri Clark's "I Just Wanna Be Mad" seemed to fit the night just fine. I hung up my coat and went straight to my room without even saying a word to Tressa or Rosie. I found the song on YouTube and sent the link to Jackson. Then I turned off the ringer, tossed the phone on the bed, and went back down the hallway.

"You're back early," Tressa said.

My hands trembled when I opened the refrigerator and took out sandwich makings. "Yep, we had an argument, and I'm hungry. But I was a good girl and didn't throw anything at the walls."

"But you wanted to, didn't you?" Tressa asked. "Did you at least stand up for yourself? If you ever let a man start telling you what to do and how to do it, you will lose yourself like I did."

"I'm not a submissive little woman who walks two steps behind a man," I barked.

Tressa pumped her fist in the air. "One for womankind."

"I have to admit that I considered throwing pizza at him, and it was all over a silly situation. He wanted to plan a trip so I can meet his friends, and I let my anger get ahead of me. I've always done my own planning and traveled where I wanted," I admitted. "Do you want a sandwich, or can I put this stuff back?"

"Leave it," Tressa answered. "I'd love one. And let's watch some television while we are eating. There's a marathon of *Friends* playing all week from seven to midnight every night."

I had seen a few episodes of the old sitcom, and it seemed very fitting for the evening. Watching it might even take my mind off Jackson and the kisses we shared.

"So, why are you really fighting with Jackson?" Tressa asked. "From my view, that's the straw that broke the camel's back and not the real issue."

"Trust," I blurted out. "I'm having trouble trusting him, and there's no reason for me not to do so."

"Trusting him or trusting yourself?" she asked.

I set my mouth so firmly that my face hurt. "Okay, okay. It's me. What if—"

She held up a palm and shook her head. "You taught me that there's no room for *what-ifs* in our lives. We bury the past, walk away from the grave, and step into the future."

"How did you get to be so smart?"

"If I've got an ounce of smartness, you can blame it on the short time I've been at the Tumbleweed. Don't let this anger go on too long, or you might lose the best thing that could ever happen to you."

"Okay, Dr. Tressa, I hear you loud and clear. Let's eat and watch some episodes."

A couple of hours later, I yawned. "This has been fun, but I'm tired, so I'm going to bed."

Tressa stood up and stretched. "I barely kept my eyes open on the last episode."

I turned off the television. "I've been dozing for an hour. See you in the morning."

When I reached my room, I moved my phone from the middle of the bed to the nightstand and was about to set the alarm when I saw that I had a text from Jackson: One lyric in the song says that you love me. I'll take that. You can call me when you get through being mad. He ended it with a smiley face.

That one little emoji took what was left of the anger out of me.

Chapter Twenty-Five

On Wednesday afternoon, Scarlett laid a hand on my shoulder and asked, "Are you all right? You've been checking your phone every hour for the past two days. Are you and Jackson still not talking?"

"I'm fine," I answered. "Jackson and I are giving each other some space, but we might see each other tonight."

"Okay, but if you need to talk, I'm here," Scarlett said.

"Thank you. How's things going with the new house?" The quickest way to move her to a new subject was to get her to talk about all the excitement of the wedding or her new home.

"Since the loan has been approved, now it's just a matter of paperwork. The previous owner gave us permission to repaint the walls and put down that plank flooring. It's like a dream come true that we get to start off in our own home and not a rental."

I must have frowned, because she quickly said, "The Mendoza family all pitched in, and we had the painting and flooring finished yesterday. We close on Friday afternoon when I get off work, and we'll start moving in on Saturday." She checked the dining room to see where Tressa and Rosie were, then whispered, "We are only going up to Cloudcroft for a couple of nights, but we don't want anyone to know that we're coming back to our own home on Monday."

"Why is it a secret?" I asked.

"We want to spend a couple of days together in our new home before we both go back to work. If the family would stay away, we would probably even forget the nights in Cloudcroft. We just want some mornings to wake up late, have mind-blowing sex, and then start all over again."

We had gone back to work when Tressa came from the kitchen with a broom in her hands. "Rosie invited me to go to Mass with her this evening," she said as she started sweeping. "I haven't been to church or to confession in ten years."

On Thursday, I got a text from Jackson: Are you still mad?

I sent back one that said: Workin' on it.

The next one from him asked: Can we try for pizza and beers again on Saturday night?

I'll let you know, and added a smiley face blowing a kiss to him.

On Friday, Ada Lou came in that morning and ordered her regular late breakfast—or brunch, as she liked to call it. Then she narrowed her eyes into slits and stared at me.

"You look like warmed-over crap. What is going on?" she asked. "Are you and Jackson still arguing? What was that fight about, anyway? Girl, you need to wake up and smell the bacon."

"I thought it was 'the roses'—and we have not made up yet," I answered before I hung her order through the service window. "He wanted to tell me what to do. I'm a grown woman who has been basically taking care of myself since I was eight years old."

"I like Jackson. He's a good man," Ada Lou said. "But hold your ground. If you start letting him run you like a toy train, then you'll be giving up pieces of yourself."

"And pretty soon, you won't even know who *you* are," Tressa added.

Women empowering women came to my mind like it did so often when I thought of all the ladies who were now my friends. Going back to my old lifestyle and leaving them behind would break my heart. I couldn't do that to them.

My phone pinged. Have you thought about it long enough?

I wiped my eyes and typed I have, and the answer is yes. Pick me up at six?

I'll be there. I've missed you, Carla.

I sent one back that said Ditto!

I spent all day Saturday dealing with a merry-go-round of emotions. By the time Jackson arrived promptly at six, a tangle of nerves the size of a beach ball had settled into my stomach. I slung my purse over my shoulder, stepped outside, and just stood there staring at Jackson.

"What?" he asked. "Did I grow an extra eye in the middle of my forehead?"

I stood on tiptoe and brushed a kiss across his lips. "If you did, you would still be sexy."

He took my hand in his, and together we went to his truck. "What happened to my Carla? What have you done with her?"

When I was in the passenger seat, I flipped the console up and moved over to sit close to him. "She is ready to talk about the other night now, and she knows what she wants."

"Have we survived our argument?" he asked as he drove toward the trailer.

"I hope so," I answered. "I will always be independent. It's who I am. I don't need you to take care of me. But I do need you to love me unconditionally and support me. I will do the same for you."

"I can do that," he said. "But I have to tell you, that sounds a lot like something my mother would say."

"Then she is a smart woman. Do you still want to move forward even after I pitched a hissy fit? If not, tell me now, and we won't waste any more time."

"Up front. Honest. And blunt as hell." He parked the truck in between the trailers like always. "And, darlin', I love you and I very much want to go full speed ahead with us. I'm here for the long haul, no matter how short or how long that is." He tipped up my chin and kissed me.

I swear I heard bells ringing off in the distance, and my words came out between short breaths. "What you see is what you get. I won't change, and I don't ever want you to."

"Deal," he said.

When we got inside, I noticed a calendar on the wall beside the door. Today was January 31. Instead of just a month since I'd arrived at the Tumbleweed, it seemed like at least a year. "What a fitting way to end my first month," I muttered.

"What was that?" Jackson asked.

"Just how hot is that makeup sex you've been teasing me about?"

He scooped me up in his arms and carried me to the bed. "You can decide," he whispered as he removed his shirt and tossed it to the side. He slid the pocket door shut, putting us in a little bubble all our own.

"No one is in here," I whispered.

"But there might be someday, so we might as well get into the habit now."

I didn't care if he was talking about children or visitors or even a couple of cats. I just wanted to feel his body next to mine.

Chapter Twenty-Six

Seeing the bride before the wedding was bad luck. If the Mendoza family believed that Grady and Scarlett should not spend the night together the night before the ceremony, I was not one to argue the point. Lady Luck proved that I was more than a little bit superstitious.

We wanted to close the café on the day of the wedding and give Scarlett the time off, but she protested. If she had to stay home all day, she declared that she would bite her nails to the quick and walk the shine off the floor in the new house. Besides, what would those poor folks on the buses do if they couldn't use the restrooms and get a bite to eat?

It was business as usual, but we managed to get things cleaned up and close the café half an hour early that afternoon. We gathered what we needed for the wedding and rushed up to Scarlett's new home with only three hours until she was supposed to be at the church.

Ada Lou's truck pulled out behind us when we passed the trailer park, making a short convoy of four. Scarlett was the first one out of her car when we reached the white-framed house with a wide front porch and a fenced yard. It was uncanny how much it reminded me of the house where I had grown up, right down to the white wrought-iron gate that squeaked when she opened it.

She motioned for us all to follow her, and she unlocked the front door. "Y'all come on in. We still don't have a lot of furniture, but the

Mendoza family all helped us get the walls painted and new flooring put down."

"Honey, all that can come later," Nancy assured her with a pat on her back.

Ada Lou brought in a pan of still-warm cinnamon rolls. "Right now, the important thing is a bed. You'll get bruises if you have sex on the floor. And a table to put these on. You have to remember to eat."

Rosie shocked us by saying, "Women cannot live on sex alone. Scarlett must have food."

"I cannot believe you said that," Scarlett gasped.

"Me neither," I said.

Tressa giggled, and soon all of us were laughing.

When the noise died down, Rosie said, "I'm not a nun. I know what sex is, and I should warn you that if you try it on the kitchen table, you will get splinters on your bottom."

"Have you been drinking?" Nancy asked in a low voice.

"Spoken like a true smart aleck." Ada Lou held up a palm and high-fived Nancy.

"Not a drop," Rosie said. "I'm helping Scarlett get over her nerves. Laughter is good for a bride on her wedding day, as well as it is for the soul. Now, I'll put on a pot of coffee, and we'll have a cinnamon roll. Then Scarlett is going to take a shower. Carla, your first job is to be sure that she puts on deodorant. We can't have a sweaty, stinky bride walking down the aisle in that beautiful gown."

"Yes, ma'am," I said. "I'll personally hand it to her and watch while she uses it."

Scarlett set a wooden mug tree with six mismatched cups hanging from it on the table. The scent of coffee blended with the cinnamon rolls. "I thought we might need a little jolt of caffeine, so I got it ready to go before I left this morning." She brought out a stack of paper plates and napkins. "We will buy real dishes when—"

Her phone rang, and she pulled it out of the hip pocket of her jeans. "Hello, darlin'. I'm home and the ladies are here with me."

Everyone sat down around a table with six chairs except Tressa. She waited for the coffeepot to stop gurgling and filled all the cups. By that time, Scarlett had ended the call and joined us.

"Grady told me that it's a good thing we haven't bought a lot of stuff, because there are already two tables full of gifts and there's more coming," she said. "I can't take all this in."

"You are marrying into a family and community that loves you," Ada Lou said. "Now, let's get busy on these rolls. Scarlett doesn't want to be late for her own wedding."

In that moment, much like the revelation I'd had at the church, there was no doubt that Lady Luck had not deserted me but brought me to a new family and community—exactly like she had all the women sitting around the table with me. This was where I wanted to live the rest of my life and raise my and Jackson's children.

Scarlett and Grady's wedding was the exact opposite of Frank and Paula's, which had been held at Aunt Minnie's house. The whole congregation seemed to be bursting at the seams with love and smiles. No one was half lit like they had been the day that Frank stumbled over his vows.

The front pew had been reserved for our family—Ada Lou, Nancy, Rosie, Tressa, and me, with enough room at the end for Jackson.

"Do you still want to go to the courthouse?" he whispered.

"I do not," I said without a split second's pause. "And now I understand what you mean about raising a family here."

"Are you ready to do that now? The church is decorated and the preacher is here."

"This is Scarlett's day, not mine—and besides, I want your mother to like me someday. I don't see her in the crowd, do you? She might throw a hissy fit if her only son gets married in a small place like this, but she would definitely never forgive me if we didn't let her be a part of the ceremony."

"You've got a point there," he said with half a chuckle.

The background music from "When I See You" by Aaron Watson filled the church. The words had already begun when the preacher and Grady came from the choir section to stand between the two candelabras. All the lights were switched off except for the spotlight at the very back of the church. Candles in the windows and at the front of the church gave a warm glow to the small building. Then the back doors opened, and there was Scarlett, standing there like an angel in white bathed in the spotlight.

Grady slowly walked down the center aisle toward her, mouthing the words to the song the whole way. When he reached her side, the preacher raised his arms in a gesture for everyone to stand. Grady tucked Scarlett's arm in his, and together they made their way down the aisle, arriving in front of the preacher at the very moment the song ended. Scarlett handed her bouquet to Rosie, and the couple turned to face each other. They held hands across the space separating them with their eyes locked on each other. I wondered if they felt like they were the only people in the sanctuary.

"Who gives this bride to be married to this groom?" the preacher asked.

"Her family and I do," Rosie said.

As if he knew I would need it, that was when Jackson handed me a handkerchief. I dabbed tears away from my eyes. He let go of my hand, slipped his arm around my shoulders, and drew me closer to his side. I listened to every word of the ceremony and needed the hankie more than once, but I wasn't the only one sniffling on that front pew, or even in the crowd behind us.

"Grady, you may kiss your bride," the preacher said at the end.

The groom wrapped Scarlett in his arms and sealed the vows they had made to each other with a long and passionate kiss.

"May I introduce for the first time, Mr. and Mrs. Grady Mendoza."

The applause was so loud that it could have raised the roof right off the building. When it died down, and Grady and Scarlett had started down the aisle, the preacher said, "The families of the bride and groom have requested that all of you join them at the school cafeteria for a reception."

"I love you," Jackson whispered. "And when you are ready, just say the word and we'll have a wedding like this."

"I love you, too—but, darlin', I want the whole enchilada, so you have to do the bended knee before I say the word," I whispered.

Epilogue

Five years later

Like Rosie told me five years ago, January was the worst month in the year for tumbleweeds. We had to deal with them when Jackson and I got married on New Year's Eve right there in Dell City. A week after our first anniversary, we had to kick them out of the way to get to the hospital in El Paso to give birth to Henry, our son.

I swore that I would never have another baby in January, but Lady Luck laughed and laughed when I got pregnant and had Emily a year and six days after Henry's birthday.

When I told Rosie that number three was due right after Emily's first birthday, she said, "And there is the product of Carla's boasting. The Tumbleweed has blessed you with three children, all born during the season."

Someone once said change is like being born all over again. I believed that when we got all three children settled into the back seat of our new SUV. Clara Williams died in that poker game in Tucson, and Carla Wilson came to life the moment she walked into the Tumbleweed.

When Jackson used the toe of his cowboy boot to push tumbleweeds out of the way to make room for a double stroller that cold January evening, the lyrics of the song "Made for You" by Jake Owen came to my mind. The words said that front porches were made for kissin'. If that was true, then the tumbleweeds must have been made for me—to remind me of all my blessings from that first day when I arrived at the café.

Change had happened, and yet everything stayed the same. I still loved Jackson, even though we argued—and had makeup sex—while we built a ranch-style house on the acreage he'd bought south of Dell City. When we were designing it, I really thought we'd never need four bedrooms, but I was wrong. Sometimes, when the kids were all asleep, I would start a small argument to see if the makeup sex was still as hot as ever, and it was.

I was still working at the Tumbleweed Bus Stop and Diner, but Rosie now lived in Jackson's trailer and was happy to be close to Ada Lou and Nancy. Ada Lou celebrated her eighty-fifth birthday, but she declared that after eighty, a person gets to go backward, so we only put seventy-five candles on her cake.

Scarlett and Grady have had two precious little girls and still live in the same house. We have turned the trailer into a day care center for all our children and Tressa's two adopted little boys. She married the doctor—a widower—who moved to Dell City to work in the brand-new family clinic a year ago. With the marriage license, she got twin sons in the deal and couldn't be happier.

"What are you thinking about?" Jackson asked. "The last time you were this serious is when you told me number three was on the way."

I leaned over the console and kissed him on the cheek. "You need to stop calling her that, or I'll name number four Wild Card Armstrong whether it's a boy or a girl."

"Okay, then, when you told me *Julie* was on the way, and honey, you can't name a baby that. She would be teased her whole life, and besides you are *my* only good luck wild card."

"Thank you for that, and I was thinking of the last five years," I finally answered. "They've been the best in my life, and I'm so grateful for them."

"Even the tumbleweeds?" he asked as he drove us to the tiny municipal airport to get on the company plane to fly to Dallas for the weekend.

"Even those wicked things," I answered. "But most of all for you, my family, and my chosen family. Life is good. No complaints. Not even about the tumbleweeds."

Acknowledgments

Dear Readers,

I have a sign in my office that says MY LIFE IS FILLED WITH ROMANCE, DANGER, LOVE, AND DUST BALLS THE SIZE OF CATTLE. That sign became my muse as I wrote this book—only I changed the last word to *tumbleweeds*.

As I finish this story, it's winter in southern Oklahoma, and most mornings it is colder than a stepmother's stare. It's not difficult to imagine the wind blowing the tumbleweeds every which way out in West Texas. Or to think about a blizzard with nothing to stop the blowing snow but cactus plants and barbed wire fences. You might have read *The Wild Card* in the same kind of weather—unless you live far enough south to have sunshine and warm days. I hope you brewed up a pot of coffee, some hot chocolate, or maybe a cup of tea, then grabbed a warm blanket and enjoyed getting to know Rosie, Ada Lou, Carla, Scarlett, and all the folks at the Tumbleweed Bus Stop and Diner.

As I've said many times, it takes a village to get a book ready to put into my readers' hands. I'm grateful to each and every one of those who have helped the process along the way—all the folks who take an idea to a manuscript and through several edits, as well as cover designs and promotion, make up my village. I owe special thanks to Folio Literary Management for representing me, and to my agent, Erin Niumata, who has been on this journey with me for more than twenty-five years. Let's hear it for my publisher, Montlake, for continuing to believe in me. Then a round of applause to Krista Stroever, my developmental editor, who takes a lump of coal and helps me turn it into a shiny diamond. Thanks to my family, who have all stood beside me through the ups and downs of life. And a very special toast to my readers, who encourage me every day to keep writing. All of y'all have made me the author I am today, and I'm sending out virtual hugs to each and every one of you.

Until next time,
Carolyn Brown

About the Author

Photo © 2015 Charles Brown

Carolyn Brown is a *New York Times, USA Today, Washington Post, Wall Street Journal*, and *Publishers Weekly* bestselling author and RITA finalist with more than 140 published books. She has written women's fiction, historical and contemporary romance, and cowboys-and-country-music novels. She lives in the small town of Davis, Oklahoma, where everyone knows everyone else, knows what they are doing and when, and reads the local newspaper on Wednesday to see who got caught. She and her late husband, Mr. B, are parents to three grown children and too many grandchildren and great-grandchildren to count on the fingers and toes of one person. For more information, visit www.carolynbrownbooks.com.